Mermaids of Eriana Kwai
Book Three

ICE
KINGDOM

Rogue Cannon Publishing
Canada

First published in Canada in 2017
Rogue Cannon Publishing, Abbotsford, BC

tianawarner.com

CHAPTER ONE - Meela
Reefs, Rockfish, and Reinas

Three days as a mermaid and all I'd managed to learn was how to not die.

So far, I could swim, breach, and speak. Skills beyond that were taking longer.

Drifting somewhere between Eriana Kwai and the Aleutian Islands and surrounded by empty murk on all sides, Lysi was teaching me about layers and currents.

"Stick to the faster ones, unless there's something big in your way."

"How big?"

"Whales. Sharks. Trust me, you do not want to take on one of those."

I gave a "hmph", which materialised as a large bubble that I swatted away. I remembered vividly the terror of being nearly capsized by a pod of orcas.

"Also, don't go below the twilight layer unless you're prepared to rise slowly," said Lysi. "It hurts to depressurise too fast."

I followed her into the flow of a quick, warm current, where the rich taste of plankton met my tongue. Something crackled far below.

"We're over top of a reef," she said. "If you focus, you can sense the bottom."

"Coral?!"

I looked down eagerly. Would the novelty of the ocean ever wear off?

That was when I saw it: the cutest creature alive. I squealed and took off through the water, leaving Lysi shouting behind me.

"Mee, where are you—?"

The creature tried to flee, but I shot out a hand with a speed I'd never known myself capable of and cupped it in my palms.

"Lysi! Look!"

She caught up, pushing mats of coppery-blond hair and seaweed from her eyes. "Mee, would you pay atten—oh, that is cute."

It was a plum-sized purple octopus—or maybe it was a squid—with overlarge, googly eyes and rows of tiny suckers on each tentacle. If it hadn't been swimming—and it had a ridiculous way of doing so by flapping little wings on its head—I would've thought it was a bath toy.

"What is it?"

"It's a stubby squid."

I brought the little thing to eye level and peered at it. "Even your name is cute."

"Feel the way his suckers are moving?" She placed a hand under mine, bringing my attention back to our 'How to Be a Mermaid' lessons.

I closed my eyes. In the cloudy underwater world, I was supposed to rely less on my vision and more on my other senses. I could pick up smell, taste, sound, and feel from incredible distances—revealing the size, shape, and even chemical makeup of everything around me. When I concentrated, I picked up every whirl in the current. At first, it had been hard to cast my senses past the constantly rushing tide and gurgling bubbles, but I was getting better.

My eyes flew open. "I feel his suckers suckering!"

Lysi laughed. Below the water's surface, my hearing better than I'd known as a human, the sound travelled pleasantly down my spine. My heart thrummed.

She kept her hand beneath mine, holding my gaze with startlingly blue eyes.

"I can also feel your pulse," I said, noticing the way it quickened when she touched me.

She blushed. I looked down at our hands—mine over hers, brown skin against white—something that, until three days ago, I had thought I would never see again.

It felt strange to finally be allowed to be together. Nobody was around to tell us we couldn't hold hands, couldn't love each other, couldn't even speak to each other.

But then, nobody was around at all.

The situation was both lucky and frustrating. Sure, none of King Adaro's armies were chasing us down—and they'd undoubtedly been ordered to do so after the king himself had failed to finish us off three days ago. But our isolation also meant we were nowhere near finding the rebel group we were searching for. How were we supposed to find allies when all we had for company were a bunch of fish?

At the thought of Adaro swimming freely with Sisiutl under his control—my people's sacred legend, the power that should have been mine—the pressure in my eyes built, the world reddened, and I knew I'd transitioned to demon mode. I let it happen. It was easier to see through the dark depths this way, to blend with the green-grey sea, and to make tight turns with the new webs that stretched between my fingers.

The current stirred as something large moved below. It was a shape and rhythm I hadn't encountered yet. In a single motion I pulled away from Lysi, let go of the stubby squid, and plunged. I beat my tail a little harder than I intended and had to push out my webbed hands to stop myself from face-planting against the bottom. My hair whipped past me, and I flung the braids back over my shoulder before they could tangle around my neck.

Rockfish—big, ugly, orange things with underbites—cleared out of my path as I pushed clumsily along. Under my new fingers, the texture of rock and sand was wonderfully intensified. I followed the vibrations over my skin, which told me that somewhere ahead, a fish the size of my upper body lay hiding. I sped up. A prawn scuttled away, half-swimming, half-running, looking like a pompous galloping horse.

"Found it!"

My target darted away before I got there. He was strangely flat, with eyes on top of his face like he had evolved sideways.

I watched him go, deciding the ocean was insane.

"What was that?"

Before Lysi had even caught up, I spotted a cluster of plants to my left and zipped over to them.

"What are these?"

Palm-sized, mossy blobs clung to the rocks alongside starfish, and little white trees with fluffy tops.

I poked one of the moss blobs. It turned out to be un-mosslike, and what I thought was fluff was actually needles. I wondered if I'd discovered some sort of underwater hedgehog. The needles moved, convening around my finger as though to grab it.

"Urchins," said Lysi, sounding out of breath.

I moved on to another blob beside it. These tentacles looked soft, swaying with the current.

"Anemones," said Lysi, before I could ask.

I poked it. This one was squishy. The sticky tentacles wrapped around my finger and clung to it like tape.

"The cavity in the middle is so it can digest—"

Something silver glinted in the corner of my eye. A school of herring the size of a house floated nearby, noses to the current.

They darted away before I got there.

I chased them, concentrating on beating my tail in long, powerful strokes.

"Mee, wait! You need to—oh, for goodness' sake."

I burst into the cloud of fish, reaching for them as they scattered. They were quick, but I was quicker. Maybe too quick. My reactions outstripped my thoughts, and I found myself in the middle of an explosion of fish before I knew what I'd do with them. I grabbed one in each hand and bit them behind the skull like Lysi had taught me.

A hand closed around my arm and hauled me back into the open.

"You can't burst into a school like that," said Lysi. "Baitball, remember?"

I offered her one. "It still worked."

"But if you were hunting with a group, you would've totally ruined everyone else's chances."

I watched the herring fleeing in every direction. I supposed she had a point.

"Watch." She darted after them and made a wide circle, rounding them up.

After a lifetime on land, I'd never seen anything move with so much grace. An eagle's wings couldn't match the fluid coordination between Lysi's powerful tail, slim body, and the mane of coppery hair flowing behind her.

Not for the first time, I wondered how it was possible for anyone to be so perfect.

"Then you spiral in," said Lysi.

I hurried after her with considerably less grace, ignoring the heat blooming in my cheeks. It didn't help that my brain still tried to separate my tail into two kicking legs. I tried not to let it frustrate me, but I hoped Lysi never watched me as closely as I watched her.

We pushed the herring in a cluster against the water's surface. They bumped into each other, pushing to the centre and shoving the others to the outside. The effect was a pulsing silver ball that I thought looked quite pretty.

"Now it's safe to grab them," said Lysi, catching one easily.

Ripples hit us from behind. We turned to find a pod of Pacific white-sided dolphins approaching.

I swiped two more fish and we surfaced for breath, letting the dolphins take over the meal.

"Would you get out of demon mode?" said Lysi. "You're scaring me."

I flashed Lysi my smile of needle-sharp teeth before letting them retract. The pressure released from my eyes as the blood drained, my seaweed skin reverted to its golden brown, and I opened my fingers to watch the webs shrink.

"You transition way too often," said Lysi.

I shrugged. "I was just thinking about stuff."

"Adaro is nowhere near us."

At the mention of his name, my eyes threatened to redden again. "For now."

Lysi reached for my hand. "And for now, we're calm. I like it when I can see the green in your eyes, and when your smile doesn't say, *I'm going to decapitate you.*"

I grimaced. "As long as I get to decapitate a certain someone."

Decapitate, or run a spear through, or poison, or suffocate, or set sharks on …

I inhaled deeply—a breath that would last me the next three hours—and dove. I kept hold of Lysi's hand as we continued along, satisfying myself by considering all the ways I might eliminate King Adaro.

"You know it's going to be impossible," said Lysi.

I looked away, wanting to deny it, but she was right. Adaro had the leviathan for his bodyguard, which legend said was indestructible, and he himself was impervious to iron. Together, they made an invincible duo.

The thought was unnerving, but I refused to let it discourage me. I would find a way to break him.

"Whatever plan the Reinas have, I hope it involves the biggest army we've ever seen," said Lysi.

The Reinas. That was what she called this mysterious rebel group because of some code phrase she'd heard. The problem was that we didn't know where they were, who they were, how many, or what they were truly called. She only knew they'd shown up during an assassination attempt on King Adaro, and then again near Eriana Kwai, where they'd invited her to find and join them.

"As long as they let me do the honours," I said.

"Sure, of course," said Lysi, smiling.

She didn't seem to grasp how important this was to me. Vengeance aside, this was about controlling the Host of Eriana. The serpent's power was passed by blood; whoever killed its master would gain control. So while I was glad to hear of a movement against Adaro, I was terrified that someone else would get to him first.

"Did the Reinas tell you anything about their plan?" I said, voicing one of the many concerns needling at me.

"There wasn't time."

At my silence, she added, "I know they're from the Moonless City—that's in the South Pacific—and they were taking a northwestern current when we crossed paths. That's why I think they're headed to Utopia."

I chewed my lip. Adaro probably wasn't even in Utopia. He was probably on a battlefront somewhere, or the Pacific coastline, or sinking ships he happened upon in the Gulf of Alaska. He could be anywhere.

Days ago, when I'd been trying to find a giant serpent on Eriana Kwai, I'd thought the tiny island was too big. Now we had an entire ocean in which to find this rebel group. The world suddenly felt overwhelmingly vast.

I imagined Adaro swimming towards his next target, the serpent undulating behind him, her fangs stained with the blood of the day's victims.

My teeth prickled with the urge to transition. I willed myself to stay calm.

"They could have at least told you where to go," I said.

"They probably thought I already knew."

"Or they didn't trust you enough."

"Well, they knew nothing about me."

"And we know nothing about them. What if we're making the wrong decision? Every day we spend trying to find them, people are dying."

"I know, Mee. But even if we find out where Adaro is, it's not like we can just swim up and kill him. We need a plan. We need their help."

I sighed, expelling another large bubble. I smacked it away irritably. She was right. I'd need the Reinas' help if I wanted to avoid death by leviathan and a thousand soldiers. The serpent might have had two heads, but she wouldn't be able to catch a whole army swarming at once. Would she?

"I already have a few ideas as to where they might be," said Lysi.

"Here I was thinking your plan was to just ask someone if they'd seen a group of traitors flapping around."

She tossed back a lock of coppery-blond hair. "I didn't spend my whole childhood exploring forbidden places for nothing."

"Something I'm thankful for, or I'd never have met you." I kissed her cheek.

Lysi guided us down various currents, taking the most discrete path to Utopia to avoid encountering anyone. We made a few detours, Lysi mumbling things to herself like, "No, didn't think so," and, "Had to try."

I felt tormented, knowing that Adaro had the serpent. My people were no longer his only target. Everyone was vulnerable, but no one knew it yet. Only my friends back home and I knew the true story of the Host of Eriana and how its power was passed.

My insides clenched with a wave of homesickness at the thought of my friends. I was forever separated from them, which made the ache even worse.

They were the reason I had to defeat Adaro. My people had lived in poverty for decades because of him, and now he was more dangerous than ever. I gripped Lysi's hand tighter. She was my comfort in this world that was, admittedly, a bit lonely and frightening.

Maybe I was imagining it, but I thought my emotions had intensified since becoming a mermaid. My love for my people and for the mermaid swimming next to me had become a physical sensation in my skin—a permanent rush of affection.

The sky darkened, summoning tiny glowing things— copepods, Lysi called them—from the depths. The low moan of a whale echoed somewhere ahead.

We travelled a long time without speaking, heading west. I brooded over Adaro the whole time, how much I hated him, and how satisfying it would be to finally kill him. I kept imagining Sisiutl turning her allegiance over to me, her new master. A thrill bloomed in my chest at the thought of controlling something so powerful.

When I turned my senses outwards, I picked up a gloominess about Lysi. I watched her perfect face, gaze fixed ahead, worry pulling at her features.

"What's wrong?"

She glanced to me, quickly smoothing her expression with a smile that didn't reach her eyes. "There are others I'd like to find, too."

"Your friends?"

She'd told me a bit about the group of friends she'd made at the battlefront over the last few weeks. Without having met them, it hurt to know they had all been either killed or forced to scatter after their attempts to get to Adaro. They had been through war together and had protected Lysi. As far as I was concerned, they were worthy friends.

Whenever I asked about them, though, Lysi evaded my questions. She kept saying we had more important things to attend to in a tone that made me feel like I was a recovering hospital patient, even though I kept telling her to stop worrying about me.

Sure enough, she said, "Finding the Reinas and ending this war is more important."

I frowned. She had loved ones at stake as much as I did. At least my parents, friends, and all my people were on Eriana Kwai. I knew exactly where they were. Lysi's were scattered. Her parents were in Utopia—at least, they had been the last time she saw them, months or even years ago. Her brother was battling in the west, if he hadn't been killed. Her few surviving friends from the battlefront could have been anywhere.

I squeezed her hand. "We'll find them."

She avoided my eye. I wondered what she was keeping from me. Was she more worried about her family than she let on? Or was it something else—something about her friends?

Abruptly, she grabbed my arm and pulled me towards her, snapping me out of my thoughts.

"Whoa, hi—"

She clapped a hand over my mouth. "Listen."

Something was drifting below us. Its shape on the current resembled a squid that was at least my size. Was that it? I tuned my senses to our surroundings.

There. Something was approaching from the north. It was more substantial than a school of fish, like a pod of whales. But no. These auras were more distinct than whales.

Lysi and I looked at each other. After three long, frustrating, but glorious days without encountering a soul, it seemed our isolation had come to an end.

CHAPTER TWO - Lysi
Curfew

Whoever this approaching group was, something about them was off. A darkness seemed to drift down the current.

I pulled Meela in the opposite direction.

"We need to move."

After everything we'd done to try and kill King Adaro, I had no doubt we were wanted dead or alive. The question was how wide the news of us had spread.

"Lysi, who are they?"

I hesitated. "I don't know."

I would have sooner drowned than let anything happen to Meela. I'd brought her into this civil war, and I owed her more than this.

"Army?" she whispered.

"I don't think so. I feel both mermaids and mermen." As I said it, I doubted myself. Adaro might have split his armies by gender in the past, but now that he had the serpent, I had no idea what his strategy was. I stopped. "Wait."

The group was approaching from far behind us, but there was also someone lingering up ahead.

"This way." I took off in another direction, dragging Meela with me.

"Couldn't we just act casual and hope they pass?" she suggested half-heartedly.

"Mee, we're enemies of the crown. If someone recognises us …" I shook my head. I had to keep us from being discovered. It was too dangerous. "Let's dive."

We plunged deeper into the blackness.

To my horror, the distant bodies followed. Several figures drew closer, and fast. Were they closing on us?

It was no question. When we turned, so did they. An icy feeling engulfed me.

"They're tailing us," I said. "Go."

We put on a burst of speed. Meela kept pace, making long strokes like I'd taught her.

A landscape of coral sprawled ahead, breaking the emptiness. We plunged in, weaving through the peaks and valleys. The terrain would stop our pursuers from feeling us on the current. Unfortunately, it also prevented us from feeling them.

I listened, but the crackling reef muffled outside noise. Everything was a jumble of activity as the reef fish cleared out of our way.

"Lysi," said Meela, voice breaking, "what are they going to do to us?"

My heart gave a painful squeeze. Fear had turned her eyes blood red. I wished I could tell her something other than the truth: that they probably had orders to take us to Adaro by any means, in any condition.

If we could find somewhere to hide—

We rounded a boulder and I expelled a breath in surprise. A square-set merman blocked our path, eyes blazing through the dim light. His reptilian mouth was creased in a snarl.

He raised his spear. There was a heartbeat of silence. Then, reacting on instinct, I shoved Meela aside.

The spear shot between us and embedded itself in the coral.

"Lysi!"

It was too late. A net had been attached to the spear. The merman had hold of the other end and jerked it across me with one flick of his wrist. I was trapped beneath it, beating my tail against the rocks in blind panic, sand and plants whirling around me.

"Go, Meela!"

She lunged for the merman and sank her teeth into his arm.

My scream was drowned out by his roar of pain. He swung a fist but Meela propelled herself backwards just in time.

I struggled against the net. The sight of the merman trying to attack Meela sent hot anger through me, a tight pressure building in my chest.

I found an opening and ripped myself free. My tail got caught and I spun to untangle it, hands trembling from the panic of being stuck. I wriggled loose and shot towards Meela, only to slam straight into another mermaid. She grinned, revealing a missing front tooth.

"What do you want?" I shouted, trying to yank free from her grasp. Had Adaro promised a reward for our capture?

In answer, the mermaid swung a mace at my head.

"Coral, Meela!" I said, dodging the weapon.

She would be no match for a merman in a battle of strength, but agility was another matter—even for a new mermaid like Meela. She could lose him in the maze below.

"You'll follow?" she said.

"Yes!"

She dove, and at once the merman gave chase.

The mermaid with the missing tooth swung at me again. I grabbed the mace handle, stopping it before its jagged end could strike. I was a nose away from her snarling lips. She was so beaten and grimy, I wondered what had happened to her. Then I slammed my tail into her gut and knocked the air from her lungs.

I spun and took off after Meela.

They had vanished from sight, but faint ripples hit me as the merman crashed into walls of coral. I followed their wake, dipping and weaving between the rocks.

How could I have let this happen? I should have kept Meela safe instead of exposing her to this emptiness where anyone could sense us. She was still too inexperienced in her new body.

I slowed for a moment, casting my senses. My every fibre vibrated. I'd lost them.

Then a terrible scream echoed through the coral—not from ahead, but behind.

I whirled around and shot upwards, rising above the coral to scan the area. It was empty and silent, save for the crackling reef. Her scream dissipated on the current.

Suddenly Meela burst from the coral, panic on her face. When she saw me, her mouth opened in surprise. She was alone.

There was a laugh like grinding stone. "Aw, they did think it was each other. That's so cute."

The toothless mermaid rose behind her.

"Look out!" I shouted.

Meela darted upwards—a mistake she had not yet learned from. Toothless chased her to the surface and cornered her easily against it. In one fluid motion she grabbed Meela's tail and slammed the mace into her stomach.

I streaked towards them, ready to break the mermaid's arm, but Meela let loose a roar and spun, punching her face and neck with trained skill.

Something slammed into me from the side, knocking precious air from my lungs. My energy was draining, the exertion depleting the oxygen I had left. Before I could orient myself, a thick hand wrapped itself around my throat.

I thrashed wildly, but the merman squeezed tighter, pulling me into a headlock. I pried on his massive arm, his hand slowly crushing my windpipe.

I searched for Meela and found her still near the surface, a whirl of fists and teeth. Toothless was backing off, arms thrown up in defense.

Amid the chaos, a blonde mermaid who looked no older than fourteen snuck up behind them. She was tiny, scarred and beaten, but there was something fierce about her. Clenched in her webbed fist was a black blade.

I tried to shout to Meela, but the words came out as a croak.

The young mermaid dove into the fray and emerged soon after, dragging a roaring Meela by the hair.

"Sounded like you needed help over here," she said in a high, youthful voice.

"We had them," said Toothless, clutching her throat where Meela's punch had landed.

The large group we'd felt approaching drew nearer. I sensed the presence of at least a hundred mermaids and mermen.

The young mermaid jerked Meela's hair. "Who are you?"

My heart pounded. Did they not know? Why had they been after us, then?

Meela opened her mouth, but I choked out a couple of syllables before she could speak. The merman loosened his grip.

"What?"

"We're in His Majesty's army," I coughed.

"Ha!" said Toothless. "Then what are you doing so close to Utopia?"

"We're on our way back from the Battle for Eriana Kwai."

The young mermaid pointed her blade at me. "I'll skin your face for lying. That battle ended long ago."

"Fleeing, no doubt," said the merman, his voice loud in my ear. "Bet they're former humans."

The young mermaid studied us. Her eyes lingered on Meela. I wondered if they could tell by her aura.

Either way, we would be better off if they assumed we were fleeing because of that—and not because we were traitors to the crown.

"You had fair warning about breaking curfew," said Toothless. "You're coming with us."

Curfew? Had I heard that right? Since when did Utopia have a curfew?

The approaching group finally closed in, engulfing us like the mouth of a blue whale. The merman released my throat and I rubbed at the tender skin, glancing around.

No, this was definitely not an army. The crowd was weaponless and had a fearful aura. They were mostly older merpeople. The weedy scent of ungroomed bodies wafted through the water.

Surrounding them were armed guards and at least a dozen black marlins. Wherever they were going, these merpeople were being moved against their will.

Meela eyed the marlins.

"Keep your distance," I whispered. Twice the size of a mermaid, their solid, streamlined bodies and pointed beaks were made for hunting.

The merman who'd been strangling me sneered at Meela. "Not from around here?"

Meela shot him a blood-red glare.

Our captors fell into position among the surrounding guards. I glanced to their weapons, the marlins, and then to Meela. She gave me a meaningful look. I shook my head once to indicate it would be unwise to try and escape.

"Keep going," barked the young mermaid.

The group travelled southwards, taking us with them. An elderly couple with silvery hair fell in behind us, watching us cautiously.

Heart still pounding, I seized Meela's hand, determined not to be separated. She squeezed back, but her attention was elsewhere.

Her eyes flicked from guard to guard. We would have to find an opportunity somehow—maybe when we stopped to rest. But for now we were surrounded on all sides, trapped between shallow floor and sunlit surface.

After some time, a low chatter picked up among the guards, and I risked a small whisper to Meela.

"Are you all right? How's your tail? Is anything sore?"

The merman on Meela's other side overheard me and eyed her. "What's wrong with your tail, 'ey?"

He had sunken cheeks, long, grey hair, and a tremulous voice that cracked like driftwood.

"Nothing," Meela snapped. "I'm fine."

She went back to observing the group. I raked my senses over her and decided she was telling the truth.

I peered across her to the merman. He was casting an appraising glance over us.

"Why is there a curfew?" I said.

He glanced shiftily to me, then fixed his beady red eyes ahead as though he hadn't heard me.

"We've been on the battlefront," I said.

He didn't respond. His shoulders were getting more hunched, making him look ancient and frail. I might have felt bad for him if I wasn't so desperate to know what was going on.

When I kept staring, he said, "We have to be ready for anything, don't we, 'ey? What with His Majesty's armies on the move."

On the move?

"Has he started advancing on the Atlantic?"

"No."

"Where is he now?"

The merman twisted his fingers, eyes darting as though searching for an escape.

"Come on," I said. "We're allowed to talk about what's happening, aren't we?"

He glanced at the guards, pressing his lips firmly together. Was any discussion of the king discouraged, then? So much had changed, even in the few tidecycles I'd been away from Utopia.

The silvery mermaid behind us spoke up. "Everything else is united under the crown. Now he's using the, uh—serpent—to move humans away from the coast."

She pronounced *serpent* as though speaking of the incarnation of death. I supposed the thing was even more terrible to those who didn't know where it came from.

Then again, apart from witnessing its reawakening on Eriana Kwai, did I even know where it had come from? The real legend was as much a mystery as how it could be destroyed.

"The entire coast?" said Meela, her attention now on the conversation. She still hadn't reverted to a normal state.

"That's his plan, last we heard." The mermaid looked to the merman next to her, presumably her husband. He offered a reassuring smile.

"And the Atlantic," I said.

She nodded.

"When?"

She glanced to her husband again. He gave a feeble shrug.

How close was Adaro to ruling the seas? Had he really taken over everywhere below surface except the Atlantic? The day he decided to move in on the Atlantic would be a critical one. That was the last kingdom, and the largest. Queen Medusa was the remaining chance at stopping him.

"Where are we going, then?" said Meela.

I glanced at the miserable faces around us. The merman beside her finally spoke. "We're helping His Majesty's expansion."

Meela looked around. "By doing what?"

"His Majesty needs a powerful force to get rid of all humans between here and the coast."

"More powerful than the Host?"

The merman squinted at her. "'ey? The what?"

"The serpent."

"You called it a Host—"

"I meant to say serpent."

"Why—?"

"Never mind," I said. "What's he doing with us?"

The merman puffed himself up—a less-than-impressive gesture. "Something to annihilate as many Pacific humans as possible."

"Okay," I said slowly. "How?"

"Can you think of nothing that would span half an ocean with its power?"

Meela shuddered beside me. She was staring at the merman with an odd expression.

"What is it?" I asked.

"A tsunami," said Meela.

I scoffed. "You can't control a tsunami. They're caused by earthquakes."

"Yes, and what causes earthquakes?" said the merman.

"Shifting plates," said Meela.

He nodded. "There's a boundary near the Moonless City where plates converge. If we can shift the pressure by relocating the rock—"

"You can't *cause* an earthquake!" I said.

"You forget, girl, how far into the crust the deep sea goes."

My insides felt like ice. Adaro had growing armies, he had the serpent, and now he was planning to bend nature to his will. How many humans would die if a tsunami of that magnitude hit the Pacific shores? Would the humans retaliate? Could they?

"But this doesn't explain where we're going," said Meela.

The answer dawned on me, and I stopped moving. The silvery mermaid crashed into me, setting off a chain reaction behind her.

"I'm sorry, love," she said, smoothing my hair as if to repair damage. "Sorry," she added to the line behind her.

Meela grabbed my hand and pulled me onwards.

The guards hollered at everyone to keep moving. Meela waited until they'd averted their attention again before speaking.

"Lysi, what?"

Her expression told me she felt my fear. I tried to calm myself. She didn't need to know the extent of Adaro's labour camp. It would only scare her.

"Nothing."

"Not *nothing*!"

To my dismay, the silvery mermaid whispered, "I hear there's magma. It keeps killing everyone, erupting in random places. Gets worse, the more they dig."

"Dig? Who? You mean us?" said Meela.

"He gets non-military civilians to help," I said. Now it made sense why most of these captives were older. "I knew about the camp, but—I never knew what they were doing."

The silvery mermaid said, "I hear it's so deep that the only light comes from those trench fish. You can't eat those, obviously, so everyone's starving."

"Plus, the guards have tempers like tiger sharks," said her husband. "The pressure and rationed air is enough to drive them mad. They'll kill anyone who's gotten too bloody to keep digging."

I wanted to reassure Meela that these were just rumours. But when it came to Adaro, rumours usually turned out to be true. I recalled the stories of deaths and disappearances growing up—rumours that turned out to have disturbing patterns.

The situation was devastating. The labourers were miserable, the guards were miserable, yet all of them would keep obeying orders. They would stay down there until they died. Of course, if everyone revolted at once, there'd be no stopping them. But that would never happen. There was too much fear, too much uncertainty about whose side anyone was on. That was why the armies kept fighting. That was what kept everyone at the labour camp. That was what kept us fighting this war.

The merman beside Meela scoffed.

When we all turned to look at him, he said, "It might be a hagfeast down there, but we all know the reason, don't we, 'ey?"

I raised my eyebrows.

"Why is Utopia facing food shortages?" he said, seeming to find new energy. "Why are we losing lives every time we go near a beach? Who is brutally attacking us with iron? I'm ashamed I was ever one of them."

Meela gaped. I wanted to cover her ears before they could spew more horrors at her, when the last thing he'd said sunk in.

"You're a former human?"

The treatment of former humans had come up a lot lately. Under Adaro's reign, the subject was taking a terrifying direction. Resistance to this had been what unified the guys who'd tried to assassinate Adaro with me. They'd all been related to former humans who had been mistreated. One of them was a former human himself.

My stomach twisted. I still had not told Meela about Nilus. The knowledge that her big brother was alive swelled in my conscience, growing worse with each passing day. After finding out days prior, I'd sworn I would tell her as soon as I got a chance. Now, several chances seemed to have come and gone, and still I couldn't bring it up. All these years, Meela had assumed her brother was dead. I was the only one who knew he was alive and that he was a merman.

The problem was that I didn't know where Nilus was, if he'd been captured, or worse. What if I told Meela he was alive and then we found out he'd been killed since I last saw him? I would be dropping a bomb on her for nothing. She had already been through so much in the last few days—forced to abandon everything she knew and everyone she loved. I couldn't put more stress on her.

"We're all former humans, aren't we, 'ey?" said the merman.

"You are—I mean—we are?" I said.

"Except maybe her."

He nodded towards the end of the group, where a mermaid with a bright orange and blue tail swam a little apart from everyone else.

My heart leapt. That was a southern mermaid. She was like the ones I'd seen from the Moonless City. Like the Reinas.

"Wait," said Meela, apparently struggling with her thoughts. "How can you … Sure, people are overfishing, but you said Adaro is keeping everyone in Utopia on a curfew. Food shortages in Utopia have nothing to do with humans—"

I jabbed her in the ribs. This wasn't the time for anti-Adaro arguments. She waved me away and pressed on.

"The reason people are killing mermaids on beaches is because the mermaids are *trying to eat them!*"

"Meela," I said sharply.

"What? You don't think this is—?"

"We can talk about this later. Just shut up."

She shot me a glare. I glared back. We didn't need to get ourselves or anyone else in trouble for conspiracy. By the looks of it, these merpeople had already experienced brutal treatment. My heart ached for them. Soon, in the painful depths of the labour camp, things were about to get a hundred times worse.

We had to get away from here. We needed to find the Reinas before Adaro did irreversible damage.

Meela glanced at the silvery couple.

"A former human had best learn her place in Adaro's kingdom," said the merman beside her, who was now projecting thorough dislike.

A muscle flexed in Meela's jaw.

"Mee." I tilted my head towards the southern mermaid. "I think I know her. Come on."

Our neighbours gave off a sense of relief as we drifted away. I couldn't help watching Meela push her hands out adorably to balance against the current.

"Where do you know her from?"

"I don't," I whispered. "But she's southern. An ally. I want to talk to her."

Was I naive to think she was a Reina, just because of her appearance? The South Pacific Kingdom had been here long before Adaro arrived in the north. Surely they were united in their resistance. I hoped so—and thinking about the labour camp turned that hope into desperation.

We swam slowly, letting others pass, until we drew parallel with the southern mermaid.

Her body was lean, her bones sharp, her tail long—an evolutionary difference between south and north. Blue gems pierced her cheekbones, nose, and collarbone. Her brown hair was thick and dreadlocked. She must have been in her thirties, with several lifetimes of scars across her body.

She glanced at us sideways.

"You're from the south," I said.

"Nothing deceives you," said the mermaid.

"Excuse me?"

"What would you like?"

I squinted, trying to get a read on her. Strange accent aside, her aura was hard to decipher.

"What's your name?" said Meela, picking up the awkward silence.

"What is yours?"

"Meela. This is Lysi."

"Deiopea."

"Are you a former human?" I said.

She narrowed her eyes at me.

"Everyone else here is, so I wondered—"

"No." She tossed a dreadlock over her shoulder. "I was not a human, nor am I descended from one."

As I suspected, she was taken captive because she was southern. Did that mean Adaro was trying to dispose of anyone whose loyalty didn't lie with him? I wondered who in Utopia was truly safe, and, given these prisoners' opinions of humans, what lies they were being fed.

"What were you doing this far north?" I said.

"I was searching for a new place to live."

Liar, I thought, feeling the skip in her pulse.

There was one explanation. A southern mermaid wouldn't come this far north unless she was part of the Reinas. She could take us to them.

Meela was silent.

I chose my words carefully, aware there might be prying ears. "If you're up north for the reason I think, we want to join you."

I watched her closely, but Deiopea showed no sign of recognition. She fixed her gaze ahead. "You are speaking nonsense."

"I met some southern merpeople a few days ago," I persisted. "Right near Eriana Kwai. They helped me. I said *para la rein—*"

Deiopea clapped a hand over my mouth. "What is the matter with you?"

Triumphant, I pushed her away. "I knew it."

Her eyes flashed red. "You do not just blurt such things!"

"So you believe us, then?" I whispered. "We're on your side."

Deiopea studied me for a long while before saying, "I cannot tell you what you wish to know."

Despite her stubbornness, my heart jumped. She knew where they were.

I nodded towards Meela. "Do you know who this is?"

Meela glanced furtively at me.

"Please enlighten me," said Deiopea flatly.

"This is Metlaa Gaela, descendant of Eriana. Do you know what Adaro has control of at this moment?"

Deiopea hesitated. She seemed interested despite herself. "They are saying it is the most fearsome being in the world, and it rivals the power of the original Medusa."

"It's true."

I paused. An idea had been smouldering in the back of my mind, and at her words about rivalling the power of Medusa, it glowed a bit brighter. I pushed the thought aside for later.

"Deiopea, the serpent came from Eriana Kwai. Meela is a former human, and she knows more than any of us about it."

Deiopea squinted at us. "You are making this up."

"I'm not."

"He tried to kill me to get it," whispered Meela. "He tried to kill Lysi."

After a moment, Deiopea said, "He has tried to kill many. It has not stopped any of you from fighting loyally for him."

"Ever since Adaro came to the Pacific," whispered Meela, "my people have been descending further into poverty. We can't fish. We can't leave by boat. We can't go near the beach without getting attacked."

Deiopea stared ahead, appearing disinterested.

"Every spring," Meela continued, "my people send a ship to Utopia to try and win back our freedom. We call it the Massacre. Every spring, Adaro has killed our warriors. He killed my friends, my allies. My brother."

My stomach clenched. A voice in my head scolded me, telling me I was a terrible friend and girlfriend, and dishonest, and a coward.

"He tried to kill you, too?" said Deiopea, turning to me. "Why?"

Because I tried to assassinate him twice, I thought.

I shook my head and muttered, "Not here."

Deiopea narrowed her eyes, her lips tightening at the corners. I would need to do better if I wanted her to trust me.

I lowered my voice to barely a whisper. "There was a group of us. The first time was at the mine. You probably heard how that ended. The second time, we tailed him and tried to use iron. Several of our group were killed."

Deiopea turned to look at me properly for the first time. The pain on her face betrayed so much more than her guise.

"I don't know where my mom and dad are," I said in a hollow voice. "Or my brother. Considering the crime I'm wanted for, I wouldn't be surprised if they've been captured."

I had been trying not to think about my family. There was nothing I could do to help them.

I felt Meela's gaze on me and looked away.

Matching my barely audible tones, Deiopea said, "When Adaro's troops invaded the Moonless City and took the queen, we rallied against him with all we had. We barely had a military. There had been no need. Adaro took the city far too easily. My husband and son were killed the same day he invaded."

"I'm sorry," I whispered.

"That's awful," said Meela.

"I have nothing left to lose, now. When he imposed the curfew and forbade anyone to leave the city, I fought. When he reduced the food and supplies coming in, I fought. When we were ordered to report any former humans so they could undergo a screening—" She huffed, expelling a large bubble. "The Moonless City is sometimes called the City of Colour, did you know?"

I blinked at the change of subject, shaking my head.

"I've never seen it less colourful than it was before I left. Adaro's occupation drained all life from the coral, the fish, the buildings. It was so quiet. No one knew what would happen to us. Would he force us to fight his war? Would he keep us there until we starved? Kill us all for resisting?"

She glared at the ocean floor. Rage and vengeance seemed to fill her like a pufferfish.

"I will not drift idly by while that happens. He cannot strip the colour from my city. He cannot take away my queen."

"You're right," said Meela. "He can't. That's why we need to get to—to where we want to go."

Deiopea looked at her sharply.

"Come with us," I whispered. "When we …"

When we escape, I thought, letting it be implied. There were too many potential ears listening in.

Still, we must have given off an air of conspiracy because the nearest guard, a pale, dark-haired mermaid with an expression like someone had shoved a dead fish under her nose, shouted, "Enough whispering!"

She twirled her mace. All conversation died.

I raised my eyebrows meaningfully at Deiopea. She fixed her eyes ahead and swam in silence for a moment. When the guard finally turned away, Deiopea glanced at me, quickly, just long enough to nod once.

CHAPTER THREE - Ben
Kodiak, Alaska

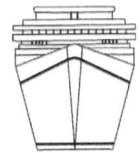

Benjamin Reeves had trained for disaster scenarios for the greater part of his life. Earthquakes, forest fires, storms, and tsunamis. Terrorist attacks. He was prepared to help in any situation. Except this one.

He was cruising the long way home in his pickup truck, windows down, summer breeze lifting the hair on his arms. His mind was still on the matte black twin-engine helicopter that Bagh had just shown him—the latest addition to the air wing.

"LM-80 Cormorant. Long-range enough for a medevac from the middle of the ocean. This thing's designed for anti-submarine, anti-ship, search and rescue, cargo lift, special ops, you name it."

Reeves was wondering whether said special ops included him when he noticed the group of people gathered in the harbour.

They were pointing at something in the distance, which he at first took to be a huge pod of orcas. Several people were taking pictures.

He rolled to a stop in an empty intersection and squinted through the sun's glare.

His mouth slowly fell open. Not whales.

The vast shape in the water rose and fell through the surface in a connected wave, bigger than his mind could comprehend.

Sitting in the idling truck, Reeves scrambled to regain his slipping hold on reality. He clung to one certainty like a buoy: this thing, whatever it was, was heading for shore.

He shut off the truck so he could listen. People were beginning to panic. He could hear them shouting. He wrenched his seatbelt off and flung open the truck door.

By the time his feet hit the pavement, the thing was already in the harbour. Reeves cursed as a shower of seawater erupted like a mine.

Several people screamed. Dogs pulled at their leashes, barking frantically. The crowd began to sprint away from the shore as the mammoth creature crested the waves.

On the passenger's seat, Reeves' phone rang. He stood in the intersection, frozen by what he was seeing, when the scream of a child cut through the noise.

Propelled into action, he dove across the seat for his phone and then sprinted towards the shore with trained agility, phone at his ear.

The voice on the other end was frantic. "Reeves, I need you to get to the harbour—" It was his superior, Officer Miller.

The screaming girl's mother scooped her up. She took off towards the parking lot.

"I'm here, sir."

"What the hell is going on?"

"I was hoping you'd tell me."

"All I know is we got a distress call from the coast guard, and then we lost contact."

The tsunami siren erupted, an unceasing wail from the top of several masts along the shoreline. At this, people burst out of nearby homes and shops.

"Sir, it's unclear what—"

At the end of the docks, something rose out of the water that made Reeves stop in his tracks. It was a black serpent's head, as large as the moored speedboats, a flare of horns at the back of its skull. A blast of seawater rained from nostrils the size of basketballs. The serpent tasted the air.

"Reeves, you there?"

The serpent closed in, crushing the sailboats in its path and sending swells of water high enough to capsize the rest. Several people on the docks vanished beneath the waves.

Reeves lowered the phone and raced closer to the beach.

"Get out of the water!" he bellowed.

The dock shattered beneath the serpent's weight. It did not seem to feel the shards of wood and fibreglass dragging under its scales.

People on the shore were running and screaming. Reeves stopped briefly to usher an elderly couple up the steps leading to the parking lot, then turned back in time to see the creature reach land, not a hundred feet away. The scrape of its scales across the pavement rose above the wailing siren and the noise of the crowd.

He pulled civilians back from the shore, shouting at them to get to their vehicles and to pile in as many people as they could.

A series of shrill barks rent the air and Reeves looked around, eyes landing on a border collie that had been left tied to a bike rack. He pelted across the beach and ducked next to the dog, its breath hot and fast on his neck as he freed its collar from the leash. The border collie fled without looking back, nails skittering across the pavement.

There was a deafening boom.

Reeves threw himself behind the bike rack and peered up through the bars.

The serpent's great head had shattered the boathouse with the force of a crashing meteor. Its horns caught on the roof and peeled the rafters off, throwing them across the beach like twigs in a windstorm. Reeves flung his arms up, protecting his head as one soared towards him. It crashed over the bike rack and snapped in two, the pieces landing on either side of him.

The slit pupils narrowed further as the serpent peered down on the chaos, as if inspecting its own efforts.

Further out, three men shot across the water in a speedboat, fleeing in the opposite direction. The small boat powered over the swells and whirlpools left by the serpent, and for a moment, Reeves thought they would escape unharmed.

Then a second serpent breached the water.

Its massive head shadowed the speedboat like an eclipse. The water cascading off of it was enough to flood the boat, which rocked violently under the deluge. The screams of the men on board carried faintly on the wind.

Reeves scanned the water, breathing hard. Was there an entire pack of them?

The immense jaws hovering over the boat opened with a noise like splintering wood. Saliva and seawater dripped from fangs that were each the size of a man's arm.

Two of the men dove off while the driver cowered beneath the wheel. None of it mattered. When the serpent struck, its jaws closed over the boat and all.

Reeves watched the men disappear with mounting horror that numbed his body.

Finished with its meal, the second serpent swung around and followed the path of its mate onto the beach. It reached the shallows and—

Oh, no. The two heads were connected to the same body. This was a single leviathan, a head at each end.

The breath caught in Reeves' chest. Dimly, he realised he was still clutching his phone and lifted it to his ear.

"Reeves! God dammit—"

"I'm here, sir."

"We're sending help. We need to nuke this thing before it takes out all of Kodiak."

Reeves sank to his knees behind the bike rack, heart pounding. He'd spent his whole life training for this—from Cadets, to the Navy, through every screening, assessment, and boot camp, topping it all off with survival training at the Naval Special Warfare Cold Weather Detachment. So why did he feel so ill-prepared all of a sudden?

He looked at the serpent's body, studying the hundreds of coal-black scales that glittered like armour. His gaze drifted to the water.

"What the hell is the procedure, here?" said Officer Miller. "Is this a natural disaster?"

There. Reeves' eyes locked onto something that sent a chill through him. Perched on a rock next to a hazard buoy and watching the chaos unfold, black hair dripping beneath a black crown, was an enormous merman.

As Reeves watched, the demon raised and lowered his arms repeatedly. What was he doing? Reeves studied the odd movements, then turned back to the serpent in time to see one of the heads close its jaws around a parked SUV and crush it like it was made of spun glass.

The merman was still gesturing from the rock. Was the serpent responding to this in some way?

The merman raised his left arm as though pushing the air, and the second head moved along the shore, the great black body curling around itself.

With a glance around to make sure no more civilians were at risk, Reeves ran back to the road, staying low. The shoreline was ravaged, ghostly.

"Sir, I think this is related to the mermaids," he said, panting.

A pause. "How do you know?"

"One of them is out in the water. A male."

Over the tsunami siren, another wail pierced the air as several police cars peeled into the intersection. The officers leapt out, drawing guns and firing at once. The bullets ricocheted off the serpent's armour with a series of *clinks*. It didn't surprise Reeves that the weapons did nothing.

"I think the merman is controlling the serpent, sir. It's the way he's moving."

As he said it, he wished it wasn't true. He knew what this meant.

Sure enough, after a long pause, Officer Miller said, "You know what to do, chief."

Reeves rubbed a hand over his forehead. The siren was starting to make his head ache.

"Sir, Perseus isn't ready yet."

"She might not be pretty, but she's ready for duty."

The serpent continued to ransack the harbour. The sea demon's plan evidently involved destroying every man-made structure along the shoreline. Bullets continued to ricochet off the creature's armour.

"Sir, I think our priority should be to go straight for this merman. He's got a black crown. I think he's their king."

"All the more reason! This is an act of war, Reeves. They've broken our treaty."

"*He* has broken our treaty."

"Look, California has gotten four distress calls in the last three days from ships being attacked by mermaids. This is no coincidence."

Reeves hurried to his truck and slid into the driver's seat, the sirens muffled only slightly as he slammed the door. He squeezed his eyes shut and willed himself not to argue.

Memories flashed through his mind as though thrown into the path of a lighthouse, blazing painfully for an instant and fading just as fast. Caramel skin and dark hair. Brilliant brown eyes and a warm smile that left him feeling inexplicably safe.

He had never told anyone about her. Nights when he could not sleep found him wondering if she had even been real.

But he had survived that day because of her.

Miller was breathing hard on the other end of the phone. "I'm contacting the Secretary of State. Operation Perseus is launching as soon as we get the go-ahead. As far as I'm concerned, this is an act of war."

In the intersection, the police backed away, cast into the shadow of the advancing serpent. Reeves started the truck and threw it into reverse.

An act of war, yes. But on whose orders? Were all merpeople to blame, or this one demon?

If everything he'd ever been told about them was true, Reeves would have drowned during that storm. The icy sea had nearly swallowed him whole. He remembered the panic mounting as he realised, strong swimmer though he was, he could not fight the waves and get to the life buoy cast out by his yelling shipmates. When the veil of rain blocked his view of the ship, that should have been the end.

What that mermaid had done was not an act of war.

"Yes, sir," he said hollowly.

He couldn't prove she had been real. He couldn't prove she'd pulled him to the buoy and placed it over his head. The team had not seen it.

But he didn't think she'd been a hallucination. He should have drowned that day.

He knew, of course, that mermaids had a predatory drive and an allure that scientists tried to study on a chemical level. He'd heard about the experiments. He had always wondered if the mermaid's sweetness was a product of that allure.

Either way, he owed her his life.

He shook his head, forbidding himself to go there.

Tomorrow, he would gear up with the rest of his SEAL Team several months ahead of schedule. He would push aside that memory and do what he had been training for.

With his team at his back, he would retaliate against this act of terrorism for the sake of his country.

But he would not ignore his intuition. He had spent years learning to trust that feeling. And now, more strongly than ever, it was telling him to hunt down that merman on the rock out there, and kill him.

CHAPTER FOUR - Lysi
Deiopea's Promise

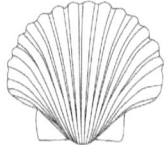

The floor dropped away and blackness took its place. Countless fish rose from beyond the twilight layer as the sun disappeared. Some of them glowed, making the world below as speckled as the sky above. Other fish were invisible to the eye. Some had tentacles so long, they stretched beyond my senses.

Meela stuck close to me.

"They won't hurt you," I whispered.

I was more concerned about the guards and black marlins on all sides.

The further we got from Utopia, the darker Meela's aura became. I knew what she was thinking. Adaro was probably killing humans that very moment, and we were moving further from the possibility of stopping him. I understood she was worried someone else would get to Adaro first, but I wished she would quit letting this consume her. Her every thought seemed focused on how to hunt him, kill him, destroy him. I worried what the obsession was doing to her.

My stomach clenched, the hunger painful. How long had we been swimming? How much longer until we had to dive to get to the labour camp?

I knew better than to say anything. On the last breach, a merman made the mistake of asking the guards if we were going to stop to sleep or eat. He got a conch shell to the face.

The guards, on the other hand, shared the meals they'd packed along. Even the marlins received portions of shrimp and cuttlefish.

Our pace slowed as our energy drained. Several times, I caught my eyes closing and shook my head to stay awake.

The guards barked at us to move faster.

"If any of you fall behind, you'll get a beating!"

The world above turned from black to a soft navy. We'd been swimming all night. Beside me, Meela grew limp, and I grabbed her before she could drift into anyone.

"Thanks," she mumbled.

"Are you feeling okay? Hold onto me. I don't want you drifting into the marlins."

"Lysi, I'm not holding onto you like a little kid."

"But what if you—?"

"I'm fine!"

She tried to pry her arm from my hand, but I held on, afraid she'd fall behind.

Deiopea spoke, voice so quiet I nearly missed it. "The last thing my husband told me was to protect our son from Adaro. He did not know our son had been killed moments before."

Her eyes flicked down to my hand. I let Meela go, realising I was probably embarrassing both of us.

"It's terrible, what you went through," said Meela.

Deiopea closed her eyes and let out a puff of air. I didn't know what to say, so I waited. After a moment her aura seemed to lighten, and she continued.

"My son died stopping a school raid. Adaro's soldiers were trying to take them to Utopia for military training. The children were fleeing through the back. My son stopped the army at the front door. That was where he died. His actions stalled the army long enough to give the children time to escape. We placed them into hiding."

"You must be proud of him," I said.

"Pride, adoration, love. Words are not strong enough to describe how I feel. But for a long time, I believed I had failed him and my husband. I let him die when I could have tried harder to protect him. Now I understand that sometimes you cannot protect your loved ones, no matter how hard you try. Life and death happen, and it is out of our control."

I said nothing. Maybe that was true, to an extent. There was a permanent ache in the back of my mind for my parents and brother. I had no idea where they were, and nothing I did could control whether they were alive or dead, or whether I would see them again.

But Meela was here with me. As much as I could help it, her survival would be completely under my control.

"Adaro's made sure everyone has lost someone they love," said Meela.

Deiopea regarded her sadly. "I am sorry about your brother, Meela."

There was that clenching feeling again. I had to tell her.

But today was no better than yesterday or the day before. I still didn't know where Nilus was. I still didn't know if Meela would get to see him again, or how she would take the news, if she would break down or be angry at me.

It's never going to be the right moment to tell her, said a voice in my head.

She had to know, eventually. Now was as good and bad a time as ever. What if the worst happened and I never got the chance?

Do it now, said the voice.

My tongue felt too fat for my mouth. Would I be able to get the words out?

Shouts jolted me from my thoughts. Something violent was happening through the darkness ahead. Currents pulsed towards us. Bubbles, moving bodies. Something huge churned the water.

Everyone, both captives and guards, flocked to the surface. A moment passed before I realised what they were clinging to. Huge, solid, and man-made, the long keel of a sailboat undulated through the water.

"Mermaids, come forwards," shouted the guards.

There was a scuffle as every female moved ahead. Deiopea and I exchanged a glance. If they were sending mermaids first, that meant—

"Come on! First ones to lure them get the free meal."

"No," whispered Meela.

Before I could stop her, she darted forwards.

"Mee!"

I chased after her. She shoved into the crowd and vanished.

The guards' weapons cracked against the hull. Mermen pushed the swinging keel while mermaids pulled themselves up, disappearing through the surface.

I hurried through the crowd, searching frantically. I didn't want Meela to see what was about to happen. Plus, if the humans had iron weapons …

"Stop!" I heard her scream. "They haven't done anything!"

I spun in the direction of her voice. A merman in my path motioned upwards.

"Want a boost?"

I snarled. "Get out of my way."

He raised his hands. "Hey, if you want to pass up a free meal—"

"Meela?!" *Where was she?*

The crowd thickened, trapping me between them and the hull.

Finally, I caught a glimpse of her at the keel, trying to stop a brunette mermaid from climbing it. I shot towards her and grabbed her arm.

"Mee, get out of there!"

The brunette shot us a terrified look, evidently afraid of being seen with anyone disobeying orders. She continued upwards.

Meela pulled away. "We can't let these attacks keep happening."

Someone bumped into her, and I drew her into me. We were much too close to the boat. How Meela expected to stop this from happening, I didn't know—but she didn't understand the risks of being so near to humans. I had to get her out of here.

Someone screamed. A sting exploded across my skin as something made of iron plunged into the waves. The scar on my waist seared. I recoiled, bumping into others.

"What is that?" said Meela, fearful now.

Burning flesh met my nose. The Battle for Eriana Kwai, the assassination attempts, every terrible memory I had burst to the front of my mind. My head clouded with panic, but I kept my hold on Meela tight. We had to get away before one of us was hit.

A gap opened below us. I dove, dragging Meela with me, but she struggled to swim back up, her attention on the crowd.

"We can't let them do this!"

I pulled hard, forcing her to look at me. "Meela, you have to be careful now. You can't trust humans anymore."

Everyone was shouting. Some mermaids still climbed the ship. Others tried to back away. Meela's mouth opened and closed as though trying to get air. My insides seemed to melt with her pain.

"I'm sorry," I said. "There's nothing we can—"

Something occurred to me. I glanced around, taking inventory. Even the guards swarmed the boat—only a few hanging back to keep the circling marlins under control.

Deiopea caught my eye.

My heart thudded faster. I grazed Meela's arm to get her attention. She cast me a distracted glance. I nodded at the boat, and then to Deiopea.

Meela's expression changed as she caught on.

The boat lurched. There was an uproar, and everyone moved in like piranhas.

I smelled blood. Moments later, a cloud bloomed near the stern.

Meela met my eyes, her face pleading—but we couldn't save those people. This was so far out of my control.

The marlins must have smelled the blood, too, because all of them began fighting their way closer. A guard swung his longblade at one but it dodged the weapon swiftly.

In a blink, all the marlins were plunging into the frenzy, ignoring commands. The guards closed in, shouting.

There was no time to consider.

"Go," I said.

Meela, Deiopea, and I turned tails to the surface and shot downwards.

For several moments, we swam headlong. No one called after us. The lightening sky overhead did nothing to help us hide. We kept going until blackness engulfed us.

The current shifted. Someone was following us—but made no sound. Unless my senses were mistaken, this was the silvery mermaid and merman who'd been behind us the night before. They fled quickly, a few fathoms closer to the surface than us.

"Bolters!" a guard shouted.

Meela grabbed my hand. "Faster!"

My senses picked up a flurry of activity, and we plunged, Deiopea sticking close beside us.

The same merman shouted, "Marlins!"

I glanced over my shoulder and a chill ran down my spine. Two marlins had broken away from the boat. They shot after the couple, a few fathoms up. The couple was weak, tired. The marlins closed in, twice as fast, twice as powerful.

Screams broke out and blood spread through the water like a cloud. The marlins were a whirl of slashing beaks and tails. They lunged at the couple again and again.

"Look out!" said Deiopea.

Another marlin sped away from the boat, heading for the three of us.

There was nowhere to hide. The water was too open. Our only option was to outswim it.

"Are mermaids faster than marlin?" said Meela, voice high with fear.

"Just keep going. Long strokes."

Despite my worry, she kept up. I didn't need to slow my pace.

We zigzagged, breaking apart and convening at random, trying to throw it off. The marlin was solid, streamlined, with snake-like agility. The sail on its back waved as its powerful body swung back and forth. Its focus was absolute.

Out of nowhere, another marlin darted at us. Meela and Deiopea screamed. We scattered. For a moment, the fish didn't seem to know who to chase. It twisted around and found the closest target, firing towards me like an iron bolt. I flipped over its dorsal fin, the rigid flesh brushing my waist. It whirled around.

Meela was several lengths ahead. Its focus landed on Deiopea.

Deiopea and I locked eyes over the marlin's sail. If that fish had been the only one, she would have had time to escape. She opened her mouth—to speak, maybe—and the first marlin slammed into her side. I hadn't felt it coming.

The pointed beak caught her arm. Deiopea grunted and rolled away. Blood seeped from the gash.

"Deiopea!" I shouted.

The second marlin lunged. It struck her dead-on.

"No," I sobbed.

The marlin's beak sank into her body. Her mouth gaped, and she hung as though suspended by rope in the water.

A lump rose in my throat. Meela and I had convinced her to come with us. Were we so selfish to risk Deiopea's life?

I wanted to say I was sorry. I wanted to take back every thought I'd had that she'd been stubborn or difficult. I wanted her to know her death meant something.

I couldn't get the words out.

Before the life left her eyes, before the blood spilled from her mouth like a ribbon, she met my gaze and said, "Kori Maru."

I had no time to consider it. A hand grabbed my arm.

"Come on!" said Meela.

The marlins were closing in on Deiopea.

With a last glance at her lifeless body, I fled with Meela.

The marlins did not follow. Sickened, I tried not to think about them feeding on Deiopea.

Kori Maru. I repeated the words in my mind, trying to place them.

Meela and I kept swimming, not saying a word. The chaos faded into the distance. We were alone.

Kori Maru. It was the name of a ship, I was sure.

We travelled at depth, following the fastest current back northwards. Sadness overcame me—and then guilt. If Deiopea hadn't come with us, she would still be alive—and those marlins might have gotten me or Meela instead. I hated myself for feeling relieved.

We swam for a long time at top speed. I wanted to make certain we hadn't been followed.

Meela whimpered. "My lungs are going to collapse."

I swore. A dull pain had been growing under my own ribs for a while. I should have let Meela breach long ago.

"All right. I think it's safe," I said weakly.

We grazed the surface, taking a quick breath with each stroke.

As I sucked life back into my lungs, I became certain Kori Maru was a shipwreck. We'd learned about hundreds of them in school. They were useful for navigating—for those who could remember all of them.

Of course the Reinas would meet at a place like that. It was perfect. Adaro's armies wouldn't go near that kind of 'human filth'.

"They're in a shipwreck," I said to Meela. "Kori Maru."

"How do you—?"

"Deiopea said it before she ..."

Meela looked around as though hoping to see the wreck. "Do you know where?"

I frowned, and then decided to attribute her lack of concern over Deiopea's death to adrenaline. Maybe it was all too much for her to consider at the moment.

"It ends in *Maru*, so it's a Japanese ship," I said.

"The Bering Sea?"

"That's what I'm thinking."

We fell silent, catching our breath with every breach.

Everything we'd left behind nagged at me—all those prisoners, those poor humans, Deiopea. Her entire family had been killed and her city occupied by Adaro's army. No one was safe—southern merpeople, former humans, anyone who might oppose Adaro. Plus, the conditions of the labour camp and what they were working towards were all worse than I'd thought. How many were dying down there each day? How long did we have until they succeeded? How much coastline would such a tsunami destroy?

That idea smouldering in the back of my mind glowed once more.

I stopped. "Wait."

Meela spun around, panicked. "Are they—?"

"No, no. Sorry. I—" I cast my senses behind us anyway to make sure we were still alone. "I was thinking, Mee. Even with the Reinas' help, we can't stop this."

"What do you mean?"

"The way they're rounding everyone up. The labour camp. All the guards, and the black marlins—and you didn't see the way he uses other animals in battle. Adaro's army won't go down easy."

"Okay," said Meela slowly. "But our only option is to try."

Her green eyes popped against the orange glow of the rising sun. It peeked over the horizon, brightening the flat, peaceful surface. I wanted to rest, to find a raft or an island and curl up there with her. But we had to keep moving.

I swam onwards, Meela keeping pace.

"Killing him is only part of the battle," I said. "What about his armies? We need to consider the bigger wars—the one between the kingdoms, and the one against humans."

"Isn't that why we're going to the Reinas?"

I shook my head. Deiopea had said the entire Moonless City hadn't been able to resist Adaro's army. How would a small group of rebels be able to overthrow him? We needed more help than that.

"There's another option," I said. "Someone who might be powerful enough to stop all of this."

"Tell me you have a leviathan hidden somewhere."

"No."

My brain worked over what Deiopea had said about the serpent. *Rivals the power of the original Medusa.* She had been talking about the Medusa of millennia past—but what about her descendant? What about the Medusa reigning over the Atlantic?

"We need Queen Medusa," I said.

Meela glanced sidelong at me. "If she has snakes for hair and a glare that turns you to stone, sure. If not, I don't see how she can help us."

I shook my head. "Adaro might have the serpent, but Medusa has the oldest regime in history and a kingdom a thousand times the size of Utopia."

"You think her army can rival Adaro's?"

"We can wait and find out with the rest of the world, when Adaro invades the Atlantic—or we can find out sooner. We can go to the Atlantic. We can get Medusa's help before Adaro becomes unstoppable."

Meela gaped. "You want us to go to the other side of the world?"

"We need her help. She's managed to keep peace in the Atlantic for her entire reign."

My tone became bolder. According to my parents, Medusa was fair, wise, and generous. She could save the Pacific.

"Lysi, you're being ridiculous. Why would Medusa, an actual queen, agree to talk to two average mermaids from the Pacific?"

"Because you're not average. You're Metlaa Gaela from Eriana Kwai, a former human and one who knows more about the leviathan than anybody. She'll want to hear it."

Meela frowned. "If she cares about peace so much, why hasn't she done anything yet to stop Adaro?"

I hesitated. I'd wondered the same thing. But we couldn't judge the queen's decision until we knew more.

"Maybe she doesn't know the extent of what's happening," I said.

"You don't think someone would have told her?"

"Adaro's army is guarding the border between here and the Atlantic. It's not easy to get past."

"And you want us to try," said Meela flatly.

"Mee, she's the most powerful queen in the oceans. Maybe ever. My parents said she speaks nine human languages and is said to have the wisdom of all her ancestors behind her throne. Plus, since her rule she's started mining the seafloor for diamonds and silver and has established a trading system with humans—"

Meela blew a bubble of exasperation. "It's already taking us forever to track the Reinas halfway across the Pacific! Now you're saying we need to take a trip to the other side of the world. We're wasting time."

"This'll all help us in the end!"

"After how long? It'll take ages to get to the Atlantic."

"Half a tidecycle, I think."

"Tidecycle? I don't even know what—"

"It's the time it takes the tides and the moon—"

"Whatever. That's beside the point."

I scowled. "Just trying to help you out."

"I didn't mean it like that," she said, softening. "But Lysi, we have one merman to find, and he's somewhere on this side of the earth. We finally have a lead with this Kori Maru thing, and we need to go after it."

"You don't think we'll have a better chance of stopping Adaro's armies with Medusa's help?"

"Our focus isn't on who has the bigger army," said Meela. "We need to get to Adaro, not start a massive war between the Atlantic and the Pacific."

"But Mee, even after we kill Adaro, we've still got all his armies and government and—"

"No. My answer's no."

She swam ahead, leaving me to catch up.

We didn't speak for a long time. Meela's aura had closed on itself, like she was too absorbed in her own mind to pay attention to anything outside it. Fixating on getting Adaro again, no doubt. I wanted to grab her and tell her to calm down, because we were doing the best we could.

I let the subject drop, but I wasn't going to give up. Killing Adaro was one thing, but we needed the most powerful force in the seas if we wanted to end the war. And we had to stop it as soon as possible—for all those prisoners, for humans, for Deiopea, and just as much, for Meela's sanity.

CHAPTER FIVE - Meela
Wrecks of the Bering Sea

The more I tried to stop thinking about it, the more my mind replayed the scene. My ears still rang with the shouting crowd, clashing weapons, and splintering boat, which seemed to grow louder as time passed. The smell of blood and iron lingered in my nose. I saw the swinging keel, the red clouds in the water.

It was the Massacre all over again, except this time I was on the other side of the surface. Somehow, I'd thought the merpeople would be reluctant to attack. Had I expected everyone to be like Lysi? Instead, they'd moved in to kill those humans without hesitation. They even seemed to enjoy it.

"You're all … prickly," said Lysi, bringing me out of the memory.

"Thinking about the boat," I mumbled.

I could feel her looking at me. I kept staring ahead. Swimming in silence through the open ocean, its emptiness felt absolute. We'd stopped to gorge on a school of fish, but since then, there was no sign that anything besides the two of us existed.

"They were doing what they've been taught," said Lysi.

"Weren't you taught to do that, too?"

"Yes, but I have you."

"So? What if you hadn't met me? Would you be into killing and, and—?" I couldn't bring myself to say it.

"Mee, our kind has spent years hearing how humans are worthless, and how we own the water and humans have no right to be here."

"And they believe it?"

"Adaro promised to unite the seas under one crown. He's doing that by uniting everyone with a common enemy."

It was working. Hate and fear were powerful enough to build a kingdom on. Thinking about Adaro's strategy made my pulse race with anger. He had trained an entire generation of merpeople to believe humans needed to be extinguished.

Desperation cinched my chest, pulling me northwards as if by a rope. The sooner we found Adaro, the sooner we could end all of this.

Lysi made a sound as though she were about to say more. I glanced at her, but she closed her mouth.

"What?" I said.

She shook her head.

"Lysi."

She cast me a sideways glance. "Well, is it any different from how you were raised?"

I looked away, taking a minute to squash the surge of outrage. My face grew hot. She was right. Everyone on Eriana Kwai believed mermaids were an invasive species that needed to be pushed back to the Atlantic. The whole purpose of the Massacres was to force them away from our home.

War was not one-sided. For centuries, humans had been overfishing anything edible, capturing and tagging anything intelligent, and killing everything else. We had made it easy for merpeople to treat us as the enemy.

"They teach us that feeding on humans is no worse than fish," Lysi said gently. "Both are made of meat. Both are a relative."

I didn't know what to say to that. The idea was beyond argument.

Lysi took my hand. "He doesn't understand the most important part of existence. The mind, the soul, everything that makes us feel."

Her touch calmed me, and I squeezed her fingers. I had to remember that Adaro's concept of the relationship between humans and merpeople was that we were all just part of the food chain. But I knew love, and I had those in my life who returned it. That we were made of flesh and bone was the smallest part of what it meant to be alive.

"Do you think anyone else feels the same?" I said.

"I think lots do. They're just afraid to say it."

We pressed on through the bluish murk, the world vacant on all sides.

Some time later, ripples told me something big was swimming towards us. I stopped. We hadn't encountered anything other than fish since leaving Deiopea and the captives.

"Lysi?"

She felt it out for about two seconds before saying, "It's fine."

I hesitated, and then hurried to catch up. "You sure? It feels huge."

"She's a basking shark."

"Shark?!"

Lysi chuckled. "I promise it's fine."

I took her word for it, but stuck close beside her.

Sure enough, when the thing materialised from the blue, I let out a small scream. Its mouth was open wide enough to swallow both of us whole, the white and grey insides resembling a cavernous ribcage.

Lysi grabbed me before I could jet away. "They eat krill and plankton, Mee. Look. No teeth."

We watched it drift past us and continue down the current, mouth gaping as if letting out a long and silent scream.

Teeth or not, the last time I'd seen the inside of a mouth that big was when the leviathan tried to eat us. The memory didn't ease my nerves.

"How are you supposed to tell if something's going to attack you or not?" I said, crossing my arms.

"It'll take practice. Try and feel her energy."

I concentrated, but felt only the vague aura of an animal and ripples as it coasted by. How could Lysi even tell it was female? Would I ever be able to read auras as well as her?

As the sun sank, we pushed harder, agreeing it would be better to find the Reinas than to stop and spend the night alone. My body was ready to crumple with exhaustion. The only thing keeping me moving was the will to survive.

As we reached the Aleutian Islands, Lysi said with enthusiasm I could tell was forced, "The Bering Sea is just over the trench."

Each time we breached and I saw those billowing volcanoes, a familiar, grim feeling closed over me. It was a hollow sadness, like the Aanil Uusha was hovering overhead, waiting to claim someone. I'd felt the god of Death every day on the Massacre, as I stood on the deck of the Bloodhound staring at those islands.

I found refuge each time we submerged. It was as though the underwater world pushed new life into me. I thought of the green ribbons I'd hung in my bedroom as a kid and wondered, not for the first time, if I'd always been destined to be a mermaid. I was in love with the sea.

I kept my feelers out for signs of the Reinas as we wove between the landmasses, determined to find something other than a basking shark before sundown.

Running aground must have been common near the Aleutian Islands, because we found two shipwrecks within an hour of each other. The first was a small battleship of sorts, resembling a block of concrete and definitely uninhabited. The second was more industrial and eerie, with the crumbling appearance of having been smashed against the seafloor. Its hull was shattered, the deck cracked. I could see the life preservers still fastened aboard. Plant life and barnacles covered the ship to such extent that it blended into the landscape, and I couldn't find a name painted on the side. Judging by the undisturbed wildlife, though, I guessed the ship had never been inhabited by merpeople.

One thing we did find was an excess of sharks—and not the basking kind. Lysi assured me the sharks wouldn't bother us as long as they didn't smell blood. Still, they had powerful, predatory auras, and I couldn't help feeling nervous as we passed by.

Continuing through the cascade of volcanoes, we glided silently over a dark trench, the depths of which might have plunged to the centre of the earth, for all I knew.

We passed another ship—this one half submerged and leaning against the shore of a small island. The waves crashed into it, sending sprays high over the rusted frame.

As the sun touched the horizon, we came upon a fourth wreck. It was wooden, a more traditional structure with two masts and a bowsprit.

"This isn't it," said Lysi. "I'm sure we're looking for a trawler."

I swam low over the deck, scanning the webs of ropes and splintered masts. The mainmast had crumbled sideways so it leaned against the foremast. This was a brig—slightly different from the Bloodhound in its rigging, but the skeleton was similar enough to send a shiver through me. On the Massacre, our loyal ship had barely survived long enough to bring us home. The thought of dying in a shipwreck in the iciest part of the ocean still haunted me.

My skin prickled, stinging faintly.

"What is that?" I said, rubbing a hand over my arm.

I turned to find Lysi a few reluctant lengths behind.

"Iron. The wood's probably laced with it."

I had a terrible, constricted feeling in my chest. Had this been one of our own Massacre ships? What if the crew had been killed, and this ship had been left to float away until it hit the islands and sank?

I scanned the side for a name, but found nothing.

A soft hand wrapped around my arm. "Come on. Don't swim so close."

"I want to poke around a bit."

"No," said Lysi firmly.

"Aren't you curious?"

"Mee, there's iron everywhere."

"I'll be careful."

She pulled hard, forcing me to look at her. "All it takes is an accidental brush across your skin and you're burned forever."

I shut my mouth, ashamed for being so tactless. Of course Lysi knew what it felt like to be burned by iron. The enormous scar across her waist was there because of me. I looked away.

"Let's keep moving north," she said.

I followed, keeping close to her tail. Lysi was right. Poking around here would be needlessly reckless.

"Should we follow the curve of the islands?" I said. "Won't there be more shipwrecks closer to land?"

"Yes, but I'm sure Kori Maru is further north."

We left the Aleutian Islands behind. The Bering Sea was cold and wild, the waves overhead more violent than anything I'd experienced. I was glad for the safety of travelling far below the surface.

Having not slept the night before, we grew sluggish. My concentration waned and every part of me felt heavy. The sky darkened to a deep navy blue. It must have been at least midnight.

"There's a wreck over there," said Lysi, "but it's wooden. Feel the texture on the current?"

"Sure," I said, too tired to bother. "Where'd you learn about all these wrecks, anyway?"

"It was part of our geography and navigation lessons. You have to learn these things if you want to find your way around. But it isn't proving very helpful, apparently."

"It's okay. I learned a lot of things in elementary school that I can't remember. Long division. Outer space. The British Empire."

"Why do humans need to learn about outer space if they don't need to keep track of tides?"

"Huh?"

"The cycles of the moon."

"Oh," I said. "No, we learned more about planets and stuff."

"What do planets affect?"

"Um. Nothing."

Lysi cast me a sidelong glance.

I laughed. "We don't learn about that stuff because it affects everyday life. It's more for the sake of, just, knowledge. Understanding the universe."

"Did learning about the planets help you understand the universe?"

I considered, thinking about our place on this blue dot hurtling through space among all those other planets and stars. I thought about how small we were in the middle of a war, and how small the war was in the context of space.

Then I looked at Lysi swimming beside me, and I decided that as long as she was there, I didn't care how miniscule we all were.

"Yeah," I said. "I guess it did."

We passed beneath a raft of wood and plastic. Strands of seaweed and ropes dangled several lengths deep. Small fish darted in and out, plucking off algae and burrowing inside.

"Let's stop," said Lysi. "We might not find another good spot and I don't want to be up all night again."

Every part of me was sore, but I wrinkled my nose at the idea of stopping.

"You know, we could just go straight to the Atlantic instead of searching all over the Bering," said Lysi.

I glared. She didn't need to tell me how hopeless this search seemed. But I maintained that it was more productive than leaving the Pacific Ocean altogether.

Lysi hoisted herself onto the raft.

I rubbed my burning eyes. "All right. Sleep."

I pulled myself up next to her and felt suddenly grateful that mermaids didn't suffer seasickness, because something told me the bobbing raft would have made me queasy at one time.

The storm had calmed, but the waves were still enormous, each one taking several seconds to rise and fall. The movement lulled me into sleepiness. I lay on my side and pulled a tangle of seaweed over me like a blanket—not out of necessity, but out of habit. The first night I'd done it, Lysi laughed at me, but now she helped arrange it over my tail.

"Warm?" she said teasingly.

"How long do you think before I forget what it was like to sleep with a quilt and a pillow?"

She kissed my cheek and lay facing me so our noses touched. I breathed in her sweet scent, hoping to bring her with me into my dreams.

"I hope you never forget that part of you," she said.

"What part?"

"Your humanity."

I offered a smile.

"Look around," said Lysi.

Perplexed, I raised my head off the raft. I let out a gasp. The sea glowed, flecked with what looked like brilliant, sapphire stars.

"Who needs outer space?" said Lysi.

I dipped my hand into the water. The blue dots glimmered, bright as lanterns, where I stirred them.

"What are they?"

"Plankton."

I met Lysi's eyes, finding sapphires more brilliant than those below us.

"Have I mentioned how much I love the ocean?" I said.

She smiled.

We fell asleep with our arms wrapped around each other, tails entwined, lulled by the motion and sound of the waves.

I dreamt I was human, on a tiny sailboat in the middle of the ocean. There was no wind so I was trying to use my hands to paddle back to Eriana Kwai.

Annith appeared wearing a sombrero and told me there was no point. The war was over and this was everything left in the world—empty water and nothing, nothing, nothing.

I awoke with a start. The sky was indigo, overcast. Lysi was asleep beside me. The waves lapped against our raft, a few wisps of plankton lingering nearby.

There was an uneven *glop*. I sat up, wincing as every muscle tightened.

Ripples spread across the water beside us. Something—or someone—had just been here. That must have been what woke me.

Rubbing my neck, I looked down at Lysi. She slept quietly, face relaxed.

I dipped my hand in the water and felt movement on the current. I concentrated harder, closing my eyes. An aura tickled beneath my skin. It was a mermaid. She was swimming away.

After congratulating myself for being able to identify her, I frowned. What was she doing way out here? Why was she alone?

She moved quickly. Without pausing to consider, I slid into the inky depths before I could lose track of her. Maybe she was a Reina. Maybe she could help us find Kori Maru.

As soon as I hit the water, the mermaid sped up. I put on a burst of speed, throwing caution aside.

"Wait!"

She didn't slow down.

"I just want to know if you can help me!"

It took every effort to keep up. My body protested with each beat of my tail.

I chased her for at least a couple of minutes before she gave up and stopped.

I caught up to find a small blonde with a northern appearance like Lysi and me. She wasn't a Reina. The iron scars across her body led me to believe she'd endured many of Adaro's battles against humans.

She held out a spear with a stone tip, stopping me from coming closer. She was in demon mode, ready for a fight.

I raised my palms in a gesture of surrender. "Do you know where I can find Kori Maru?"

The mermaid backed off more. I wondered if asking for directions to a shipwreck was a strange thing for a mermaid to do.

"Half-tide that way."

She pointed northwards, a little further west than we'd been heading, and made to leave again.

"Wait." *Half-tide?* What did that mean? I knew tides worked in day-long cycles, but then there were high tides and low tides—so did a half-tide mean twelve hours, or six? Why hadn't I asked Lysi about this?

The mermaid stared like I was something foreign. Which, to be fair, I kind of was.

But I couldn't let her leave yet. This was the first non-threatening mermaid we'd come across. Given that she had a spear pointed at my face, that was saying something about the last few days.

Several questions occurred to me at once. Desperate to keep her from leaving, I blurted the first thing that came to mind. "Where did you come from?"

The mermaid narrowed her eyes. "Why?"

"We've been travelling and haven't heard any news about the war."

Her face hardened. "Find someone else to ask about that."

"Please." I moved closer. She kept me at the end of her spear. "You were looking for a place to sleep, right?"

She didn't answer.

"You can share the raft with us, if you could just answer my questions."

We hovered for a moment in the blackness. I hoped I came across as honest and not completely desperate.

"I'm coming from Japan," she said eventually.

"Why are you leaving?"

She hesitated. "I'm going back to Utopia."

"But were you following Adaro's orders to attack?"

"What do you mean?"

"Were you in battle against humans over there?"

"Obviously—"

Something moved below, and the mermaid jerked, redirecting her spear. Even I could tell it was a fish.

I was getting a rising impression she wasn't supposed to be here.

"Where's Adaro now?" I said.

Her head snapped up at this, aura darkening. "Who wants to know?"

I hesitated. Even if my suspicions were right and she had deserted the army, that didn't necessarily mean she would take well to someone planning to kill her king.

"Never mind," said the mermaid, backing away. "I don't need a place to sleep."

As she made to turn away, I shot forwards and grabbed her wrist, my teeth sharpening so quickly they cut my bottom lip. The mermaid cried out and swung her spear at my head.

I grabbed the spear with my other hand before it could hit me.

"Tell me where Adaro is."

"I don't know!"

Something about her racing pulse, or maybe the way her aura seemed to cloud over, told me she was lying. She knew.

I snarled. "This is important. I need to find him—"

She slammed me in the gut with her tail. I grunted, a bubble erupting from my mouth. Next thing I knew, her arm had torn from my grip and her weapon slid through my other hand, spearhead catching on my palm.

Ignoring the stinging cut, I lunged after her as she took off like a bolt. I cursed, knowing I was too stiff and exhausted to catch her.

A moment passed, and the world fell back into silence. I looked down, examining my webbed fingers, then closed my eyes and forced my appearance back to normal. The threatening approach had been a total failure. I was glad Lysi hadn't been there to see it.

Then again, if she'd been awake we might not have followed the mermaid at all. She would have told me I was being reckless, I thought, remembering when my curiosity had almost led me inside an iron-infested ship.

At least we had directions to Kori Maru, now. That was something.

I headed back to the raft, wondering what time it was. Behind the clouds, the sky was still indigo—but this far north during the summer, I supposed the sky never got darker than twilight.

Ahead, something stirred. I froze for a minute, and then shut my eyes and groaned.

"Meela!"

Lysi was in full panic.

"I'm here," I called, hurrying in the direction of her voice.

The chaotic ripples paused, and then Lysi shot towards me out of the darkness.

"Mee, where—?"

"I ran into a mermaid," I said before she could get angry. "I mean, swam into. Is that an expression here?"

Lysi opened and closed her mouth. Then she glanced down at my hand, which oozed a ribbon of blood. I crossed my arms.

"Anyway, it's that way to the Reinas," I said, nodding in the direction the mermaid had indicated. "*Half-tide* further— ouch!"

Lysi punched my shoulder. "Don't leave like that! What if you'd gotten lost, or eaten, or attacked?"

"Thank you so much for your confidence in me."

She huffed, expelling a jet of bubbles. I shrugged and rose to the surface, Lysi hesitating before I felt her follow behind, grumbling about keeping track of me.

We hauled ourselves back onto the raft and I told her what had happened, glossing over the part where the mermaid had fled because I threatened her.

"At least we know which direction to go," said Lysi.

"You're welcome."

"I still think that was stupid."

I shrugged. Stupid or not, it was worth it.

We slept another couple of hours and departed at dawn. Breakfast was a school of mackerel, which we shared with a pod of Pacific white-sided dolphins.

A short while later, the water shifted from Pacific to Arctic. The waves grew even choppier and took on an icy blue tinge, and the wildlife became a lot more blubber-y.

"Ugh, no wonder they're meeting out here," said Lysi, watching the waves thrash overhead. "I thought the trek to the South Pacific was bad. Adaro wouldn't waste time sending an army through this."

"What about the mermen stationed at the Northwest Passage—I mean, the Ice Channel?"

"They wouldn't get there by travelling this far out. They'd stick closer to the shallows where it isn't so miserable."

"I don't think it's miserable," I said, admiring the way the waves looked as they frothed and churned overhead.

Admittedly, the chaotic swells made it harder to breach, and I worried about what sleeping arrangements we would have to make if we went another day without finding Kori Maru. We wouldn't be able to stay on a raft in seas as violent as this. We would need to get to land. But if my geography was right, we were about as close to Alaska as we were to Russia.

We kept swimming. Lysi didn't project any fear, and I trusted her instincts more than my own.

"I was thinking," said Lysi, breaking an hour-long silence, "maybe whenever we have time—when this is all over, or if we have free time before the Reinas execute whatever plan they have—"

"Free time? We'd better not. If we have any free time once we get there, I'm going to spend it trying to come up with a faster plan."

Lysi said nothing. A moment passed before I realised how obtuse I was being.

"I'm sorry."

She cast me a sidelong glance.

I poked her ribs. "What were you going to say?"

"I thought maybe …" She blushed. "Maybe we could go on a date."

My stomach gave a swoop, and every thought I had about finding the Reinas dissipated. I couldn't stop the grin breaking across my face.

"You're asking me out?"

She laughed.

"What do mermaids do on a date?" I said.

"Well," she said, brightening, "we could go for dinner, or watch a play, or go to a sports game—"

"Whoa. Hold up. A play? Sports? Dinner—like a restaurant? Mermaids have all this?"

"Of course! You think we hunt every meal? You think we do nothing for entertainment?"

"So you go to a restaurant and people bring you—I mean, mermaids—bring you food?"

"Uh, yeah. That's the idea."

"And plays?"

"We can go watch a show. Spio and I used to go and heckle. We got escorted out a lot, but it was worth it to see …"

Her smile faded at the memory of her friend.

"Hey," I said, grabbing her hand. "He's still out there. We'll find him."

She gave me a sad smile.

"What about the sports?" I prompted.

"There are a few different ones we could watch. My favourite is rings."

"Rings?"

"It's played with dolphins. They make rings of bubbles and push them around with their noses. Two teams of four merpeople have to chuck a stone through the moving rings while the dolphins pass them around."

I tried to wrap my head around all of this.

"Honestly, Mee, did you think we lived like fish?"

"I … Of course not."

But I felt myself go a bit hot with shame for thinking otherwise. I was like one of those people who assumed everyone in Canada lived in igloos.

"Let's go to a rings game," I said. "My brother used to let me watch him and his friends play basketball. I even joined in a few times."

A strange look crossed Lysi's face. She let go of my hand, but I'd already felt her pulse quicken.

"What?"

She hesitated.

"What is it?"

"Okay. Mee, there's something I need to tell you."

I slowed down, my mind jumping to a million possibilities at once.

"Was it the battlefront? Did something happen? Is it Spio?"

"What? No!"

With the air of someone steeling herself for an eruption, she said, "You can't get mad at me for not telling you. There's been so much going on and I didn't want to overwhelm you. I haven't found the right moment, but I'm starting to think there will never—"

"Lysi. What is it?"

She rubbed a hand across her eyes. "Okay, so I told you the guys from the rebellion each had a connection to humans, right? That was what brought them together; Adaro was victimising former humans who were close to them."

I scowled.

"In one guy's case, he took things more personally." She looked up at me. "Because he actually was a former human."

"All right," I said slowly, not sure what she was getting at.

But Lysi abruptly stopped swimming, her mouth agape. Fear washed over me before I even sensed the movements in the distance.

"Army?" I said, barely a whisper.

Lysi shook her head. She squinted ahead for a long moment. "Mee, I think this is it."

Could it be? Half a day must have passed since we left the raft. I stayed quiet, not wanting to break Lysi's concentration.

Suddenly, my heart leapt. It was distant, but its frame was so enormous and out of place that it left me without doubt. Somewhere beyond the cloudy blue water sat the ghost of a trawler. It had sunk overtop of a narrow canyon, forming a sort of eerie bridge. I felt the impurity of iron in its frame, prickling my skin like an itchy wool blanket, and the thick layer of wildlife growing over every surface.

Hundreds of bodies stirred in the canyon beneath the ship. When I concentrated, I could distinguish an assortment of fish, predators, and merpeople.

Lysi looked at me, blue eyes wide in excitement, a smile pulling at her lips.

We'd made it to Kori Maru.

CHAPTER SIX - Ben
Perseus' Last Monster

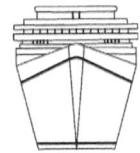

The USS Perseus hummed through the Gulf of Alaska, approaching the heart of the mermaids' city. In the bridge, Reeves scanned the empty surface, and then turned his eyes to the monitor. Several thousand feet existed between him and the seafloor. Life signatures moved far below.

Flee, he thought. *I'm giving you a chance.*

The US Navy had been monitoring the increase in mermaid activity over several years. Until now, traditional means—iron nets, helicopters, safety regulations for boaters—had been enough to keep the American people safe. With the breach of the Aleutian Treaty and the rising number of attacks in the Pacific Northwest, it was time to deploy Perseus whether she was finished or not.

Captain Larson slowed the ship to a crawl and looked expectantly at Reeves. He tugged the sleeves of his uniform, trying to relieve his sweating underarms. It was no use. The uniform was too crisp, too stiff.

His pulse pounded—but not from fear. He'd been on too many drills to feel that anymore. He'd received months of special training for Operation Perseus, and now that the time had come, an immense feeling of guilt pressed on him like a boulder.

You owe her your life.

He shook his head. He was just following orders.

But every time he closed his eyes, that mermaid's face flashed through his mind as it had done countless times—blank, bloody, lifeless.

"Chief?" said Captain Larson.

"Yeah. Give me a minute."

Reeves scanned the water, pretending to focus on something.

The mermaids had become a threat to national security, yes, but there must be a better plan than this. He'd been unsuccessful yesterday in convincing Officer Miller to investigate that merman, who obviously had power over the serpent—but how? Did he possess something that could grant anyone control?

Reeves almost laughed at himself for considering the possibility. What did he expect, a magic trident?

"Chief, every second we wait—"

"I know," said Reeves. "Hold on."

Larson rolled her eyes. Though she had more years of experience than him, she was being forced to take his orders on this mission, and she had been challenging his every move since they left. Reeves pretended not to notice the way her team gave him sidelong glances and sarcastic retorts. It wasn't his fault their teams hadn't met and trained together before Perseus launched. They were all being shoved into this mission prematurely. Besides, he was plenty qualified for this position. It was the matter of actually going through with the operation that made him want to vomit.

It had never left his dreams, the face of the one who had saved his life. And then she lay on the rocks, blood spilling from a dozen places where iron bullets had penetrated, those brilliant brown eyes wide open and glazed. He could never be sure who'd pulled the trigger on her. It could have been anyone on his team, reacting as they were trained to when the mermaids breached the facility.

She'd saved his life, and his team had shot her. He would never be able to forgive himself for that.

Reeves picked up the mic and reported their status to Officer Miller.

"Get your crew ready," he said to Larson.

He caught the second eye-roll as she turned away.

The defiance didn't bother him. He'd spent several years of grade school being the shortest guy in gym class, so he was used to his peers underestimating him. He'd grown up working extra hard to prove his abilities.

The moment the bridge door closed, leaving him alone, Reeves raised the mic before he could think and found himself blurting, "Sir, don't you think we're jumping the gun?"

Silence. Then, "Reeves, the entire Pacific Northwest is being invaded. Civilians are at risk."

He gazed across the glassy water, beautiful and peaceful. "Sir, there are whales in the area."

"Now, Reeves," Miller barked.

Reeves gripped the mic tighter. To disobey would be to lose his job. Everything he'd spent his life working towards would be gone because he was too much of a coward to pull the trigger on a few sea demons.

But was that all they were?

The ship bobbed in silence for a long moment.

Outside, shouts erupted. "Chief!"

Reeves burst through the bridge door. His soldiers stood at the railing, rifles aimed at the water. He hurried to the port side.

They were surrounded. Women—no, mermaids—poked their heads from the water, watching. They didn't try to scale Perseus' iron hull.

"Everyone back up," commanded Reeves before the mermaids could lure anyone.

His soldiers took three synchronised steps back. Reeves averted his eyes from the water, unable to face the lives he was about to end.

Perseus' deck was bare, unadorned, but the key feature was there. An iron railing in the middle formed a barrier around a coffin-like hole. Larson and two crewmates slipped between the railings and jumped inside. They hadn't waited for his orders. Reeves' tongue felt too fat in his mouth to shout at them for this.

The operative weapon was supposed to be controlled from a computer screen, but the engineers hadn't had time to implement it, so everything had to be executed manually.

He heard Larson barking orders and the clank of machinery. Perseus shuddered. The panel on the keel was opening.

Reeves scanned the members of his team. None looked nervous, but he was certain every one of them was sweating like he was—possibly terrified. What they were about to do was unprecedented, untested, and highly dangerous. The ramifications were bigger than any op he'd heard of in years.

His team, unlike Larson's, awaited his orders with an air of respect, which he returned in equal measure. They'd worked with him and become his friends over the months. He couldn't let them down.

Inside the coffin, Larson and her crewmates worked quickly. There was a click and a mechanical groan below as the launcher emerged. Reeves had seen the thing moored; it was the size of a pickup truck with twenty supercavitating torpedoes positioned in a circle, and now they would be pointing into the pure blue depths of the Gulf of Alaska.

Reeves peeked into the water. The mermaids must have felt or seen the weapons, because their peering faces had disappeared.

"Ready to fire, chief," said Larson.

Reeves' mind shut down as panic rose inside him, pulse hammering at his throat.

"*Chief.*"

"I know, Larson!"

There was nothing he could do. He was a pawn. His job was to give the order, and with all these eyes on him, it was his only choice. To back out would be to lose everything, to bring shame on his team, to become a subject of ridicule for Larson's. He would have to return to Miller and tell him what happened. He would return home to overly supportive but secretly disappointed parents, and live the rest of his life in another line of work, knowing he'd failed.

Someone screamed at the other end of the deck. Reeves whirled to find one of his soldiers collapsed, a sea spear jutting from his shoulder. One of Larson's crewmembers ran to help.

Everyone else on board had lifted their rifles and crouched into position.

Reeves cursed. He had to make the choice: everyone aboard Perseus, or the mermaids. The answer should have been obvious. A teammate had gone down. But how could he pull the trigger on the entire North Pacific Ocean? He couldn't do this.

He turned to Larson, adrenaline pulsing. He would be relieved of duty for this. He would prove her doubts correct and be a failure to himself and his team.

"Oh, for God's sake!" she shouted.

She stomped the lever into place.

"Larson!"

The ship shuddered. Beneath the hull, all twenty torpedoes would be launching in tandem.

Reeves' pulse pounded. It was too late. It couldn't be fixed.

"Brace!" bellowed Larson.

Reeves and the crew gathered in the centre of the deck and crouched at the railing, wrapping limbs around the poles and each other—because the proper safety equipment had not yet been installed.

The first torpedo exploded. Perseus rocked in all directions. An icy spray slammed down over Reeves. He gasped, taking long, slow breaths that tasted of brine and seaweed. Water thundered across the deck. The shockwave had not yet settled when the second torpedo went off.

Each one was designed to detonate at a different range than the previous. With every explosion, shards of iron would be blasting in all directions, driving shrapnel into any creature it could reach. That included mermaids, mermen— and wildlife. Nothing within miles had a hope of surviving.

The third explosion rocked Perseus more violently. The waves churned like a maelstrom. Reeves focused on holding his body tightly to the deck, thinking he might vomit. He had never been one to get seasick, which was fortunate considering his career—but the rising nausea had nothing to do with choppy waves. He squeezed his eyes shut, clinging to the railing, and for the second time in his life, he began to pray. *Forgive me.*

He waited for the fourth explosion, determined to count each one and mourn the deaths he had let happen. How was it possible that this was only the fourth missile—out of *twenty*? He should never have agreed to that many. There would be nothing left in the Pacific.

The time for the fourth explosion came and went. Reeves opened his eyes to find Larson staring at him, her brown eyes enormous, pupils dilated.

"What happened? Is it faulty?" she said.

Crack.

The ship lurched with such force that everyone was lifted into the air. Reeves watched the deck fall away. He seemed to hover in mid air for a second, and then the deck flew back up to meet him at sickening speed. He flailed, as if trying to swim, and got his hands under him in time to stop his chin hitting the deck first.

He smelled blood. He tasted it, thick in his mouth.

Thuds echoed around him as the others hit the deck, coughing and gasping.

A siren wailed. The hull had been breached.

"Larson ... find ... out—" Reeves coughed.

He sat up and clutched his chest, trying to get the wind back into his lungs.

He tried again. "Find out what's—"

A thunder rose over everything else. The deck tilted. Reeves slid down it, reaching wildly for something to hold onto. He found a cleat barely big enough to wrap his fingers around.

Waves frothed beneath him. Bodies hit the water. The spray stung his eyes as he looked around. A few crewmembers hung from the deck beside him, and beyond that, he saw only the gaping insides of the hull.

He blinked, trying to process what this meant.

It dawned on him with the same feeling of an icy swell crashing over his head. The ship had broken in half.

They were sinking.

The sky darkened. Reeves looked up and saw something else, something infinitely worse than his broken ship, which sent a chill from his spine down to his dangling legs. His brain clouded over. He was going to pass out.

The enormous black head rose from the water and gazed coolly down at them, pupils narrowing.

Useless thoughts dashed through Reeves' mind: how his life had just begun, and how he'd never be able to get married, or have kids, or take a beach vacation—not that he was especially keen on visiting the beach, ever again—and how he hadn't expected his life to end quite like this. And he'd never gotten the chance to fly the LM-80 Cormorant.

Then the other serpent head came out of the water and rose beside the first. It opened its mouth. Fragments of iron and shrapnel fell from its jaws.

The seventeen remaining torpedoes, crunched into pieces, plunged into the waves below.

CHAPTER SEVEN - Meela
Kori Maru

The shipwreck was so close I could feel it, smell it, even taste the iron on the current.

"Can't wait for somewhere safe to sleep," said Lysi.

"Can't wait to be around others who don't want to kill us," I said.

More enticing than safety and rest was the promise of allies. I needed to know we weren't the only ones below the surface who wanted Adaro dead.

Someone approached from the wreck. Lysi and I exchanged a glance and slowed.

The mermaid gradually materialised, a lone figure on a murky blue canvas. She had piercings all over that glinted in the dim light, and a green and purple tail. Her short brown hair reminded me of an urchin.

"Can I help you find your way?" she said in a clipped tone.

Lysi pushed back a lock of coppery hair and drew herself upright. "We've come to join you at Kori Maru."

"Afraid we're not accepting visitors, sugarkelp."

"Yes, you are," I said. "We're here to help."

The mermaid narrowed her dark eyes. "Help?"

"The movement against Adaro," said Lysi. "Para la reina."

The mermaid's eyebrows lifted, but she regained her composure quickly. She scanned our appearances—clearly North Pacific—and offered a wan smile.

"We have no quarrel with Adaro."

"We do," I said. "And we've been searching for you for days. So let's skip past all this."

Lysi and I were both wilted and grimy. This mermaid must have felt how tired and defeated we were. She could have helped us out a bit. Her reluctance gave me an immediate dislike for her.

She looked from me to Lysi, scowling.

"We were invited to come here," said Lysi. "I don't know her name, but …"

The mermaid crossed her arms. I became aware of how much muscle loomed in front of us—did she bench press baby whales?—but I stared back. We weren't about to turn away after all the effort it took to get here. I'd fight my way past if I had to.

"Who are you?" said the mermaid. She raked her eyes over Lysi's hair, over her body, down to her tail.

"I'm Lysithea. I'm from Utopia. This is Metlaa Gaela. She's from"—Lysi hesitated—"also Utopia."

I frowned, trying to catch Lysi's eye. Had she lied because I was a former human, or because I was from Eriana Kwai? Was she worried about how they would react to my Eriana heritage? I supposed my people had probably killed more mermaids in the last few decades than the rest of the world combined.

But the Reinas needed to know who I was. My knowledge of the serpent would be useful. She was probably being overprotective again.

"Uh huh," said the mermaid. "Capital of Adaro's kingdom?"

"Well, yeah," said Lysi, "but—"

"You kelpies telling me you got a problem with your own king? That's treason. We can get in serious trouble for associating with you."

I set my jaw, deciding Lysi was wrong. Eriana Kwai was my family, my culture. If that made merpeople hate me the moment they met me, so be it. I wouldn't erase that part of me.

"I'm from Eriana Kwai," I said.

Lysi looked at me sharply. The mermaid's mouth opened a little.

"Eriana—wait." The mermaid scanned Lysi from head to tail again. "You were at Eriana Kwai, too, blondie?"

Lysi hesitated before giving a short nod. "That's where I met a group of you."

The mermaid's hard exterior melted away. She slapped her forehead. "You're the one—you met Dione. Wow. Come with me, sugarkelp. I'm Galene."

Galene did a graceful flip and swam towards the wreck. Lysi glanced to me. A thrill of victory coursed through my chest—and a bit of smug satisfaction.

"So what does *para la reina* mean?" I said, as we followed Galene.

"Means we're acting for the queen," she said.

"Medusa?"

Galene looked over her shoulder and glared. "Evagore. The rightful queen of the Pacific. Disappeared when that scumball invaded the Moonless City."

"What happened?"

"Adaro told everyone she fled. Some say she was killed. We think he's holding her prisoner."

"Is everyone at Kori Maru from the Moonless City?" said Lysi.

"Southern, yes. We've had a few from the north like you more recently."

"How long have you been here?"

"Four tidecycles. Nearly since this whole thing started."

While Galene studied Lysi, I tried to work out a *tidecycle*. Lysi had said something about the tides and the moon. A month? The Reinas had been active for at least four months, then?

"Bet you're hungry," said Galene. "We got a stash of herring eggs you can dig into. I'll show you after you're settled."

"Thanks," said Lysi.

"Anything, sugarkelp."

She gave Lysi a secretive kind of smile. I moved up so I was swimming between them.

"There're a couple of empty grottos you can take," said Galene. "You can have the one next to mine, Lysithea. The mermaid occupying it moved out a few days ago."

"What happened to her?" I said, hoping there wasn't a high death toll here.

"We broke up." She looked pleased that I'd asked. "She moved a few grottos down. Real snapper. Little crazy, mind you. You could say I've got a thing for feisty blondes."

Her eyes traced over Lysi's hair, her perfectly defined face, and down to her waist.

I made a point of taking Lysi's hand. "Lysi and I can share a grotto. Thanks."

Galene glanced to our hands and kept swimming. "Group of guys went to monitor a nearby acoustic channel and should be back tonight with news. Dione can brief you."

Lysi gave my hand a squeeze, catching my eye. We both suppressed a smirk.

As we approached the shipwreck, the prickling of iron worsened. Lysi must have felt it, too, because her aura became subdued. I supposed all these merpeople had learned to live with the discomfort.

A canyon yawned beneath the ship, curving out of sight. The rock walls were indented with dozens of caves—whether natural or carved by merpeople, I couldn't tell. Many had wooden doors or seaweed across the entrances.

At least two hundred mermaids and mermen must have been here, judging by the number moving about the canyon. Some brought their families. Children moved in flocks—or were they called pods or schools? I had a distant memory of Lysi telling me mermaid families usually had enormous amounts of children.

Of the few here with northern appearances, I wondered how they'd come to join this group from the South Pacific. It inspired hope that the different underwater cultures might be able to join forces. And if they were happy to work with each other, maybe they could also ally with humans.

Galene stopped us at the mouth of the canyon. A group of teens beyond it turned to stare.

"Get Dione," Galene barked at them. "I have mermaids from Eriana Kwai."

They flitted away, and she turned to consider Lysi.

"Look at the state of you, poor thing. You've had such a long trip." She pulled a clump of seaweed from Lysi's hair.

Ugh. Were all merpeople this forward?

"It was tiring," I said shortly. "Think you could go grab us those herring eggs?"

Galene smiled at Lysi as though she hadn't heard me. From the canyon, a southern mermaid approached.

Dione had a regal presence about her, with dark skin, dark eyes, and dark hair. Every bone in her body was distinct, like she had been chiselled from stone. Braids floated eerily around her head, supported by kelp buoys. A row of diamonds pierced her left collarbone.

"It's you!" said Lysi. Then she seemed to come to herself and said, "I mean, hi."

Dione offered a smile. "I wondered if fate would lead you to us. The gods did not disappoint me."

She spoke in a deep, pronounced dialect that I had to strain to understand.

"We never properly met. I am Dione, member of the queen's council and lead representative at Kori Maru."

"I'm Lysithea. This is Meela." Lysi turned to me, face alight. "Dione is the one who saved me from the serpent at Eriana Kwai."

"And I expect your knowledge of the serpent will prove valuable. Please, come with me."

She drifted into the canyon. We followed, leaving Galene behind.

"You know where to find me, sugarkelp," she called after Lysi.

I snarled. Lysi laughed and kissed me on the cheek.

As we drifted nearer to the wreck, we attracted stares from everyone we passed. Either new allies seldom joined them, or there was something strange about us.

Lysi tried to smooth her hair. I took her cue and did the same to the poufy mats that had once been braids.

Dione led us into a cavern beneath the ship. Unfortunately, this was not a private grotto where we would be able to rest. Several merpeople were gathered around a stone slab acting as a table. They looked up when we entered.

They were all from the South, with tails of sundry colours and gems glinting across their bodies. Nearest to us were three young mermen who must have been my and Lysi's age, lean and muscular, not yet scarred by battle. On the far side floated a mermaid whose hair was white-blonde. Next to her was a merman with waist-length dreadlocks and a ring in his nose.

Lysi crossed her arms across her stomach, as though trying to hide how grimy and chapped her skin had become during the trek.

"This is the mermaid I spoke of," said Dione. "She has information on the serpent."

Lysi and I exchanged a glance. This abruptness surprised me. I knew the Reinas would want information about it, but I'd thought we would have a bit of time to learn their plan first. Suddenly apprehensive, I wondered how much we should tell them. All that time Lysi and I had spent alone and we hadn't once discussed what we would say, or what we shouldn't.

"Girls," said one of the young mermen, darting over. "Welcome to the Maru."

He made to sling an arm across my shoulders, but the second one elbowed him out of the way and wedged himself between Lysi and me. "I'm Creon, sworn avenger of the crown and everything gorgeous within her kingdom, so, of course, this includes—"

"Enough," said Dione, throwing out an arm before the third one could move.

The young mermen bowed and returned to the table. Lysi and I followed, leaving behind the soft glow of daylight to join them.

"When we crossed paths, I did not know the serpent was acting under Adaro," said Dione. "Not until later did we learn of his movement along the coast."

"You know where he is, then," I said.

Dione cast an appraising glance over me. "We know where he has been but not where he will go next. He has been moving along the coast at random, pushing humans from the shore."

She motioned to the table's surface where a world map had been chiselled into the stone. Everyone stopped staring at us and returned their focus to it. Gems of various colours were hammered along the west coast of North America. Rubies, emeralds, and amethysts marked several places along the coast, from the Aleutian Islands, to Eriana Kwai and British Columbia, down to Washington and Oregon. Attack sites.

"Can you follow him?" I said.

"He moves too quickly. He will be gone by the time we arrive at the site of his last attack."

I leaned closer to study the map, searching for a pattern. His attacks seemed to happen at random, if the colours were meant to indicate anything.

The cavern was silent except for the burble against the stone walls. I glanced up. Dione and the others were looking expectantly at Lysi. Lysi shifted uncomfortably.

"How did the serpent come to pursue you, Lysithea?" said Dione. "What did Eriana Kwai have to do with it?"

Suspicion rose in me at Dione's abrupt questions. So this was why the Reinas invited us here. Or rather, why they invited Lysi here. We were worth as much as the information we could provide.

The same could be said for all of you, I thought, scanning the room.

The prolonged silence broke Lysi. "Um. The serpent's been around since the beginning of time and is part of several human legends. I don't really ..."

She looked to me for help—or maybe to confirm that we should share the story.

"I can tell it." I kept my voice low, though everyone would hear in such close quarters.

Lysi nodded, and then addressed the cavern. "Meela knows more than anyone. She was the one who uncovered the legend on Eriana Kwai."

It was my turn to flush as every gaze in the room fell onto me.

I wouldn't share every detail on the Host of Eriana with these strangers, but I would need to spill some information if I wanted their help getting to Adaro. Maybe if I showed I trusted them enough to tell them my people's legend, they would trust me enough to listen to my ideas.

"The leviathan is the most powerful creature ever to exist and the only of its kind," I said. "So of course Adaro wanted it. That's why he's been obsessed with Eriana Kwai. Sisiutl, the two-headed serpent, was laid to rest on our island."

I paused, trying to quickly think of a plan. What was I supposed to tell them? I had no information that would help them destroy the serpent—and the information I did have about how control was passed by blood was not going to be shared today. Or ever.

"The serpent spent millennia destroying villages and any ship it came upon. The mortal Eriana was the only one who could control it. The Aanil Uusha—that's our god of death—he bound Eriana's soul with the serpent's so it could always be controlled. That's why Adaro calls the serpent the Host of Eriana. Eriana's soul can be freed from its host if the serpent is killed. But that's the problem."

"Does it have a weak spot?" said Dione.

"Not that we know of. It's indestructible."

"We can go for the eyes," said the first young merman, thrusting an invisible sword upwards.

"If you get that close to her face, you won't live long enough to do anything," I said.

"I'd be willing to do it," said Creon, puffing out his chest. "A sacrifice to save the crown and the gorgeousness—"

"It would be a pretty pointless sacrifice!" I said.

Dione raised a hand, and we fell silent. "Meela, you said *our* island. *Our* god of death."

"I'm from Eriana Kwai. I'm a former human."

"You are no longer human. Why do you still include yourself among them?"

"Eriana is my blood," I said. "The history, the gods, they're still a part of me."

Lysi looked between Dione and me, her apprehension so thick I wondered if she was about to jump to my defense.

But Dione nodded. "So the serpent can destroy anything but cannot be destroyed. What else do you know?"

She spoke in casual tones as though we were discussing weather patterns instead of an apocalyptic creature.

"I only learned about the serpent in the last month—I mean tidecycle. The legend was hidden for centuries."

"How did Adaro gain control?"

There it was. If I told them Adaro had killed Dani, I'd be revealing that the only way to control the serpent was to vanquish its present master. If I lied, would Dione feel it the same way I'd felt that mermaid's dishonesty at the raft last night?

I chose my words carefully.

"As a descendant of Eriana, I was able to awaken the serpent with my blood. The rest of the legend was hidden from me, and I didn't know she would fall under someone else's control after I awoke her. The legend said the one to bear Eriana's mark would become her master."

I let the implication hang, not looking at Lysi.

"Adaro is bound to the serpent through your blood sacrifice, then," said Dione. "Did the sacrifice take you from your human form? Is that why you are now a mermaid?"

I nodded.

Dione considered, absently tracing a hand over the table.

I was startled by a deep voice when the merman with dreadlocks spoke. "If the blood sacrifice did not die, but became a mermaid, perhaps this tie between the king and the serpent is not as strong as it ought to be."

Lysi twisted her mouth. "He was able to send it after me easily. Plus, he's ransacking the entire coast with it. I don't think there's a weakness here."

"If serpent and master are bound by blood," said Dione, "what happens to the serpent if its master is killed?"

My heart jumped, but the reaction was covered by Creon, who said, "It might break free from all control and go on a rampage, or avenge its master."

"Or," said Dione, "it might also die."

There was a pause. I had to take control of this conversation before they got any closer to the truth. How could I get their help while guaranteeing the serpent would end up in my hands, and not Dione's, or someone else's? My stomach churned. This group had no reason to let such an inexperienced mermaid carry out the deed. I had to convince them I was their only option.

"The problem," said Lysi, picking up the silence, "is that Adaro isn't easy to kill. We tried using iron, we tried blowing him up. That's why we need your help—"

Dione raised a hand, silencing Lysi. "Our priority is not to kill Adaro."

The words hung like a thick fog. *Not kill?* Had I heard her correctly?

"What?" I said.

"Sorry, but what do you mean?" said Lysi.

"Para la reina," said Creon, as though this explained everything.

"Everything we do is for the queen," said Dione, voice rising. "We are trying to find her, to free her from Adaro's imprisonment, to return her to her throne. She is the rightful ruler of the Pacific, not Adaro. Stopping him will come only after we have found the queen."

I dropped my gaze to the engraved table, taking in all of the attack sites. Another gemstone would surely be added in the next day or two. What were Lysi and I doing here if their goal wasn't to kill Adaro? I didn't care about finding Queen Evagore—not when Adaro was in the middle of destroying every coastal city he could get to.

"But I saw a group of you try and kill him at the mine!" said Lysi.

"We have learned since then," said the white-blonde mermaid.

"Learned what?"

"That he cannot be killed so easily."

"We lost lives in another failed attempt after the mine," said Dreadlocks. "Assassinating him will be even more difficult now that he has the serpent."

I glowered at them. "If you aren't going to use the information I give you to kill Adaro, then what do you need it for?"

Those around the table shifted. Dione raised an eyebrow.

"We can explain better if we know what your plan is," said Lysi with a warning glance at me.

Dione inclined her head. "The full plan is in strict confidence. Not even everyone at Kori Maru knows it. It is a question of security."

"You can at least tell us what the others know," I said.

"You are asking me to entrust two strangers with our war plans that have been under development for several tidecycles."

I crossed my arms. "I'm entrusting you with a legend that's been a part of my people for millennia."

Dione glanced between Lysi and me, brow furrowed. Everyone around the table became still.

For a long moment, Dione considered us. Then she said carefully, "We need to track the serpent and understand its power. Adaro needs to be at least a day away from Utopia before we act."

"So you're storming the city," I said.

She swept a long-fingered hand down the coast of North America. "As Adaro focuses on destroying human settlements, he is leaving Utopia without its king. A government is in place, of course, led by Nemertes. But this can be breached. So, yes, we plan to destroy the government and find our queen."

"I don't understand why you're going for the government," I said. "This is Adaro you're talking about, which means any government is just a symbol with no real power."

"It is the link between the king and his civilians."

"But if you're going to spend effort and resources to overthrow something, you should focus on the top of the chain."

"Mee—" said Lysi.

"The top of the chain is not a wise place to try and break," said Dione. "Consider one that binds an anchor to a ship. If you decide to attack at the top, you must sink the entire ship. If you attack the bottom, you must destroy the anchor. But to attack the middle? You simply cut the chain."

"That doesn't even—what will cutting the chain accomplish when the ultimate goal is to sink the ship?"

"I think I understand," said Lysi. "You're disrupting Adaro's rule over Utopia. By forcing yourself in the middle, you're giving yourself power over both the king and the civilians."

Dione nodded. "We are going to find Queen Evagore and place her on the throne in Utopia."

I looked down at the table, to the gap between the Canadian coast and the groove marking Utopia. It gave me small comfort to know that storming the Utopian government would lure Adaro there. That, at least, would save me the effort of trying to find him myself.

"What'll you do when he comes back with the serpent?" I said.

The window of time would be short. Adaro would return the second he found out, and with the serpent, he would move quickly.

"By then, we will have our queen and all of Utopia behind us. If, as you say, we cannot destroy the serpent—"

"We'll fight!" said Creon, pumping a fist.

The others around the table murmured their agreement.

I restrained from rolling my eyes. "You can't *fight* the leviathan."

Creon let his hand fall. They all stared at me.

"Use your army to attack, but our target should be Adaro," I said. "Don't worry about the Utopian government until the king is dead."

"Mee," said Lysi again, but I didn't care that I was being argumentative. This wasn't the time for politeness.

Dione narrowed her eyes.

"Besides," I continued, "what makes you so sure Utopians will fight Adaro with you? What if they're too scared to go against him? What if they even support him and see your attempt as treason?"

"This is not for you to question," said Dione, temper flaring.

"But—"

"Mee, stop it," said Lysi.

Dione once again raised a hand, commanding silence, then said more calmly, "We do intend to stop Adaro, but the majority voted on saving the queen as our first priority."

A majority vote? Interesting. Maybe she was trying to convince me that many of them supported this plan—but a majority meant there was also a minority. Others did not agree. But how many? Could I rally them?

"How will the coup work, then?" said Lysi with a sideways glance at me.

"I have told you enough," said Dione. "As I said, no one has the full details. It is the only way we can assure that, if someone is captured or leaks information, they will not be able to reveal everything."

"We modelled this strategy after Adaro himself," said Dreadlocks. "Those who have worked under his government tell us he makes sure no one knows everything about him—not even his closest allies."

I didn't like it, but what could I do? They'd told us the basics, as I'd told them the basics of the leviathan. And, like me, they'd withheld information—maybe even lied.

My insides twisted with frustration. Here we had a whole army ready for action, and I could do nothing. Every moment I spent here, powerless, people were dying at the hands of Adaro and the serpent.

I didn't want to destroy the chain or the anchor. I wanted to sink the ship. Lysi and I would need to have a serious conversation later.

"You can trust that once we have lured Adaro to Utopia, we intend to kill him," said Dione. "But we need your help for this. How can we destroy that serpent?"

Lysi and I looked at each other. How was I supposed to convince them to help *me* be the one to kill Adaro, without revealing why?

The silence stretched a beat too long. Dione opened her mouth—and a lie came to me in a flash. I blurted it out before she could speak.

"The legend says only a descendant of Eriana can defeat the serpent. To do this, he or she must kill the serpent's master."

They all gaped at me, including Lysi. I exhaled into the words, trying as hard as I could to believe this was true.

I need to do it. I am the only option.

"And you, as you said, are a descendant," said Dione, her stare so intense it seemed to burn my skin.

I nodded once. The glopping of water against stone grew louder in the silence.

"So you, personally, wish to be the one to kill him," said Dione.

My heart skipped a beat, but I said steadily, "It has to be me. It's in the legend."

Did she know I was lying? I cursed my inability to control my reactions. Lysi was so much better at hiding jolts of emotion than me.

"The Eriana Kwai mermaid is how we defeat him, then," said the white-blonde mermaid. "She is written in the legend."

Everyone looked to Dione with a mixture of hopefulness and uncertainty, but she merely continued to stare at me as if analyzing my every pore.

"You have a personal vendetta against him?" she said.

I was trying to come up with a way to make it sound like the white-blonde mermaid was onto something when everyone turned to the cavern exit. Something was happening outside.

"They're back," said Dreadlocks.

Murmurs broke out around the room. Dione held her gaze on me a moment longer, then turned away.

"Then let's not keep our comrades waiting."

Everyone pushed away from the table.

Noticing our confused faces, the blonde addressed Lysi and me. "There's an acoustic channel nearby. It moves between Utopia and the northern military line. We take shifts monitoring it."

We followed everyone out of the grotto to join the flocking crowd.

"What's an acoustic channel?" I whispered to Lysi.

"It's a current that sound travels down better than anywhere else. There are only a few, and the kingdom reserves them for long-distance messages."

"How long?"

"The best ones carry sound past the equator. Sometimes you can hear a blue whale from the other side of the ocean."

I gaped, adding yet another item to my list of reasons why the ocean was so mesmerising.

Lysi hummed thoughtfully. "This is probably why they picked Kori Maru. Adaro wouldn't suspect anyone of eavesdropping on the channel way up here."

We joined a growing crowd at the mouth of the canyon. The mood was light, cheerful, a pleasant tingling across my skin that dulled the itch of iron. Conversation and bursts of laughter rose over the chatter of fish and shrimp in the reef, and the colourful tails added a glow to the otherwise brown, red, and grey landscape.

Several minutes passed before the approaching group came into view.

As we waited, an odd feeling overcame me, one I couldn't identify, that brought to mind the distant past. I turned to Lysi, intending to ask her if she felt anything strange, and saw her staring open-mouthed at a mermaid floating a few lengths away.

"Lysi?"

Then someone behind us called out a greeting—I thought it sounded like *Coho*—and Lysi startled as though someone had slapped her. She shot in front of me and put both hands on my shoulders. All colour drained from her face.

"Mee, remember I started to tell you something before? The merman—the former human who was part of the assassination attempt?"

"Sure. Yeah."

Her eyes flitted away from mine for a moment. "He was from Eriana Kwai."

If Lysi hadn't been holding onto me, I would have sank.

"What?"

"I'm sorry I didn't tell you sooner. There's been too much going on."

My mind jumped to a million possibilities. Was he a former warrior? A kid who'd wandered too close to the water? Did he get lured?

She kept looking over to that mermaid floating a few lengths away. Why? I followed her gaze. The mermaid was curvy, with long black hair and caramel skin. Her attention was on the returning group. They'd arrived at the canyon and were being swarmed with questions.

I shook my head. My lips felt numb. "Lysi, who is he?"

Lysi seemed to choke on her words. It was a moment before she got them out.

"It's Nilus, Mee."

A fog engulfed my brain, disconnecting me from everything. The gurgling of the reef and the laughter and conversation died.

Could he have been lured but not killed? Was that possible?

My eyes burned. I blinked, angry with myself for grasping at such a dead hope—and at Lysi for leading me to disappointment. My brother was dead. He had been gone for over a decade. Wouldn't I know if he was still alive? Wouldn't I have felt it deep inside me?

"It can't be."

Lysi was mistaken. It was a desperate, impossible wish to think anything otherwise.

But as the returning mermen and mermaids came closer, that long-forgotten presence grew stronger. A distant emotion washed over me like a waterfall.

"He's here?" I said, the words numb on my lips.

Lysi nodded once. Her eyebrows pulled down. Pain exploded in my chest.

Every emotion rushed through me. Sadness, joy, fear—a surge of anger. Lysi knew Nilus was alive and hadn't told me? I thought back to the last few days, all that time we'd spent in silence. I thought back to when she'd met my parents on Eriana Kwai.

"Lysi, why didn't—?"

"Meela?" said a deep voice beside us.

A small cry escaped me. I didn't look. I closed my eyes for a moment, steeling myself, and then turned to face him.

Him. My big brother.

By sight, I would not have recognised him. His features had changed from human to merman—reptilian skin and face shape, overlarge red eyes, bulbous ears, and webbed fingers. Like all mermen, he was an exemplified sea demon and never reverted to a human-like state. He was worn and tired, hair long and ungroomed, stone crossbow over his back. But somewhere beneath this exterior was Nilus. I felt it in his aura. Everything about it was familiar, taking me back to my life before he left on the Massacre and everything changed.

I lunged for him and wrapped my arms around him, shouting something incoherent that sounded like, "Nil—how—ohmyg—aliv—!"

He made a faint noise, like a note of surprised laughter.

Underwater, my tears manifested as strange half-sobs and puffy eyes that were probably leaking, but I couldn't tell.

"You're a mermaid," he said in a strangled voice. "My god, how—? Lysi?"

Lysi spoke, but I couldn't hear the words through the fog in my brain. I closed my eyes, feeling Nilus' presence with every part of me. All the love I'd felt as a child, the affection that had been laid to rest alongside Nilus' memory, came flooding out.

It felt as though my heart had been transported back in time—and at once, I wished I could do just that—travel back ten years, five years, even to yesterday, to tell myself that everything would be all right, that Nilus was not dead, and I would hug him again one day.

When we pulled apart, Nilus gawked at me as if he was the one seeing a ghost.

A mermaid lingered beside us—the one Lysi had been staring at.

"Oh," said Nilus, blinking. "Meela, this is Ephyra, my wife."

"Wife?!"

Ephyra smiled, her teeth a perfect row of pearls. I managed to keep my jaw from falling open. She was curvy in all the right places, her skin smooth and tan, shiny black hair waving behind her like silk. Her heavy-lidded eyes and full lips glimmered with iridescent makeup.

That solves that mystery, I thought, deciding Nilus had definitely been lured.

Lysi cleared her throat. "When did you get here?"

"Two days ago," said Nilus, peeling his wide eyes away from me. "We went home to get the kids, and—oh, Meela, you have to meet them!"

"Kids? I'm an auntie?" I said shrilly.

I whirled as Nilus shouted for them to come over. Five miniature mermaids came zipping through the crowd, all girls, all with long black hair.

"Papa!" they all shouted, swarming him in the most adorable group hug.

I let out a sound that was halfway between a laugh and a sob. "They're all so beautiful!"

"Girls, this is your Aunt Meela."

Aunt Meela. The words were like honey.

I'd never really liked kids, but knowing I was related to these ones was an entirely different feeling. I opened my arms and was met with an enthusiastic and giggly group hug.

"This is Clio, Sedna, Halie, Pasithea, and"—Nilus put his hands on the eldest's shoulders—"Little Meela."

Her irises were the same colour as mine, her hair the same shade. She was about the age I'd been when I'd lost Nilus. My eyes burned with fresh tears.

"The next will be here in a few months," said Ephyra. She cupped a hand over her belly, which protruded so little I hadn't noticed.

"I'm an auntie," I said thickly. "My parents—oh, god, my parents! *Our* parents! I have to tell them."

I turned southwards as if I could return to give them the news right then. Then something occurred to me and I spun back to Nilus.

"You never came to us. You've been alive all this time."

His smile faltered. "No one would have understood."

I frowned. "That's not true. I would have, Nilus."

It felt strange to say his name after so long. My eyes swelled again with tears that wouldn't spill properly.

He pulled me into another hug.

I squeezed my eyes shut. "I can't believe I'm hugging you again."

All the affection I'd ever felt for Nilus raced through my veins, filling my heart so much I thought it would explode. It was as though the last ten years had not been robbed of him. Memories repressed from grief flashed through my mind: days exploring the forest, jumping in the ravine, climbing trees to get the juiciest apples, hiding inside hollow stumps, making forts out of branches, staying up late and sneaking outside to watch the stars.

Whatever was happening outside Kori Maru—whoever was being attacked or imprisoned—felt insignificant. So what if the Reinas weren't going after Adaro yet? We could stay here with everyone and help them with their coup. I didn't need to rush. Not when Nilus was here. Not when I finally felt, for the first time in so long, like everything was right in the world.

CHAPTER EIGHT - Lysi
Ruby, Emerald, and Amethyst

I didn't bother Meela with what was happening a short distance away. While she and Nilus talked, the others who'd returned from the acoustic channel whispered urgently. Panic rippled through them as if a cannon had plunged through the water.

I hovered closer to listen.

"... retaliation," said a mermaid. "Right over Utopia."

The word "iron" carried through the crowd in whispers.

Dione's eyes bloomed red. "How many casualties?"

"At least a hundred," said a bearded merman. "Sounded like there were supposed to be enough explosives to wipe out the city, but Adaro got there in time to stop most of them."

My pulse quickened. This meant humans had tried to wage war against Adaro—and failed.

"What exactly did the message say?" said Dione. "Is he planning anything?"

The volume of the conversation dropped. I made to push closer, but a hand closed around my arm. I spun to find Galene.

"We need to leave Dione to her council."

I glanced back desperately, unable to hear the conversation. The crowd pressed closer, everyone eager to know what was going on.

"Some of us have wondered if the humans would respond," said Galene. "They've been less friendly to us over the last few years."

"Meela knew the Americans would get involved as soon as Adaro broke the Aleutian treaty," I said. "It was a matter of time."

Galene wrinkled her brow, examining me. "Think there's a chance they'll be able to get rid of the serpent?"

I considered how humans had wiped out cities in wars among themselves. But the serpent had apparently just stopped something designed to destroy all of Utopia.

"I think they'll obliterate half the Pacific before they put a bruise on that serpent."

Galene kept studying my face like I was a foreign object.

I said, "I'm only relaying what Meela's told me about humans and the serpent. Adaro's unwise to—"

"I know. I believe you."

My gaze drifted over to Meela, still chatting with Nilus, the children hovering at their tails. I fleetingly marvelled that such well-behaved children could possibly be related to Meela.

"This'll get the king more supporters," said Galene, drawing my attention back.

I nodded. Adaro would seem the hero for stopping the explosives.

"The humans will look like the bigger evil," I said.

"Maybe. But I like to think most Northerners are aware of what Adaro's doing. The labour camp and all."

"What was the Pacific like before he took Queen Evagore?"

Galene's lips turned up in a half-smile. Something in her aura softened at the mention of her queen.

Before she could answer, Ephyra appeared beside us.

"May I borrow Lysithea for a moment?"

Galene nodded and backed away. "Later, sugarkelp."

Ephyra motioned for me to follow. "I want to show you something."

The canyon was deserted except for a few children left playing. We passed empty caves and mounds of coral.

The scar at my waist burned, the pain intensifying as we crossed into the shadow below the wreck. I dug my nails into my palms, forcing my attention elsewhere.

"I'm glad you made it here," I said to Ephyra.

I couldn't help remembering the last time I'd seen her, when she tried to capture me on Adaro's orders, and I tried to bite her face.

She offered a slight smile. "Same to you."

We turned into the same cavern as earlier, where the map was chiselled into the stone.

"We have been tracing King Adaro's whereabouts," said Ephyra.

"I've seen this. Dione showed me and Meela."

"Did she tell you the significance of the gemstones?"

"Attack sites?"

Ephyra placed a forefinger on the ruby at Eriana Kwai.

"Our sources from Utopia and the spies along the acoustic channels have helped us create a nearly complete map. Fortunately for us, the serpent's movement can be felt for leagues in every direction, making Adaro easy to track."

She traced her finger from Eriana Kwai to the ruby at the top of the Aleutian Islands, and then to one on Vancouver Island.

"He acquired the serpent at Eriana Kwai and then went to the Aleutian Islands before moving east again."

I scanned the rubies, committing their locations to memory.

"The next wave of attacks happened in Canada."

Ephyra traced a zigzag of emeralds. Then she moved to the next round of attacks, marked by amethysts. I took in every gemstone, determined to remember all of the locations.

"I do not think he moves in a predictable pattern," she said. "Tracking his location is a waste of time."

I looked up. "You don't think it's possible to predict where he'll go next?"

"Are you familiar with king tides, Lysithea?"

"Sure. When the full or dark moon coincides with the strongest tides. Happens a couple of times a year."

Ephyra nodded. "There is one pattern worth investigating. I noticed it when I worked for him."

"King tides?"

"During king tides, Adaro disappeared for a whole day without warning. He simply left, and no one knew where he went or why."

"Did anyone else notice?"

"I am not sure. We did not discuss it."

I considered this information. The behaviour was odd, but I had no idea what to make of it.

"What do Dione and the others think?" I said.

"They plan to leverage it. If we can expect the king to disappear, that will be a good time to attack Utopia."

"So when's the next king tide?"

"Next tidecycle."

We fell silent. I could tell Ephyra wanted to say more. I wondered if she'd been able to share a lot of valuable information about the king, having worked by his side for so long. Then I recalled Dreadlocks saying Adaro made sure nobody in his government knew everything about him.

"Why did you tell me this?"

"It is something I thought you might find interesting."

I nodded to the exit. "They aren't going to try and find him any time soon, are they?"

Ephyra hesitated. "It is not the priority."

A moment passed where we stared at each other. I saw my fears reflected in her expression, felt them in her heavy aura. All we had to work with was an odd pattern of behaviour. We were no closer to finding Adaro and the serpent.

"There are two wars happening, Lysithea."

I nodded. The effort at Kori Maru was dedicated to the civil war, not the one against humans. But the latter was leading to explosives being dropped all over the Pacific. We had to stop it as soon as possible. I didn't want to think about what might happen if we didn't.

"What do you know about Medusa?" I said.

If Ephyra thought this was a strange question, she didn't show it. "The king never spoke of her. Anyone who did was punished."

"He's scared of her?"

"Perhaps. He clearly wants us to forget she exists. He might be worried that many who followed him to the Atlantic regret their decision."

"Do they?"

"It is hard to tell. You know as well as I that no one speaks ill of the king."

Her eyes drifted to the map, but they were unfocused.

"I want to get Medusa's help," I said. "I think she's our only chance at defeating Adaro."

Ephyra seemed to consider this. She nodded slowly. "Perhaps."

Her agreement surprised me; I'd expected more resistance. Maybe I'd just spent too much time trying to convince Meela of the same.

"Meela doesn't think so," I said. "She's being as stubborn as a barnacle."

"Maybe she does not understand Medusa's power."

I shook my head. "It's not about that. It's about how long it would take to get there. I don't know how to convince her it's worth it."

A shadow eclipsed the cave entrance, and we spun around.

"Convince whom of what?" said Dione, as she and several others entered the cavern.

"Family troubles," said Ephyra with a graceful smile.

Dione looked at her a moment too long before saying curtly, "I see. Lysithea, may I speak with you privately?"

With a parting glance at Ephyra, I followed Dione out of the cavern. She led me to the surface—a place we could speak without being overheard. We breached to strong winds and a cascade of fat raindrops. Waves rolled in enormous, slow swells.

"Our meeting was cut short, but I wish to learn more from you and Meela."

"We told you everything."

She studied me, expressionless, the whites of her eyes stark against the grey sky.

"This news from Utopia requires my attention, but I will arrange a private meeting to debrief both of you in more detail."

This intrigued me. Was she trying to negotiate an exchange of information?

No matter what Dione told us, information on how to control the serpent would not be up for exchange. Meela and I agreed on that much.

"That would be nice," I said.

Dione nodded once. She seemed about to submerge, then stopped.

"Consider, Lysithea—" A tinge of red appeared in her eyes. "—that forging an alliance on half-truths and deceit would be most unwise."

CHAPTER NINE - Meela
Blood of Eriana

I followed Nilus through the canyon to his family's grotto. We kept glancing at each other with shy smiles. I was still trying to take in his appearance. Had his hair always been so dark, or did that change once he became a merman? His muscle mass had certainly increased.

I wondered what changes he noticed in me.

His daughters blitzed by us, giggling. Off on some imaginative adventure in the canyon, I was sure.

Clio, Sedna, Halie, Pasithea, Little Meela.

As soon as I got the chance, I wanted to get to know all of them. How did talking to kids work? Was I supposed to tell them stories? Maybe I should ask what their favourite animals were.

We made it to Nilus' grotto and he opened the door—a real wooden one with a knob and everything. I ran a hand up the smooth surface.

"Did you build this?"

"Me and Little Meela."

Nilus removed his crossbow and tossed it to the floor.

The grotto was roughly circular, with lumpy stone walls and an air pocket overhead. Littering the floor were a few dolphin-shaped figurines and a jumble of kelp, shells, and gems. Five starfish clung to the far wall in a perfect row. In the corner sat a rawhide bag and a pile of combs and jewellery.

"Is this everything you were able to bring from home?" I said.

"It's enough. The kids brought their favourite toys." He reached into the rawhide bag, dug around, and grinned. "Close your eyes."

I did. He grabbed my hand and put something in it. I closed my fingers around it, feeling a smooth stone on a ring.

"Is this—?"

I opened my eyes and let out a small scream. It was the onyx ring he'd once given me, the one I'd lent him as a token when he'd left on his Massacre. My fingers trembled as I turned it over. All these years, he'd kept it. It was exactly as I remembered it.

My eyes burned.

"You abandoned us, Nilus."

I looked up to see grief etched in his face.

"I never stopped caring about Eriana Kwai," he said. "Doesn't the fact that I'm here, hiding after I tried to kill Adaro, prove it?"

"I'm not talking about your loyalties. What about me, Nilus? Our parents?"

"I'm sorry, Meela. I was scared. I thought you would rather think I was dead."

"Me?"

Nilus drew a wooden container from the bag and removed the lid. He scooped a glob of dark paste and slapped it over his face.

"Maybe not you, as much. But our parents. Everyone else."

He scrubbed his face vigorously, massaging the paste into his skin.

I wanted to tell him he was wrong, but I couldn't. Until recently, maybe my parents did think transforming into a sea demon was a fate worse than death. A lot of our people hated mermaids enough to think so. But now?

I wondered how things had evolved on Eriana Kwai in the last few days. Did my people have a change of heart after what happened at the beach with Adaro and the serpent? Were my friends and parents making efforts to help everyone see the truth about merpeople?

"Well," I said, "they were fine with my transition."

Nilus froze in the middle of scrubbing his face. He peeked through his fingers with an expression as though I'd told him our father had decided to become a professional ballerina. "They weren't upset?"

"They were sad I had to leave, of course, but they were happy for me."

Nilus said nothing. He slowly lowered his hands, his red eyes flitting around the room. I picked up the quickening in his pulse as he considered this.

"So, you're going to go visit them the first chance we get," I said, and I was surprised at the anger in my voice.

I couldn't help feeling abandoned, even if it wasn't his fault he was lured. Part of me was also angry at Ephyra for taking him from me—for using the allure against him.

"Do you even love Ephyra?" I said.

"Of course I do! I wouldn't have married her if I didn't."

"She gave you no choice!"

"If she hadn't changed me into a merman, I would have died, Meela. She wouldn't have done that if she didn't love me."

We stared at each other, suspended in the cavern. We'd both abandoned life above water to be with a mermaid, but we had taken very different paths.

"I'm not asking whether she loves you," I said. "I'm asking whether you love her. Allure isn't the same as true love."

He examined the webs between his fingers. "Whatever it is, Meela, I'm happy."

"But how do you know it's not—?"

"Because when I look at her, it feels … it feels like my heart is expanding. I love everything about her, every part of her, both inside and out."

When I kept staring, stone-faced, he continued.

"Whenever I see her, I feel happier. I want to hug her and kiss her and protect her from everything bad in the world. Any day I'm not with her, I miss her, and I wish I could talk to her. I can't imagine how I lived my life before, and I can't imagine going back to that. I'm a better version of myself when I'm with her. From the day we met, I wanted to have all these crazy adventures together, and I kept picturing the future and how we would spend the rest of our lives. If that's just the allure, then I don't care."

My eyes burned with tears. I dropped my gaze, following the idle path of something bioluminescent near my tail.

"Nilus, I've spent half my life without you, and it's been horrible. I was an only child in a family that should've had a son."

"None of this would've happened if I hadn't been sent on the Massacre."

"I know that's not your fault. Things ended up this way, and I don't blame you for that. But it would've been a comfort to know you weren't dead."

I was still squeezing the onyx ring between my palms. I passed it back. Nilus held it delicately between his webbed fingers, examining the stone.

"It hurt every day," he said, "to be separated from you— from Eriana Kwai. I've missed everything about it. I'd love one more run through the forest. I want to feel moss under my feet, and smell cedar … I know it can never happen again. I wouldn't trade what I have now, but man, I miss that forest."

I knew what he meant—but that was where I'd always felt different. I'd loved the sea most of all, ever since I was a kid.

"Our people will always be a part of us," I said. "Even if we can never run through the forest or climb a maple tree again, Eriana is still in our blood."

Nilus grabbed a comb from Ephyra's corner to resume his grooming. "That's poetic of you."

"No, really. Eriana's our ancestor. Papa told me."

I hesitated. Though I'd sworn not to tell anyone about the serpent, I wanted to make an exception for Nilus. We might have spent the last ten years apart, but he still felt familiar, like someone I could trust the most after Lysi. Besides, Lysi had worked with Nilus during their assassination attempts. He could be trusted.

While Nilus tore through his matted hair with the comb, I told him about my Massacre, and how I had learned that Adaro was attacking Eriana Kwai because he was searching for the leviathan, Sisiutl, and how my friends and I searched for it where Adaro couldn't.

"Why did you give it to him?" said Nilus.

I scoffed. "I didn't *give* it to him. I wanted to find it and use it to kill him."

"But?"

"Dani ended up having control, not me."

"Dani? The girl you went to school with?"

"You remember her?"

He laughed. "She asked me on a date when you guys were seven. I told her she was a bit young for me. She didn't take it too well."

I let out a breath. The bubble rose to the cavern surface with a small *pop*.

That explained a lot.

"Well, I was able to wake the serpent," I said. "Only a descendant could do it. We're the blood of Eriana, you and I."

Nilus stared at his hands as though I'd told him he had magic powers. "Cool."

"Then Lysi saved my life by turning me into a mermaid."

He glanced back up, gawking. His face broke into a grin. "I knew I liked her."

I beamed.

Nilus finished on his hair and offered me the comb. I shook my head, not wanting to bother untangling my braids.

"How did Adaro get control, then, if Dani freed it?" said Nilus.

Though Dani and I had always hated each other, grief and pity twisted my gut. I glanced to the door, feeling for signs of life. Nobody was hovering nearby.

"He killed her," I whispered. "Control is passed by blood."

A moment passed in which the reality of the situation weighed more heavily on us.

"So ... you kill him, you get control?" he whispered.

"That's what I'm planning to do. I'll keep her tame until I figure out how to destroy her."

"Why do you refer to the leviathan as female?"

"She's more than a serpent. She's ... she's Eriana. The goddess. She's a part of the serpent. There's a whole legend behind it."

Nilus' mouth opened in a perfect O.

"The problem is that she makes a pretty good bodyguard," I said. "We can't get to Adaro."

"Even if you get past that thing, I still don't know how you'll do it. We tried twice. There's been at least one other attempt since then."

"There must be some weakness. We just haven't found it yet. I was hoping for power in numbers by coming here."

Nilus considered this. He poked absently at one of the starfish on the wall.

"The focus here is on seizing Utopia before Adaro returns. They believe Evagore is—"

"The rightful queen, I know. They think Adaro took her. What do you think happened?"

"I think they're right. Adaro is to blame for whatever her state—captive or dead."

I nodded. That was what I thought, too.

"What are the chances anyone here will help me get to Adaro?" I said.

"If you can prove your plan will get their queen back, they might help you."

"But if we can't—or if she's dead—Lysi and I are on our own?"

"Not entirely on your own. You'll have me."

I smiled.

"If Eriana is part of the serpent," said Nilus, "can I ask why you want to destroy her?"

"Destroying the serpent means freeing Eriana's soul from its host. The legend is complicated. But—" I glanced around and lowered my voice again. "Nilus, I might not even have to."

He looked at me sharply. I pressed on.

"If I can keep her under my control, I can use her to make sure nothing like this happens to our people ever again. This is what Eriana used the serpent for in the first place. I'd be continuing her legacy."

Something worked behind Nilus' expression. I couldn't tell what it was. Did he agree, or did he think I was crazy? A long-forgotten desire for my big brother's approval bubbled up inside me.

I was beginning to wish I hadn't said anything when Nilus looked at something over my shoulder, and I turned to see Lysi and Ephyra in the doorway.

"Sorry to disturb you," said Ephyra, "but the sun is setting, and these girls don't have a place to sleep."

Nilus threw an arm across my shoulders. "Priorities! Let's get you settled."

The four of us swam a short ways to an empty grotto. We covered the entrance with kelp weeds and used a rawhide bag to pull down a fresh pocket of air for the ceiling.

After saying goodnight to the others, Lysi and I stayed awake. Though we were far enough north that night would not fall at this time of year, the curtain of seaweed and depth plunged us into blackness.

"I found out something from Ephyra," whispered Lysi. "Up here."

We surfaced inside the air pocket to stop our conversation from carrying outside the grotto. There, Lysi relayed in a whisper what Ephyra had told her about Adaro disappearing during king tides, and that the Reinas were planning the attack around that time.

"Wait, I don't get the pattern," I said. "I thought tides cycled every twenty-eight days with the moon."

"They do."

Lysi raised a hand above the surface. Water trickled from her fingers. I felt through the darkness and placed my palm against hers.

"So what's a king tide? Why is it only a couple of times a year?"

"It's about the moon's orbit and phases. Tides happen because the moon and the earth are attracted to each other. The moon tries to pull the earth towards it." She closed her hand over mine and pulled me in so our noses touched. "But the only part of the earth that obeys is water."

Slowly, she pushed me away, and then pulled me in again. Water sloshed against us and the rock walls.

"The strongest pull marks a new tidecycle. But the moon's phase also has an effect. When the moon is full or dark, it has a stronger pull than usual. High tides get higher; low tides get lower. When a new tidecycle coincides with a full or dark moon, the tides are extra strong. This is a king tide."

I stopped her pulling me in again. "And Adaro disappears for a day every time this happens."

Lysi dropped my hand. "Yes."

I stared into the blackness. What were we missing? What did the combined pull of a new tidecycle plus the moon's phase mean? I'd never properly learned about tides, except for the tracking I'd done as a kid so I could meet Lysi at low tide.

I grabbed her hand again, sorry her explanation was over. I pulled her close so I could feel her breath on my face.

"How long until the next one?"

"It's going to happen next tidecycle—and after that, not again until winter."

I chewed my lip. That meant we had a month until the Reinas would storm Utopia. It wasn't soon enough. Adaro could destroy the entire coast by then. We needed to act now.

"They're using us," said Lysi in barely a whisper. "The serpent is the only reason Dione wanted me here."

"I know."

"She wants to talk to us again. What do we tell her?"

"Nothing. Not without the promise that they'll help us get to Adaro."

"They won't."

I wondered if Nilus knew anyone who would be on our side. Would it be enough to stage a rebellion within a rebellion? It was a fragile plan, I thought. Too dangerous. We would have to change Dione's mind.

"Mee, the more I think about it, the more convinced I am that we need to go to Medusa."

I sighed. "I knew you would bring that up. No."

"But they don't trust us enough to listen to us! And they won't tell us any more than we need to know to help their coup. Besides, Dione knew you were lying."

"Shh!"

"Well, don't you agree? We're worth whatever information we have to share."

Lysi might have been right, but agreeing would give her an excuse to push harder for us to leave Kori Maru.

"You're being paranoid," I said.

"You actually think we have a shot at changing their plan?"

"If Evagore is alive, and if we can find some way to help them get her back, they'll help us in return. Nilus agrees."

Lysi scoffed. "How is finding Evagore faster than going straight to Medusa? At least with Medusa's help, we'd have a chance at stopping his armies from advancing. Meela, he's one move away from ruling everything below the surface."

I glowered into the darkness. "I'm not leaving, Lysi."

"Come on!"

"First you don't tell me about my brother, and now you're trying to get me to leave him behind. Do you even care that he's my family?"

Lysi spluttered. It was a moment before the words came. "I told you I was sorry for that!"

"You had days to tell me, Lysi."

"It wasn't that easy. There was too much going—"

"And what about my parents? You could have told them about him. Now they might never know, if the worst happens."

"Don't—" She huffed. Her anger pulsated towards me. "You're saying that to get at me."

I gave a half-shrug. It might have been true, but I couldn't stop the anger from flooding out.

"I'm sorry, all right?" said Lysi. "It was a mistake not to tell you right away."

"You should be sorry."

I waited for her retaliation. It didn't come.

After a pause, she said, "I don't want to go to the Atlantic, either. But I'm trying to do the right thing for everyone."

"Leaving behind the only family I have down here doesn't feel like the right thing."

Before she could respond, I submerged.

I crossed to the far side of our cavern and curled up against the rocks. Lysi stayed where she was.

We didn't speak again that night. I spent so many hours trying to fall asleep that I ended up sleeping well past dawn. By the time I awoke, Lysi had already left.

I peeked through the curtain of seaweed to find the canyon bustling. Mermaids and mermen flitted in and out of caverns while children played games and chased each other with kelp weeds.

Deciding it was safe, I emerged into the canyon—and was almost bowled over by a group of mermen carrying a stone slab. I ducked out of the way just in time. I followed the curve of the terrain, pausing to watch a group of kids throwing shells and stones into hoops. They asked if I wanted to play, and though I did, I shook my head. "I'm looking for someone."

As I moved along, I thought I could feel eyes watching me, but when I looked, everyone was minding their business. Was I being self-conscious? Lysi had assured me several times that I was doing fine, and it was hard to tell I'd been a human only days ago.

"Morning, little sis."

I whirled, face splitting into a grin.

Nilus looked better groomed and rested, crossbow slung across his back like he was ready to hunt.

"Breakfast?" He offered me what looked like a string of seaweed with fish eggs stuck to it.

I accepted it hesitantly.

"Don't do what I did and refuse to eat anything but salmon," he said. "You need your vitamins."

"Thanks, brother."

I plucked off a few eggs. They were decent—less fishy than some of the other stuff Lysi had gotten me to eat.

"I was thinking," said Nilus. "You'll need a weapon. What kind do you want?"

I nodded to his crossbow. "Is that even a question?"

He beamed. "I'll show you how to make one."

He led me along the canyon, which stretched further than I'd thought. We rounded a bend and came to an area that looked like a bomb had recently gone off. Mountains of objects were piled everywhere. Dozens of merpeople were gathered around work surfaces, including Lysi and Ephyra. The mermen who'd been carrying the stone slab were positioning it in the midst of it all.

"Welcome to the armoury," said Nilus. "Chert, slate, argillite." He pointed to the piles of rock. "Bone, sinew, shells, things humans dropped—that's useful for ropes and stuff—and that's ironwood. Don't worry, it's not actually iron. It makes for a lighter weapon, but it's still strong. We've got other wood up there." He pointed to the surface, where a timber raft was tethered to the shipwreck some distance away.

"I want to make mine out of ironwood," I said.

We approached an empty worktable. Nilus placed an ironwood log and a stone chisel in front of me.

"You'll find the crossbow a lot different from what you're used to. It took me awhile to get accustomed to the weight, and the aim is all off underwater."

"Oh. Should I make something else?"

"No. Once you get the hang of it you'll be as skilled as before. Assuming you could shoot straight before, anyway."

I jabbed him in the ribs. "Anyo said I'm as good as you. Maybe better."

Nilus smiled sadly at the mention of our old training master.

Galene's laughter boomed across the canyon. She was leaning over Lysi, watching her chisel a slab of argillite.

"I told you, I haven't made my own longblade before," said Lysi.

"Clearly. Here, hold it like this."

Galene reached her muscular arms around Lysi and adjusted her hands over the chisel and argillite slab. Lysi tensed. She glanced up, caught my eye, and pulled an exasperated face. I smirked and returned to my ironwood.

"Jealous?" said Nilus.

"I trust her."

He hoisted a slab of chert onto the table. "She's a good kid."

"Does she get the big brother stamp of approval?"

"I'm more concerned about your influence on her."

I stuck out my tongue.

Nilus filed pieces of stone into bolts, while I built my crossbow. He paused every so often to guide me.

"Don't get carried away with the shape of the bow yet," he said as I carved. "Finish the stock first, and we'll add the lever."

"Aye aye."

I whittled the stock, trying to copy the shape of his, which I'd placed on the table for reference.

A roughly shaped crossbow and a pile of bolts later, Nilus said, "I hear you won't agree to go to the Atlantic."

I glared, offended that he and Lysi obviously had a conversation about me while I was still asleep. "You're taking her side?"

He tapped the end of his bolt-in-progress, considering, then honed it more. He kept his voice low as he said, "Meela, you're not working towards the same goal as everyone else here. They're going to quickly realise that, if they haven't already."

"What, then? You want me to leave?"

His fingers slipped from the bolt. He caught it before it landed.

"Meela, of course not! Don't even—"

"Sorry. I know." I put down my carving knife before I cut myself. "I don't want to be separated from you again, Nilus."

"It won't be permanent. We managed to find each other after all this time, didn't we?"

"It took ten years! How's that supposed to make me feel better?"

He stalled, chiselling carefully. "Even if you found a way to make these guys agree to go after Adaro—we need more than that to take down his entire regime."

I glanced at the mermaids and mermen working around us. I would have found it hard to believe this many merpeople couldn't make a difference, except I'd seen Adaro's power on the Massacre, and I'd seen the power of the Host of Eriana. I knew Nilus was right. Adaro had a government, loyal followers, and armies all over the globe. This group at Kori Maru wouldn't be enough to stop them.

"I've heard a lot about Medusa in my time as a merman," said Nilus. "Everyone speaks highly of her. She's ruled that half of the world for decades."

"But if we go all the way there, we're wasting time we could be spending trying to get to Adaro."

"Time you're using so preciously right now?"

I glared at Nilus. He pursed his lips.

I picked up my knife and resumed whittling somewhat aggressively. "He can't be that hard to find. He's only got the largest snake in the entire damn world with him."

"Yes, but the Pacific is the largest ocean in the entire damn world. He could be anywhere between Alaska and Chile."

I almost smiled.

"Besides," said Nilus, "what'll you do if you find him? You expect to just swim up and kill him?"

I shrugged.

"You need to stop and plan, Meela. You're blinded by revenge. Think about what needs to happen. You need Medusa, and you need her army."

"But how are we supposed to convince her to help us? How are we supposed to even talk to her?"

"You have an inside source from Adaro's kingdom. Lysi knows things from training—attack plans, strategies. And you know more than anyone about the leviathan! You know where it comes from and how to control it. Don't underestimate yourself. Plus, Medusa might not even be aware that Adaro is planning to invade her kingdom any day now. You can go with a warning."

I growled in exasperation.

"I can't come with you," he said. "But I can help you leave, if you decide to go."

I searched his face. My heart swelled when I found the brother who'd disappeared from my life so long ago.

"Promise me one thing," I said.

"Yes. I'll come with you to Eriana Kwai after. To Mama and Papa."

I smiled.

We finished making my crossbow and bolts, and I fired a few test shots into a stone face. It took me three shots before I got the aim right.

"Uh, not bad," said Nilus with forced casualness.

I cast him a sideways grin as I lined up the fourth. "Don't tell me I picked it up faster than you."

He said nothing.

The weapon fired with surprising force considering the water resistance. My fifth bolt shattered into pieces on impact.

I slung my crossbow over my back and stuffed the pile of bolts into a quiver. Nilus made me take all of them, assuring me he would make himself more tomorrow.

I went to rescue an exasperated Lysi from Galene.

"You must get this all the time, but you have beautiful eyes, Lysithea."

I stopped behind Galene. "Can I borrow my girlfriend, please?"

They turned, Lysi giving off a definite air of relief. She followed me without a word.

I pulled her into a divot between two boulders, glancing around to make sure no one was near.

"So," I whispered. "How are we gonna get there?"

Lysi stared blankly. Then, slowly, her frown turned into a hint of a smile. "North is quickest."

"Through the Arctic?"

Lysi nodded.

I imagined all the ice floes, blizzards, oil rigs, and gigantic creatures we'd have to face.

"You sure?"

She shrugged. "That's how everyone got here from the Atlantic in the first place."

I chewed my lip. I wasn't trying to be difficult, but I wasn't sure about crossing the Northwest Passage. I'd spent a unit of social studies learning how treacherous that was. Granted, that was for humans, not mermaids, but it still didn't sound fun.

"Could we go south?"

"Medusa's in the North Atlantic. Going around South America would take too long."

"What about the Panama Canal?"

"You mean that man-made channel between North and South America? I'm sure that'll go over well, a couple of sea demons gliding through. We'll just ask nicely if they can let us pass and hope they don't shoot us in the face."

"All right, all right."

"Besides, American vessels are waiting to blow us to pieces if we go south or west."

I thought for a long moment, weighing the many things that could go wrong no matter what we decided to do.

"How will we sneak into the city once we get there?" I said.

"We don't need to sneak. The city's huge. No walls, no border."

"That seems … unsecure."

"Before Adaro, merpeople had a peaceful history. There are a small number of kingdoms, and the queens kept to their respective oceans. We never went to war, so there was no need to build walls."

I slumped. "All right. But if I freeze to death …"

Lysi smiled, her eyes glinting in the rock's shadow. "I'll keep you warm."

Galene was right, I thought, as a wave of heat rose in my cheeks. Lysi did have beautiful eyes.

CHAPTER TEN - Meela
Laws of Fae

We left for the Atlantic in the middle of the night. Nilus diverted anyone who happened to be awake so we could sneak away without having to explain where we were going, or why. He vowed not to tell Dione he knew anything about our disappearance.

We carried our new weapons: my crossbow and Lysi's black longblade. She'd sharpened the edge so thoroughly that I wondered if she stripped it down to molecular levels.

"We might have a problem at the Bering Strait," she said, once we'd travelled out of hearing distance. "It's only about sixteen leagues across, and Adaro said he stations the army there to keep the Atlantic out. But he wants to keep all of us in just as much."

She said 'sixteen leagues' as if referring to the length of a bathtub, but I supposed merpeople could sense up to a league away in the right conditions. It would be easy for an army to guard the entire Strait.

"We're going underneath, then?" I said.

"Uh, it's also less than thirty fathoms deep."

I didn't like where this was going. "Don't tell me we're trying to force our way through."

"We're going over top."

I raised my eyebrows.

"Part of the Strait should be covered by ice," said Lysi.

I squeaked. "We'll literally be fish out of water!"

"First of all, never call a mermaid a fish unless you're trying to insult her. Second, we'll be fine. Nothing will be able to get us. Well, unless we encounter a ship. Or whales breaching through the ice. Or a polar bear. Or—"

I groaned. "Why did I agree to this?"

She kissed my cheek and pulled me along.

We travelled in silence, keeping our feelers out for anything strange. The sun rose. Our path was crossed by squid, cod, and the occasional whale. Chunks of ice formed overhead, small and slushy, reminding me of the shaved ice Annith's mother made.

It pressed on the back of my mind that we would need to discuss what, exactly, we were going to ask of Medusa. Lysi would probably feel differently about how much we should share with the Atlantic Queen. But I was too relieved that we'd stopped arguing to bring it up. Lysi must have felt the same, because the sun crossed the sky and touched the horizon, and still, neither of us had mentioned a plan. We might as well have been taking a holiday, for the lack of discussion about the business we'd have to attend to once we got to the Atlantic.

The temperature dropped significantly by the time we parked on a tiny island for a few hours' sleep. I was uncertain about stopping. Though my new body handled the cold impressively, I worried a chill would set in if we stopped moving. Maybe I was being ridiculous, but I didn't want to ask. I tried to gauge if Lysi was afraid or worried.

She caught me staring and smiled.

I frowned. "Why is your aura so hard to read?"

"What do you mean?"

"I can read Nilus' mood so much more easily than yours."

"Nilus is your family."

"But you and I are ..." Heat crept into my face. "I thought there would be a special connection between us."

"Life is not that poetic."

I rolled over, studying the sky, searching for constellations that wouldn't appear. I hated this lack of nightfall and wondered how anyone got a proper sleep all summer around here. I was both exhausted and wide awake.

"You'll be able to pick up everything more easily in time, Mee. You can't expect to be an expert at this right away. It's all a practiced skill."

"I guess."

Lysi shuffled around a bit. Her face appeared in front of mine. "What do you say we practice some other skills?"

I laughed. "Smooth."

I pulled her towards me.

We slept for three hours at most before continuing northwards, swimming between a steadily rising floor and thickening ceiling of ice. Our meals consisted of whatever clams and shrimp we found along the bottom.

When the depth grew so shallow I could see both surface and floor, Lysi stopped. Nerves twisted my gut. The army would be close, now.

"We need to climb, don't we?" I said.

The ice had grown thick enough to support us, though it was broken and necessitated careful navigation.

Lysi reached for my hand. Without another word, we found a crack and hoisted ourselves out.

The above world was flat and empty. Beneath the moaning wind were gentle creaks of broken ice and waves glopping below.

We pulled ourselves across, balancing on the unsteady floes.

Feeling like I was navigating a minefield, I prayed that all the natural movement and groaning ice worked in our favour. Maybe our relatively small bodies wouldn't be noticed from below.

"Let's decide now what we're going to tell Medusa," said Lysi with the air of someone playing a game of distraction.

"Sure," I said casually, as though I hadn't been obsessing over this since we left.

"I'll tell her how Adaro's closing in on the Atlantic," she said. "The locations of all his armies."

"Make sure you tell her everything you can remember about your time serving. Attack plans, strategies. Plus we can relay everything Kori Maru had on that stone table. We know exactly where he's been and when. That's a lot of valuable information."

"But it's like Dione said, isn't it? We know where he's been, but not where he'll go."

"But we still know more about Adaro's strategies than most. We would be like the queen's spies."

Lysi didn't share my enthusiasm. "We need more than that if we want her to ally with us."

"Can't we ask for her help in exchange for this information?"

"Mee, the Atlantic Queen is not going to strike a deal with two mermaids from the Pacific, even if we do have information about Adaro's movements. She owes us nothing, and she definitely won't send her armies to battle based on that."

When she put it like that, my optimistic little fantasy sounded stupid.

I sighed. "Fair point."

We were quiet for a few minutes while we pulled ourselves along. The waves rose and fell, sending long ripples beneath the broken sheets of ice.

"If we have to tell her we know about the serpent," I said, "I think we should tell her what I told Dione, how I have to be the one—"

"No. We aren't lying to the queen. If she realises, we're done. We have to tell the truth."

"We *can't* tell the truth about the serpent—"

A shadow passed beneath us. We stopped moving at once, holding our breaths. I watched Lysi for a reaction. She stared through the ice, brow furrowed.

After a moment, she said, "Whales."

I relaxed, but Lysi stayed tense. I wondered if she was worried the whales would mistake us for seals.

We waited until their shadows disappeared before continuing on.

Lysi was right that lying to Dione did not work in our favour, and lying to the Atlantic Queen would be risky. The best bargaining power we had was knowledge of how to control the deadliest weapon in the world—but spreading that information around was also dangerous if it ended up in the wrong hands.

"There has to be another way to go about this," I said.

"Mee, the potential to control the serpent is the only thing that will get the queen's attention. Why else would she get involved in a war that's not her own?"

"But it is her war!"

"Not yet. Adaro might be preparing to strike, but he hasn't. We're asking Medusa to initiate the war between Atlantic and Pacific by striking first. That's a big decision, and it had better come with a high return."

"If she's the queen everyone says she is, she'll want to stop the war regardless."

Lysi wilted. "I guess."

"Besides," I said, "if we tell her the truth, she'll take what we say and go after the serpent."

"We can make sure we get to the serpent first."

"And what if she kills us to ensure that doesn't happen?"

Lysi hesitated for a fraction of a second. "She won't. Besides, even if she does end up with the serpent, I'm sure we'll be a lot better off—"

"No. We're not taking it out of his hands only to put it into someone else's. We need to finish this."

Lysi gave a deep sigh, her breath clouding in the air.

We continued in silence for a long while.

When a grey mass rose in the distance, I nodded towards it. "Land?"

"Diomede Islands. We're going between them where the ice is thickest."

I tried to mentally locate myself on a map. I'd taught myself geography from one of Tanuu's high school textbooks. I remembered reading that these two islands marked the border between Russia and Alaska, and the International Date Line put one island nearly a full day ahead of the other—but I couldn't remember anything useful, like what kind of population these islands had.

The ice thickened enough that ridges rose where the breaking floes pushed against each other. Icicles formed in Lysi's hair. My braids solidified down my back. Thankfully, while I recognised the cold, it wasn't uncomfortable in my new body. The goose bumps prickling up my arms seemed purely aesthetic—something I pointed out to Lysi, and which she didn't find as exciting as I did.

We kept going, and going, and going. It seemed as though the Diomedes would never get here. I fell into a trance, eyes on the ice, one hand in front of the other. The friction against my tail stung like sandpaper. Every time I turned my head, my icicle-braids pressed heavily against my shoulders.

So when we emerged onto to a flat plain, I was startled to find we'd made it to the islands. We moved between them—Big Diomede on our left, Little Diomede on our right. We would definitely be over top of the army now, if we hadn't passed it already.

The wind blew hard. With the pure white landscape, hollowness in my ears, and numbness beneath my skin and scales, I felt an odd sensory deprivation. I vaguely wondered why I hadn't turned into a mermaid-shaped ice sculpture.

The ice continued to thicken until even the slow rise and fall of waves was subdued. The thickest ice was closer to Little Diomede, so we stuck to that side of the pass.

Abruptly, Lysi stopped.

Sensing her panic, I grabbed my crossbow. "What is it?"

She tilted her head, listening. The hollow wind whipped around us.

"Load your crossb—"

A crack split the air. I spun, a hiss escaping my lips.

A couple of lengths away, a spear jutted up from the ice. A head followed with red eyes and ice-encrusted hair.

Before I could process this, the merman raised his arm.

"Down!" said Lysi.

We flattened, rolling out of the way as the spear flew towards us.

Without considering, without choosing to act, I sat up and let loose a bolt.

It grazed the merman's ear, catching a lock of hair. I cursed. I'd forgotten to compensate for the weight of the ironwood.

Another crack rang beside us. Lysi ducked in time to avoid a flying dagger.

The first merman shouted, voice rough. "It's them! Don't let them get—"

I fired. My bolt hit him in the chest. Blood splattered over the snow, shockingly red. He sank out of sight.

His words echoed. *It's them.* Was the army instructed to watch for the two of us?

I spun to the second merman and found him already pinned beneath Lysi, her blade pressed to his throat.

A dark shape appeared in my peripheral. Someone had erupted from behind an ice mound. I flattened out as something soared over my head.

Three figures raced towards us, roaring.

Humans.

At the same moment, more mermen pulled themselves up through cracks in the ice.

I turned my crossbow, not knowing whether to aim at humans or mermen.

There was a squelch and the overpowering smell of blood. I whirled to Lysi, heart wrenching. The merman beneath Lysi went limp as the longblade drew across his throat.

In my moment's hesitation, the nearest human threw something—and it hit my stomach.

Lysi screamed. I gasped, falling onto my back. In the next second, Lysi was bending over me.

"Meela!"

I clutched my stomach, panicking. "Did it go through me?"

Lysi yanked my hand away. She examined my stomach, wide-eyed.

"Oh, it's okay! It was stone, not iron. You're fine."

I looked down. Not even a mark.

I had no time to feel embarrassed in the chaos erupting around us. At least a dozen mermen had pulled themselves from the water. But with the humans advancing, all focus turned to them.

The nearest human fell back, blood spurting over the snow through a gash in his sleeve. The other two drew closer. I couldn't tell if they were men or women behind their parkas and covered faces. They hurled dagger after dagger at the mermen.

Lysi and I backed away, ducking to avoid the flying weapons. Blood stained the snow from the falling humans and filled my nostrils. Screams and roars echoed off the ice.

Before anyone could notice, Lysi and I pulled ourselves behind the ice bank. We found a pile of man-made weapons—none of them iron—plus three backpacks and pairs of snowshoes. We retreated further away from the scuffle as fast as we could.

I was surprised at my agility above the surface. Though I'd seen mermaids move on land and experienced how shockingly fast they were, I'd somehow expected to feel slow and helpless.

I prepared for more mermen to pursue us and burst through the ice on all sides. But we kept going, scraping across the surface towards isolation.

"Those poor people," I whispered.

If the Diomede people hadn't known to use iron against merpeople, that meant they must have been new to this war. Like the Aleuts, they probably hadn't had problems with merpeople until now. Adaro had been too busy focusing on Eriana Kwai to attack them.

Now, everyone was in danger.

Either Lysi didn't hear me, or she didn't know what to say, because she remained silent. I wondered if she was considering the merman's words—"It's them." We were being hunted; it was no question.

The noise of the scuffle disappeared into the wind. Minutes passed, and then an hour. Nobody followed.

My skin tingled as it dried in the cold air, and every part of me craved returning to the saltwater. We'd been above the surface for so long.

After at least two more hours, the wind dried my skin so thoroughly that the tingle was replaced by a growing burn.

What happened if a mermaid stayed out of water for too long?

"Lysi," I whispered. "My skin."

"I know. Hold on a bit longer." Her voice was high, broken.

"How much?"

"Less than a quarter-tide. I want to make sure we're past the army."

I groaned. What was that, three hours? I couldn't make it that long. My arms were ready to fall off, the muscles searing, and my whole body felt like it had been roasting in the sun for days.

I decided I'd take a quick dip at the next break, regardless of what Lysi said.

But the next break didn't come. The ice had become too thick.

The sun crawled across the sky. The landscape became a tundra. The bright white snow and icy mounds hurt my eyes. I longed for the dark, blue-green depths.

"Lysi?" My raspy voice barely made it past my tongue.

"Next break in the ice," she whispered.

Panic clouded my thoughts. Would we die up here? Would my body shrivel up and be left to scavengers? What a lame way to go, after everything I'd been through.

"Can we break a hole?" I begged.

"No. We'll attract attention if we start smashing the ice. Don't worry, it shouldn't be much longer."

But her voice sounded weak, scratchy, like my skin felt.

"You've been saying that for ages."

I'd reached a point at which I did not care about attracting attention when a dark shape moved below us. My heart jumped. This meant the ice had thinned enough to see through. It was a seal, and it was making a beeline. Was it heading for an air pocket?

I followed, digging my nails into the ice to pull myself faster.

Yes, there was something ahead, tall, thin, and spiralling. It poked through an opening in the ice. Then several more poked up beside it.

I stopped.

Yep, you're dying, I thought. *Now you're hallucinating unicorns.*

"What's wrong?" said Lysi.

I squinted ahead, not wanting to voice what was happening in my brain.

"Oh, that's nothing to be scared of," she said. "They're narwhals."

I looked at her sharply. "So they're real?"

She cracked a smile. "Yes."

"And they're breaching?"

"Told you we'd make it."

She'd barely finished the sentence when I took off, clambering towards my unicorn saviours with every last bit of energy.

"Mee, wait!"

I ignored her. My skin seared. I needed to get back into the water.

"Meela!"

Whatever she had to say could wait. She had just told me narwhals were nothing to be afraid of.

Below, the dark shape of the seal was still racing towards the hole.

The narwhals must have felt me coming because they submerged. All of the horns disappeared so abruptly that I wondered if Lysi and I had shared the same hallucination.

I was a few lengths from the hole when fingers clamped around my tail. I shrieked in surprise—and a bit of pain—and rounded on Lysi.

The pressure built in my eyes as they filled with blood. "What's the matter with—?"

The ice vibrated. I whirled. Something heavy, four-legged, bounded towards us.

A puff of air sounded as the seal poked its nose up.

In a blink, a polar bear pounced on the hole and its head disappeared beneath the ice.

Red bloomed across the surface. The bear withdrew its head, jaws clamped around the seal's neck. It lifted the limp seal from the water and dragged it across the ice, leaving a streak of blood across the snow. The red was blinding against the stark white surface.

Lysi grabbed my jaw and turned me to face her. Her eyes were red, her teeth bared. "You need to wait, Meela! How many times do I have to tell you to use your brain before you do something stupid?"

I pulled away. "Would you stop smothering me? It's not like it would've killed me. Only iron can—"

"You can still be killed by a predator!"

I opened and closed my mouth. *Oh.*

"Fine," I said stubbornly. "But I still wish you'd back off a little."

"Don't listen to me, then. It's not like I know what it's like to be a mermaid."

The polar bear continued to back up, dragging the seal away from the hole. Behind it, two cubs gambolled out from a snowy mound. They were new, no bigger than raccoons and clumsy on their paws.

My anger melted.

"Aww!"

Lysi gave me an exasperated look.

The cubs pounced on each other, bringing to mind a young Nilus and me, while the mother watched us between gory bites. Her white legs, chest, and snout became soaked in blood. I wondered how she would ever wash it off.

Lysi led us in a wide, careful arc to the hole. The bear's eyes followed us, but she showed no interest in pursuing two bony, blubber-less mermaids.

At long last, we reached the opening and plunged into the waves. I groaned at the blissful feeling of the water against my dry skin, like rubbing oil on chapped hands.

"I'm sorry," I mumbled.

"It's okay," said Lysi, calmer now. "But you need to have patience around here, all right?"

I pursed my lips, knowing she was right. At the same time, I hoped she wasn't going to get mad at me for every mistake I made.

"Well, we made it up the Bering Strait," she said, more defeat than victory in her voice. "Now we just have the Arctic Circle to cross."

I looked around. Sheets of ice and deep icebergs formed a maze in front of us.

"That was terrible! And we have to do that again coming home."

"At least then it'll be with the help of Medusa's army," said Lysi.

I hoped that was true.

The narwhals, who had submerged in a hurry at the polar bear's arrival, went back to breaching. There were ten adults and two babies, all black and white with long, lumpy bodies. I watched them with interest, trying to figure out how they didn't all stab each other with their horns. Then I wondered why only some had horns, and decided those must have been the males. I tried to feel the difference in their auras.

"They're gentle," said Lysi. "Not like orcas."

We watched them pass us as they headed northwards.

My excitement from what felt like a lifetime ago flooded back. "Can we swim with them?"

To my surprise, she considered. "I guess they'd help camouflage us. But if they get aggressive or if anything feels off, we're jetting out of there, all right?"

"Deal."

The pod watched us curiously as we approached, but showed no signs of annoyance. We swam alongside them, and soon they seemed content to ignore us.

Icebergs rolled and cracked, melting in the sun and drifting with the tides. It dawned on me that I was unable to sense what waited in the distance. The ice interfered with the currents.

I would have been nervous about being unable to sense oncoming threats, but the surrounding pod gave me a sense of security.

"Why can I be killed by a predator but not a human?" I said. "And why can I kill a merman now with wood and stone, but I needed iron to do it when I was a human? Are humans just weak?"

"No. Well, I don't know. It's one of those laws of nature."

I considered this, but found the answer too vague. "But look at the force of a wooden crossbow compared to—"

"You're thinking of numbers and calculations," said Lysi. "It's more like, why do fish lay eggs but we have live young? Why do salmon only live a few years but turtles get to live to be a hundred?"

"What does that have to do with it?"

"It's the way nature is. You're talking about an ancient law of fae."

"Law of fae?"

"We learn about them in school. This one says fae can kill other fae, but humans can only kill us with iron."

I'd never considered that before. The idea gave me inspiration. "Is a giant serpent considered fae?"

Lysi's mouth twisted in a smile. "Why? Do you know of a second one that we can use to kill this one?"

"Not quite, but maybe there's some other law that can help us here."

Lysi's brow furrowed in thought. "Maybe."

The Arctic was vaster than I imagined. It was hard to track where we were and how long we'd been travelling, since nightfall never came. Our pod followed a jagged gap in the ice coverage to ensure easy breaching, which served Lysi and me well.

Part of me wished I could pretend to be a narwhal for the rest of my life. Their auras were so friendly and carefree that they lightened my mood.

It saddened me to think pods like this were at risk because of us. If people kept trying to take out mermaids in one swoop, everything nearby would be affected. Mothers, babies, all of the ocean's creatures would pay for this war that had nothing to do with them. It was blood that could never be washed off. I would do everything in my power to protect them.

Congratulating myself on distinguishing our new friends' auras, I spent an afternoon coming up with names for all of them. I decided on plants from my mother's garden.

I caught Lysi smiling at me and raised an eyebrow. "What?"

"I like it when you're like this."

I glanced around. "A narwhal?"

She laughed. The sound brought a smile to my lips.

"Your aura," she said. "There's something about it these last few days. It's more familiar than it's been in a while."

I didn't quite know what she meant, but her smile stripped away the need to respond.

The icebergs became so deep that I had to strain to sense their bottoms. I didn't know whether to feel smothered by their size or awed by their resemblance to enormous ice castles. The currents had chiselled them into incredible shapes, their bottoms all pillars, caverns, spikes, and pockets. I grazed my fingers over the smooth, cold surfaces as we drifted past. The ice was like glass, and filled with bubbles.

"Why does everything look so green?" I said, admiring the glow on my skin.

"It's the algae in the ice. See?"

Lysi ran a finger along it, peeling off a layer.

I hardly believed how much wildlife was here. I'd expected the Arctic to be sparse, like an underwater desert. But all around us, the narwhals snapped at cod fish, and in the distance, a high-pitched chorus of squeaking, chirping, and whistling bounced off the glaciers. If we weren't underwater I would have thought it was a flock of songbirds.

"What is that?" I said.

"Belugas." Lysi snatched a cod in each hand and offered me one.

I whirled around to look. I'd never seen a beluga. The noise grew louder, and I caught a glimpse of their blindingly white bodies passing some distance away.

Grinning, I took the cod from Lysi. If the Pacific was my favourite place in the world, then the Arctic was my second favourite.

I couldn't tell how much time passed, and whether it was day or night, but the time came when our pod veered too far north. Right after I'd taught Lysi all their names, too.

With sadness, Lysi and I broke away.

"Bye, Parsley!" I called as the last tail disappeared into the blue.

Lysi shook her head and kept swimming.

The world fell into deep silence but for the groaning ice, as melancholy as the wind had been when we'd crossed the Bering Strait.

The pod had been a comfort through the barren landscape, but now we had to make our own way to the Atlantic. Would Medusa listen to us? What if the Atlantic Kingdom had already been taken over by Adaro, and we didn't know it? Thinking about all the things that could go wrong once we got there churned my stomach.

I took Lysi's hand, deciding that as long as we had each other, we would be all right.

CHAPTER ELEVEN - Ben
Myths and Gods

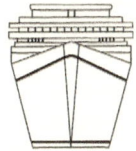

Reeves hoisted himself from the pool and sat on the edge, catching his breath. He lifted his goggles to his forehead and wiped an arm across his eyes. He checked the clock before he could stop himself. Forty minutes.

He reminded himself his time didn't matter today. This was about getting back in the water. He refused to let it become a PTSD trigger.

Personal victories, he told himself.

Still, he should have been faster.

In the lane next to him, Bagh splashed to a stop and pulled off his goggles, panting.

"You good?"

"Yeah," said Reeves. "Thanks."

Their voices echoed in the empty building.

"Beer pong tonight. You in?"

Reeves could hardly imagine playing drinking games at the moment, but he said, "Maybe."

"It's okay, I get it. You're afraid I'll kick your ass again."

He laughed. "I'm positive you'll kick my ass, Bagh."

"We could play something you're good at. I don't know, a game where you have to do math to make the other person take a shot?"

Reeves shook his head, grateful for the cause to smile.

Across the pool, the hum of the hot tub beckoned him. "I'm gonna hit the jets."

He left Bagh to continue his laps—where he would most certainly do better than forty minutes.

Reeves peeled off his swim cap and was about to sink into the hundred-and-four-degree tub when he heard a distant ringing. He jogged carefully across the tiles to grab his phone.

"Hi, sir."

"There you are," said Officer Miller.

"Sorry. I was doing laps."

"Running?"

"No."

A pause.

"Swimming?" said Miller. When Reeves didn't reply he said, "Jesus. Take a rest."

"Yes, sir."

Perhaps the officer had a point, given that Reeves had had to spend four terrifying hours treading among Perseus' wreckage before anyone found him. But to Reeves, ten days was enough recovery time.

He sank into the hot tub with the phone pressed to his ear.

"Listen, you don't have to do this anymore," said Miller. "You can retire with a generous reward for your service."

Retire? He wasn't even thirty yet, and the man wanted him to retire?

"I appreciate it, sir, but I can't accept. My entire team—" He ground his teeth. Saying it aloud sounded so matter-of-fact. No words could describe it properly. He drew a breath. "My team died because of me. And Larson's."

"There was nothing you could do."

"I could have refused to let it happen."

"You would have been disobeying orders. You had no choice."

"Every action a man takes is a choice."

Miller fell silent. Reeves shifted so the strongest jet hit his left shoulder blade.

He didn't even mention the mass destruction the Gulf of Alaska would have undergone if all twenty torpedoes had launched. He had never been much of an environmentalist, but he couldn't believe how close he had come to destroying an entire ecosystem. His kids—if he ever had any—would never have been able to see a whale, and it would have been his fault.

"We can't fight the merman with depth charges," said Reeves. "Not when he has a leviathan in his power."

"We've got choppers and satellites tracking the thing until we figure out what to do."

At least they were taking a more calculated approach. Still, it had taken a lot of wasted deaths for this to happen.

"Did you relay the message he gave me?" said Reeves.

The word 'me' was bitter on his tongue. He wished the merman had chosen someone else to deliver the message— one of his crew, who deserved to be alive instead of him.

"Every vessel is on its way to shore," said Miller.

"What about the international ones?"

"Them, too."

Reeves closed his eyes and leaned back. *Good.* Those lives, at least, he could save.

After a long silence, Miller sighed. "Look, why don't you take a vacation somewhere. Go on one of those college cruises. You've been through a lot and need time to recover. Physically and mentally."

Reeves drew a breath of chlorine-infused steam. After everything he'd been through, every award he'd received, they didn't trust him.

"We have marine experts advising us over here," said Miller, as if reading his thoughts. "Scientists. Biologists. As much as I hate to admit it, this is out of our expertise."

"It's not. You said yourself this is an act of terrorism."

Miller hesitated. "The line is fuzzy."

Officer Miller was right that Reeves was completely exhausted. In fact, he was too exhausted to argue any longer.

"All right. I'll look into a vacation."

"Good. I hear Dominican is real nice. My niece went there on spring break. She's about your age."

Reeves drove home from the pool in silence, not even allowing the radio to distract him. He would have to research Norse legend. He remembered reading about the Midgard Serpent as a teen, when he and his friends were on a fantasy role-playing campaign. He was a Paladin, back then. God, how things changed. How would sixteen-year-old Ben react, knowing he would live his dream and become a Team Chief in a few years' time? Would he be proud to know the path he'd followed, the decisions he'd made?

The Midgard Serpent was one myth he would investigate, but other cultures must have had legends of sea monsters and serpents, too. One of them surely had information on how to kill it—or how the merman managed to gain control of it.

When Reeves got home, he defrosted the most generous portion of spaghetti he had and topped it with half a block of cheese. He then crossed to his bookshelf and pulled down the twice-opened King James Bible his grandma had given him. He would start his research here. He seemed to recall something about a leviathan in the Bible.

What's gotten into you? said a voice in his head. *A few near-death experiences and you've turned into a praying man who spends Friday night reading the Bible.*

He pulled out a barstool, took a mouthful of spaghetti, and cracked the book open.

He didn't care. He would keep praying. On the brink of whatever this was, he needed a god to turn to.

CHAPTER TWELVE - Lysi
The Atlantic Kingdom

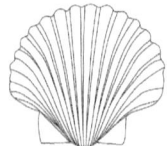

If we had to spend one more day in the Arctic, I would go insane. The sun taunted us, circling our heads and bouncing off the horizon without setting.

We must have travelled for half a tidecycle; it was hard to track.

When we made it south enough that twilight finally darkened the sky, I nearly cried in relief.

"I never want to see another iceberg," said Meela.

I grimaced. Mentally, we were diminished. Physically, we were disasters—bony from the long days of exertion, and moving with the agility of a couple of sea cucumbers. Meela's hair, like mine, was packed with plant life. It had reached the point where she could no longer undo her braids. Thankfully, her green eyes still sparkled when she looked at me.

"Is that it?" she said, running a hand up her arm. She must have been talking about the activity on the current.

"Should be."

I tried to smile. It came off nervously. Except for my deployment to the South Pacific, which hardly counted, I'd never been to another kingdom. I wondered how much we would stick out as foreigners.

We followed the activity, nerves tightening with every stroke. And then we were in the midst of it. One moment, we were surrounded by coral, and the next, merpeople bustled on all sides. They talked and laughed and went about their business.

I gaped at Meela. *We made it.*

My shock gave way to awe. Ahead, kelp archways lined the main street, swaying with the current. Beyond it, stone buildings loomed so high they broke the surface. Every structure was alive with plants, starfish, coral, and algae, reminding me how ancient the city was.

Meela's mouth was open, her eyes enormous. I let out a laugh. I was making the same face.

"Why are *you* surprised?" she said.

"Utopia's nothing like this!"

As we passed a large tower that was full of grottos, I rolled onto my back to see the top of it. Merpeople climbed out and plunged back in. It opened to a plateau above the surface, and I wondered what the plaza must look like, if it was full of sunbathing mermaids.

The majority of civilians looked northern like us. I'd thought our haggard appearances would draw attention, but everyone's style here was so different that, for all anyone knew, Meela and I looked like this intentionally. In the realm of hair alone, I saw intricacies like spikes, spirals moulded with clay, and complex braids laced with jewels. Some mermaids wore clothing, spanning everything from live sea creatures to human-made items like bikinis and fishing nets. Like South Pacific merpeople, many had piercings and gems embedded in their skin.

I'd never known Adaro's kingdom was so, frankly, boring. Was it because Adaro had forced it to be that way? Was it about order, structure, and obedience? Or was everyone just too afraid to be different?

A noisy family with six children passed, each trailing a glowing blue squid on a leash.

"Should we ask for directions to the queen?" said Meela.

I struggled to get my brain working. One of the children with the squids stopped to stare at us. We were blatantly acting like outsiders.

"No. Don't talk to anyone." I scanned our surroundings. "I think we keep following this."

The street we were on proved to be an artery that flowed through the city, with branches leading to buildings and more plazas.

"Three pounds for unlimited time!" shouted a merman at the base of a tower.

He caught my eye and grinned, motioning upwards.

"Highest open-air waterfall in the Atlantic, girls!"

Curiosity ate at me. But even if we had time to stop and lounge, we had nothing to pay with. Since being enlisted, I hadn't seen a single coin, never mind three pounds.

We passed through a market, everyone selling what they claimed were the boldest styles and tastiest snacks and most beautifying makeup. Meela tried to politely decline everyone who waved us over, until I grabbed her elbow and pulled her along faster. "We'll never get anywhere if you keep stopping."

Night was falling. It must have been nearing midnight. What were we supposed to do if we couldn't see the queen tonight? Where would we sleep?

Something loomed ahead, huge enough to block the currents beyond. I first thought it was a natural ridge in the landscape—but it was a palace. Ancient and built from stone, it was blanketed in coral and starfish. Four towers framed either side of the entrance, which was a circle large enough to fit a blue whale. Where the towers broke the surface, blurry outlines told me they rose to magnificent peaks.

I felt nothing beyond it. The impenetrable wall stretched from floor to ceiling.

Meela and I slowed as we neared the door, which was blocked by several guards. Their broad chests were encased in stone armour that looked impractically heavy. I couldn't see any weapons, but that didn't put me at ease.

In Utopia, anyone who wanted to see the king had to report to Nemertes—not that anyone ever did. But we knew the procedure. What were we supposed to do here? Who did we talk to?

With no better plan, I approached one of the guards. "Excuse me, sir. We'd like to speak to the queen."

Meela swam up beside me. The guard squinted at us.

"Do you have a summons?"

"No," I said, at the same moment as Meela said, "Yes."

The guard looked between us, saw Meela glare at me, and laughed. It wasn't a malicious laugh, more like he thought we were being cute.

"I'll check if she can squeeze you in tomorrow."

"We've come with important information—" said Meela.

"Of course you have."

"—from the Pacific."

He stopped grinning. "You what?"

His tone should have given me pause. Maybe I was too tired from our trek, or maybe I was emboldened by Meela getting to the point, because I said, "We're from Adaro's kingdom and we want to talk—"

There was a flurry around us, and before I could turn, several large hands grabbed me.

"Wait!" said Meela.

The guards had closed on us. I tried to reach for Meela to pull her away from them, but it was too late. They hauled me back, gripping hard enough to make me cry out.

"We just want to talk to Medusa!" I said. "We have information on Adaro—"

Something bashed me on the head. The world became jagged. My longblade was torn from my grip.

"Take them to the cells."

"No!" I said.

"We want to help Medusa!" said Meela.

I struggled, desperately trying to keep track of Meela. The shock of being seized so quickly settled over me. I should have seen this coming. If Adaro didn't like anyone mentioning Medusa, then of course Medusa wouldn't like anyone mentioning Adaro.

"Let us go, then," I said, though I knew it was too late to backtrack. "We'll get out of the city."

The guards dragged us around the side of the palace. We entered an empty alley that was so removed from the rest of the city it felt as though we had entered a different part of the ocean. The floor angled downwards and into an underground cave.

"Listen to us," said Meela. "This is important!"

They pushed us into a vertical passage. It spiralled straight down, too narrow to turn around in. All daylight vanished after the second turn. The tiny space pressed in on me. I had to force myself not to panic.

"Tell the queen we want to share Adaro's plan," I said. "Please tell her that."

We emerged into a pitch black room. My senses told me the walls were rough stone, lined with cells barely large enough to turn around in. None of them were occupied.

They threw me into a cell and slid the door closed behind me. I whirled and grabbed the bars, determined to break them. They, too, were made of stone, and they groaned feebly under my efforts.

Another door slammed. They had shoved Meela into the cell beside mine.

"Wait!" I said.

But they left without explanation, without telling us how long we would be there or what they planned to do with us.

I cast my senses around and was relieved to find a pocket of air overhead. They hadn't put us here to die. I rose and drew breath, trying to think. My head was pounding from where the guard had struck me. How had this gone so wrong so quickly?

Still, I didn't know what else we could have done. Maybe we shouldn't have mentioned Adaro—but then how would we have gotten in? Maybe we should have pretended we were here about something else until we were past the guards.

We obviously weren't dispensable, considering we were still alive. Maybe they wanted to hear what we had to say before making a decision on what to do with us.

Or maybe they were saving us for a public execution.

Couldn't they have told us *anything*?

In the cell beside me, Meela was panicking. She slammed her body against the door, each impact pushing air from her lungs.

"Take a breath," I said softly. "There's air above you."

"Don't tell me to take a breath!"

"Fine," I snapped. "Suffocate, then."

There was a resounding thud as she slammed against the stone. "We can't be stuck here! We're the only ones who can stop him!"

"Mee, calm down."

"No! I came all the way here for you, Lysi."

I ground my teeth. Was she really blaming me for this? "You didn't come here for me. You came here because you decided this would be the best way to get your revenge."

"What if he's on his way to my people? My parents, my friends, even Nilus and my nieces—they're all in danger, Lysi! He'll kill all of them. I need to—"

"What, you need to kill him back?"

"I don't have a choice."

"You have a choice about how it affects you. You can kill him because you have to, but you don't have to let it do this to you."

"Do what to me?"

"This ..." I waved a hand. The right words escaped me. In truth, Meela had been scaring me lately. Except for a brief time when we'd swum with the narwhals, her aura had become so dark.

"Obsession," I said. "You don't care what sacrifices you need to make to get to him."

She didn't respond.

I waited, wondering if I'd been too harsh. Was she that oblivious to the way she'd been feeling and acting lately? Or did she really not care who she lost in the process?

After a moment, she said, "You think I like what this is doing to me? It's like my mind is spending so much time with the thing I hate most that I'm starting to hate myself, too. It's eating me from the inside."

I couldn't think of anything comforting to say. Her confession didn't surprise me.

"I need you," she said. "You're the balance that keeps me sane."

"Is that the only reason you want me in your life? You need a balance of love and hate to keep you from going insane?"

"That's not what I mean." She hesitated. "I don't even think hate is the opposite of love anymore."

"What's that supposed to mean?"

"I mean … they share too many traits to be opposites. Both are all-consuming, keep you awake at night, give you this crazy feeling in your gut. You know what I mean?"

Maybe it should have been sweet, if she was describing what love did to her—but it wasn't, because she was putting me on the same plane as Adaro.

"You're saying it's all just obsession," I said.

"I don't know. Never mind."

I let it drop, my heart aching too much to continue the conversation.

In the never-ending blackness, I couldn't tell how much time passed. Stomach pains told me we'd missed several meals. My eyelids grew heavy. I might have dozed off, though there was little difference between closing my eyes and the pressing darkness.

Finally, activity flowed down that spiralling well. I jolted into alertness. A pair of mermen entered.

The water stirred as Meela rushed at her cell door.

"Listen," she said. "We're working against Adaro. Our names are Metlaa Gaela and Lysithea—"

"Quiet," said one of the mermen.

"—and we've come here to tell Medusa what we know. We weren't sent by anyone, and—"

"Mee, shut up!"

She did shut up, but I suspected this was because they'd begun to open her cell door.

A scuffle told me she tried to flee past them. At this, my anxiety reached a point where I thought I might throw up.

"Her Majesty wishes to see you," said a guard.

"She does?" said Meela.

I let the other guard grab me. They hauled us out of our cells. Medusa wanted to see us? I couldn't decide whether to be excited or afraid. Had something convinced her to hear us out? Maybe the guards had relayed our purpose to her, after all.

Still, the idea of a public execution floated at the back of my mind. If we were in Adaro's kingdom, maybe—but I hoped I was right in thinking Medusa was better than that.

We spiralled back up the passage and into the world. The daylight, though dim, was blinding.

Rather than turn back to the entrance, they pulled us towards the palace wall. We passed through a stone door, small and hidden beneath weeds. Two guards flanked the other side. They nodded as we passed.

My heart pounded. We were inside the Atlantic Queen's palace. Never in my life did I expect to be here. A thrill of excitement ran through me despite the trepidation I felt. I wished I could tell Spio, or my mom and dad, or my brother, or anyone. I committed every detail to memory. If we ever got out of here, I would want to remember it.

The palace was a maze of hand-built stone walls—rough, ancient, impenetrable. Even the outside noise was muffled, so only our movement and the crackling coral on the walls tickled my ears.

We rose two floors through more of those spiral wells. Some were exposed to the daylight above; others were speckled with holes and had tiny jellyfish in the ceiling so we were never plunged into blackness.

We passed by windows, which tapered so they were easy to see through but wouldn't be obvious from the other side.

Corridors branched off in all directions. I glimpsed vast rooms with dozens of merpeople inside, meeting or working or whatever they were doing. I tried to catch some of their conversations, but we were moving too quickly. We took turn after turn in a pattern I would never remember.

"Let me do the talking," I whispered to Meela.

"You think I'll say the wrong thing?"

It sounded like a real question, not an accusation.

"Yes."

First, as far as I was concerned, she had entered crazy mode and I had no idea what she would blurt out. Second, the way she interacted with others was still too human. I'd never thought of human culture as being so different, but now that Meela and I had spent more time together, I realised how much adjusting she had yet to do. I couldn't quite describe it, but something about even the simplest interactions was different, like the way she saw authority, and relationships, and freedoms.

The corridor widened into a vast, empty cathedral. It smelled earthy and green, every surface teeming with plant life except for the far wall. Into its bare stone were carved dozens of faces: mermaids, with serpents in place of hair. They looked eerily alive in the soft blue beams of sunlight rippling in the water. In the centre of the wall was the face I recognised from artwork: the original Medusa. Her mouth was open in a scream—just wide enough to fit one at a time.

My heart thudded faster. I knew who waited for us on the other side.

Meela's guard went in first, pulling her through after him.

Meela hissed, yanking her hand away. "I'm coming, for gods' sakes!"

My guard pushed me through and followed close behind.

We emerged to an enclosed grotto. It felt like being inside a giant egg with clay walls. The upper half, above-surface, was flecked with holes to let in daylight. A continuous roar against the surface told me waterfalls ran down the sides.

I wondered if there was a secret passage somewhere in the walls. There must have been. I couldn't imagine having this high-security room with a single entrance.

The guards led us across the grotto, keeping close to the floor.

"Your Majesty," said Meela's guard. "Metlaa Gaela and Lysithea from the North Pacific."

At the back of the room was a throne, pure black and shaped like a massive lion's paw shell. In it sat Queen Medusa.

She was northern, her greenish-brown tail draped over the edge, fin fluttering on the current. To call her beautiful would have been like calling a blue whale "kind of big". Beauty seemed to emanate from her bronze skin, tangible and absolute.

Her black hair was done in dreadlocks that brought her lineage to mind. Jewels and kelp buoys were braided into the ends, which swirled like snakes in the passing current. A translucent crown sat atop her head.

Her eyes, a vibrant orange-brown, raked over me and Meela. I had the impression that meeting her gaze would, in fact, turn me to stone. When she spoke, I half-expected a forked tongue to emerge.

"I understand you come with news of Adaro."

"Your Majesty," I said, finding myself breathless. "King Adaro's troops are—"

"Why?"

I hesitated. "I beg your pardon, Your—?"

"You risk your lives coming to me. I could easily have you killed. Barring that, you are now traitors to Adaro's crown and risk capital punishment."

I forced myself to meet her eyes. "King Adaro is a danger to the rest of the world. Something needs to be risked in order to stop him, Your Majesty."

"And you want me to risk something?"

"No," I said quickly—though I was unsure if it was true. "Your Majesty, you're the only one who can stop him."

"Adaro's war is happening on the other side of the world. It does not affect my kingdom."

"Your Majesty, his armies are stationed at the Ice Channel, South America, and in several places east of here. He's preparing to invade—"

"You think I do not know that he surrounds the Atlantic?"

I clasped my fingers together, resisting the urge to fidget. "Of course, Your Majesty, but I thought you might be able to use what I know from my time in his service."

"I am aware of the inner workings of his army."

"Yes, Your Majesty."

My stomach churned. So she didn't care what we had to say about Adaro's army. That was one piece of information rendered useless.

But why would she bring us here? She must have wanted to hear us out.

I tried to read her aura but got nothing. I felt Meela's gaze on me like the sting of iron.

The queen inclined her head to the guards who'd brought us in. They backed away. She watched them until they disappeared back through the entrance, and then returned her attention to us.

"I hear he has the Host of Eriana."

I opened and closed my mouth. So the queen had known about it.

"Yes, Your Majesty. It's under his control."

Medusa shifted, tail rippling on the current. "How is Adaro doing? Does he seem well?"

"Um ..." *Does he seem well?* That was an odd question to ask of the merman who was violently seizing every kingdom.

Meela gave a low scoff, which I felt more than heard.

The queen turned her orange-brown eyes onto her. "How many have died at his hands?"

Meela glanced to me. I gave a slight nod.

"We don't know," said Meela. I was relieved to hear a gentle tone. "He's been attacking the coast but we have no indication of numbers."

"Surely, as a former human, you have some idea of how many of your people have been lost."

I felt the jolt in Meela's pulse. Her eyes flicked to me, and back to the queen.

The queen's lips twisted, not quite a smile. "Where are you from, Metlaa Gaela?"

"Eriana Kwai."

For a moment, the queen looked intrigued, even excited. Then she sank back in her throne, composure regained. "Do you know how to return the serpent to Eriana Kwai, then? Is there a way to lay it back to rest?"

Meela looked to me, lips pursed.

If it were up to me, I would have told the truth about passing control. But Meela would never forgive me for giving away this secret. I hoped desperately that the queen would help us without knowing the full story.

"Meela has to kill its master, Your Majesty," I said. "For that, we need help."

Medusa's eyes narrowed. "Is there another way?"

"No, Your Majesty. It's indestructible."

She studied us so intently that I crossed my arms over my stomach. Did she know I was withholding information? Or was she considering whether to help Meela?

Finally, she said, "I do not agree with Adaro's position on human relations, nor with the way he governs the Pacific. But I wish to target the Host, not its master."

"It can't be one or the other, Your Majesty," I said. "They're bound by blood."

"The Host is the most dangerous force, here. That is where I am interested in focusing my efforts."

I bit my tongue, suppressing my outrage. The serpent was only as dangerous as its master. Did she not realise how destructive Adaro had been before the serpent came into his power? How could she think he wasn't the core of the problem?

"Even without the serpent, Adaro's still about to destroy the whole coast," said Meela, the words seeming to burst from her lips.

A flicker of confusion crossed Medusa's face.

Oh. She didn't know about the labour camp.

"Your spies haven't told you?" said Meela.

The queen opened and closed her mouth. She seemed to struggle with herself, too curious to be offended.

"He's going to cause a tsunami, unless we do something to stop it," said Meela.

The queen stared at us for a long moment. "How?"

"He's digging into the earth, Your Majesty," I said, heading off Meela before she got carried away. "There's a massive labour camp in the deep sea. He's rounding up civilians—Queen Evagore's kingdom, former humans, anyone who opposes him."

Medusa looked between us. Barely perceptibly, her shoulders slumped. For the first time, I saw the ordinary mermaid beneath that translucent crown.

"You must understand," she said. "I am hesitant to offer information that would lead to Adaro's death."

"Why?" said Meela.

I looked sharply at her in warning.

The queen hesitated. "Because Adaro is my son."

The words took a moment to sink in. Meela looked as stunned as I felt.

"Your son? But he's so ..." I trailed off, not sure how to end the sentence without insulting her.

"I have known for some time that my son is leading himself to an untimely end. When I heard about his South Pacific expansion and the disappearance of Queen Evagore, I feared for the Pacific Kingdom. I have tried to contact him, to send advisors, even to send troops to resist his expansion. I have come to accept that my efforts are futile."

"You're giving up?" said Meela.

"I will not order my civilians to fight a war that is not theirs."

"This war affects everyone!"

I put out a hand to silence Meela, but she pressed on, voice rising.

"Whether he's your son or not, you can't ignore how many deaths he's causing. These are merpeople who once belonged to your kingdom. These are the humans you claim to care about!"

Queen Medusa's eyes flashed red. "Do not doubt my loyalties, girl."

"Then what are you doing to protect those innocent lives? What happens when the tsunami wipes out every coastal city and you've done nothing to stop it?"

"Meela," I whispered, grabbing her arm.

Yes, I'd expected more from the queen who was supposed to rule with compassion. But Meela's tone was too severe, too dangerous to be addressing royalty.

"What she means, Your Majesty," I said, "is that the kingdoms are all connected. King Adaro's actions might affect our relations with humans worldwide."

The queen looked to the far wall. I glanced back to find the entrance vacant. We were alone with her.

"While I can help you, I will not mobilise my army," she said.

Meela opened her mouth, but stopped when I squeezed her arm and cast her a warning glare.

My heart pounded. Something in the queen's demeanour had changed. She was less defensive, now. Was the concern she showed for her son, or for the innocent lives at stake?

She traced her hands along her throne, seeming to weigh her words.

Meela glanced between us, tense.

"When I was sixteen," said Queen Medusa carefully, "I met a human from Finland. I visited him every day. We grew serious in a short time, and he swore we would find a way to be married. Against everyone's warnings, and against his wishes, I chose not to change him into a merman. I loved him the way I met him—from his blue eyes to his feet. I did not wish to take him from his natural state."

Guilt squeezed my chest at these words. That had been how I felt about changing Meela. I hoped Meela would never forget that. I tried to catch her eye but she was busy staring at Medusa.

"I was seventeen," said the queen, "when I became pregnant."

Meela said, "You mean Adaro's father is—?"

"A human, yes. When I told him, that was the last time I saw him. He did not meet me the following night, or the night after, although I continued to visit our beach until the day I gave birth."

I scoffed. "What a cod."

"I do not hold it against him, but at the time, I was hurt. Even more, I was terrified. I did not know if my baby would be born a human. I was afraid to ask for advice. My dear friend agreed to pretend he was the father to avoid scandal—but I gave birth alone, and on land, just in case."

"Wow," I breathed, feeling like she deserved some kind of single mother award.

She stared at us for a long moment. I couldn't tell if she was waiting for us to say something, or deciding whether to continue.

Finally, she said, "I wish for you to understand why my son is this way. He spent his childhood trying to find his father, despite my attempts to stop him venturing near the coast. He went through too many guardians to count. At fourteen, Adaro was captured by sailors. They put him in a cage meant for livestock, intending to bring him to land. Of course, you know humans have tried to capture merpeople many times, and it always ends the same. My son escaped, and none of the sailors lived to tell about their prize catch."

A killer at fourteen. That didn't surprise me. Plus, I imagined the experience had soured Adaro's opinion of humans even more.

"My son grew angry with me. He did not understand how I had fallen in love with a human, and worse, how I could be so cruel as to bring a child into the world as a half-breed. He argued with my position on human-merpeople relations, believing humans had no right to be in the seas.

"Adaro was always charismatic. He found a group of friends who felt the same about humans—I suspect after he'd convinced them so.

"At fifteen, they attempted to take over my throne. I admit, the plan was clever—albeit gruesome. He and his

175

allies murdered a mermaid and adorned her in my jewels, then used her decapitated head to convince my council that I had been killed.

"He was on my throne when the plan disintegrated. I was on my way to a meeting and learned of the news. The pieces came together: the meeting was a setup. I avoided what surely would have been my assassination."

"Your own son tried to kill you?" I said, barely audible.

Medusa gave the tiniest of nods. "Upon my return, I had his allies executed for treason. But Adaro was still the prince, so I imprisoned him. I assumed he was going through a nasty rebellious phase—and rightfully so, growing up without a father and suffering humiliation in his efforts to repair that relationship."

"That's no reason to try and murder your mother!" said Meela.

Medusa offered a wan smile before continuing.

"During his time in prison, his allies grew in numbers. A campaign of anti-human messages had amassed a following of hundreds. I did not know the extent of it. I released my son from prison after a year, believing his words of remorse.

"When Adaro was seventeen, an oil spill happened off the coast of America. It took the lives of an entire community in the Nares. Adaro used this to spread a message about humans. He promised to lead merpeople to victory against them. With this tragedy as leverage, Adaro gained a following of thousands. They grew large enough to be, for the first time in hundreds of years, a political party in opposition to the crown.

"Then the Ice Channel melted and a passage opened that summer. He left me without goodbye. He and his followers crossed to the Pacific to begin a new kingdom. My understanding is that he made a temporary pact with America while he focused on doing what he needed to secure the Pacific."

"Yeah," said Meela. "He needed the serpent—the Host—from Eriana Kwai."

"I don't doubt he had a careful plan. My son is clever. I do not approve of his war against humans, but it takes noble blood to be able to do what he has done."

Meela opened her mouth, anger pulsing from her.

I said quickly, "And noble blood is the only thing that can stop him, Your Majesty. Please."

A tinge of red seeped into the queen's eyes. "I have told you what you need to know about Adaro's condition. Now you can end the tyranny destroying the Pacific."

Condition? She hadn't mentioned any—

It dawned on me. My heart skipped a beat. But how did this help us? What was I missing?

Meela looked at me sharply. "What?"

"He's half-human," I said.

"So?"

I lifted my gaze to the queen. "I knew someone. She had a baby with a man—but it was stillborn."

"Adaro was not expected to live past infancy." Medusa closed her eyes, a heaviness about her. It seemed as though it cost her a great effort to speak her next words. "His body was born wanting to be human, but he is cursed with a mermaid's venom. When the tide pulls strongest, his body will attempt to complete a transformation. He must seek the protection of land until the venom transforms him back to a merman."

A silence hardened between us like ice.

"When the pull is strongest," said Meela weakly. "You mean, during king tides?"

The queen dropped her gaze.

Meela whirled to me, her pulse so strong I felt it on the current.

My mind raced back through time, making other connections. His disappearances. His hatred of humans. What about our failed assassination attempts?

"Your Majesty, is this why he's resistant to iron?"

"I presume his human genes have to do with it. He discovered it when he was captured by those sailors. He had, of course, spent his youth under the assumption that it would affect him the same as anyone else."

Maybe he couldn't be killed as a merman—but did this mean what I thought?

"So when he's in human form ..." I said.

"He is vulnerable," said the queen, barely a whisper.

All this time, we had assumed he was invincible.

This was how we would kill King Adaro.

Behind us, activity stirred in the entrance. I turned to find the guards who had taken us from our cells.

"You have what you need to make peace in the Pacific," said Medusa. "Now you will be escorted back to the Ice Channel. I implore you not to attempt to enter the Atlantic again."

"Wait," I said, feeling like I was trying to shove a giant boulder around in my brain. "What about Adaro's armies? What about the labour camp?"

"I have nothing to gain by helping you further," said Medusa. "I will not be burdened by this."

"You can't ignore what's happening," said Meela. "When the Atlantic is being invaded, you're going to regret—"

"That is enough!" Medusa rose from her throne, stretching to her full and considerable length. Her eyes shone red, her dreadlocks resembling snakes more than ever.

A hand seized my arm. I whipped around to find the guards closing around Meela and me. I raised my hands in surrender.

"These maids are not permitted to stay in my city," said Medusa. "Take them to the Ice Channel."

They dragged us to the door. I twisted to face the queen, panicked.

"No! Wait!"

Sure, we knew how to kill Adaro, but we were no closer to getting to him. He still had an enormous army, and we had no way of stopping it.

We had one last piece of information to bargain with. It was our one option. Letting Medusa have the serpent was better than not getting her help at all.

"Control is passed by blood," I shouted from the door. "You can be its master if you kill him."

Queen Medusa raised a hand, and the guards stopped. Meela shot me a blazing glare. Her lip curled, like she was ready to bite.

"It can switch allegiances?" said the queen.

I nodded stiffly.

"But it should be destroyed," said Meela, struggling against her guard. "It's too dangerous."

"With the wrong master, perhaps," said the queen.

"If you help us, you have the option to control it," I said. "If you don't, you're leaving it to him—or to us, and we intend to destroy it."

There it was. Our last, desperate hope.

A long, heavy moment passed. I avoided Meela's eye—though I could feel her fury. Whatever she thought, this was essential. This was our one chance with Medusa, and we needed to share everything we had.

The queen drifted back to her throne. She caressed the edge of the shell with long, webbed fingers. Her demon form was equal in terror to the beauty I'd seen moments ago.

When she spoke, her voice was calm.

"I stay by my decision. I am concerned enough by my son's actions to help you restore peace to the Pacific—but I will not join your war."

My insides plummeted. The guard pulled me onwards.

"No!" I said, struggling. "Please, Your Majesty. Any day, Adaro's going to invade the Atlantic, and then it *will* concern you. Why not get ahead of him?"

The queen sat back, settling into her throne.

"You can't just sit here while humans and merpeople kill each other in the Pacific," I shouted. "It isn't right!"

She raised a hand in farewell. "Good luck, Metlaa Gaela and Lysithea. Give Adaro my best when you find him."

CHAPTER THIRTEEN - Meela
Glacial Problems

A wall of ice towered over us, so pure and blue that I could hardly tell where water ended and ice began. It reached high above the surface and deeper than I could sense. I didn't remember this glacier from the way over—but the maze of ice and currents made following the same path almost impossible.

We swam adjacent to the wall and eventually found a gap where the glacier had broken. The chasm, though wide enough to fit a ship, made me feel claustrophobic. Unless we wanted to dive beneath the ice and risk being unable to find an air hole, we would be stuck following the gap until it ended.

Lysi hesitated for a fraction of a second before entering it, determinedly silent.

"You're certainly being quiet, for someone who couldn't keep her mouth shut earlier," I said.

Lysi glared.

"It was the one piece of information I asked you not to share," I said.

"Oh, stop it, Mee! It's not like you listened to me either, shouting at the queen like that."

She pushed faster, far into the chasm. I adjusted the crossbow over my back, checking the bolts in my quiver once again. At least Medusa's guards had returned our weapons before throwing us out. It was a small comfort.

We'd debated whether we should try sneaking back into the palace, but decided against it. If we were caught, we would probably face consequences much worse than simply being escorted out. Besides, the queen had made it clear she would not be convinced. Our best option was to get back to the Pacific as quickly as we could if we were going to find Adaro before the next king tide.

The disappearances Ephyra had noticed made sense now. If Adaro turned into a human during king tides, he would be extremely vulnerable. He would have no hope against me. But getting to him at the right moment would be difficult.

Lysi said we had half a tidecycle at most. Two weeks. Somehow, we had to make it back to the Pacific and find Adaro before then—not to mention finding a way past his army and the serpent, and tailing him until he left the water to transform. And we had to do all of this before the moon's orbit and phase matched up in that perfect way.

I glanced to the cloudy sky, hoping to see the moon. I didn't let myself think what would happen if we didn't get to him in time. The world could not afford to spend another six months at his mercy.

Something groaned in the distance, deep and rumbling. Lysi didn't seem bothered, so I ignored it. I watched her body wave in a smooth rhythm as she swam a few lengths ahead.

"You know you put everyone at risk, throwing around that knowledge," I said.

"The promise of controlling the serpent was all the leverage we had. We'd have been stupid not to tell her."

I huffed. "You're lucky she decided not to act. It's better than having her join the fight with the intention of getting the serpent."

"Ugh, are you serious? You think it's better she's not helping us?"

Admittedly, it did bother me that Medusa had refused. If she was as great a queen as everyone said, she would have cared about the war in the Pacific. Sure, this war had yet to affect the Atlantic directly, but lives were in danger, and she had the power to save them. Adaro might have been her son, but he was out of control, and she owed the world as queen to place those thousands—millions—of lives over his.

"She's a coward," I said.

"She's not a coward. She told us how to kill her son."

"You're defending her?"

"I'm saying she has to make hard decisions that we probably don't understand."

The groaning noise came again, filling my head, like a manifestation of my anger.

At least the queen had made one noble decision. With or without help, we had the information we needed.

Now I had a merman to kill.

The canyon widened, the glaciers on either side looming silently. They reminded me of running through towering sequoia trees, surrounded by the smell of dirt and pine and wildflowers.

A lump formed in my throat. I supposed no matter how much I loved the sea, I would always miss what it felt like to be human. And right now, when even Lysi's company was lonely, I realised I was homesick.

There was another, louder groan. Lysi glanced around this time. She caught my eye and turned ahead, continuing resolutely.

I imagined thousands of Adaro's followers making this trek all those years ago, leaving the Atlantic behind to build Utopia.

Lysi's parents had been among them.

"Why did your parents follow?" I said.

She glanced back, brow still furrowed in anger. "What?"

"Your parents followed Adaro to the Pacific after all his anti-human messages."

"It wasn't that simple. My mom said Adaro made a lot of promises that sounded better than what Queen Medusa offered. Wealth and unity and—"

"But did they not care about his anti-human messages, or that he tried to assassinate the queen?"

"I know what you're getting at, Meela. They aren't anti-human—"

The groan swelled louder than ever. A wave of apprehension pulsed from Lysi.

"So they don't care enough about humans to let that affect them," I said.

"What? No. I think Adaro quieted down about those views for a time to gain more followers. Anyway, can we not talk about my mom and dad? It just gets me all worried about them, and …"

The noise grew into a long, low rumble. I couldn't tell how far away it was, or even which direction it came from. I blamed that on my inexperience with my new senses.

"What's doing that?" I said.

Lysi lifted her gaze to the wall of ice on our right.

It hit me. The rumbling wasn't in the distance. It was all around us.

Lysi's eyes locked onto mine, wide, dilated, bluer than the ice suffocating us from all sides.

"The glacier," she whispered.

The glacier was rumbling? How? What did that mean? The noise intensified, stirring the water until I found it difficult to stay still.

"Lysi, what—?"

"Dive!"

I reacted in the same instant as the surface exploded in a great splash. A chunk of the glacier had crashed down on us. We flew downwards. An icy swell pulsed from the impact, pushing me faster.

My teeth jabbed into my lip as my body transitioned into demon mode.

I didn't need to look to know an unfathomably large wall of ice was chasing us downwards, ready to smash us with enough force to kill. We couldn't slow down.

The world was all churning water and ice. The rumbling deafened me as pieces continued to break away from the glacier and plunge towards us.

How deep was the water here? I couldn't feel past the chaos enough to tell. What if we hit the bottom and had nowhere to go?

Lysi shrieked. A chunk of ice drove between us, separating us.

I used my hands to straighten out, determined not to veer away.

I heard her shout to me, but her voice was distant and muffled.

The world became dark. The walls of ice on either side were still thick, leaving me nowhere to go, still, but down.

My entire body ached with exhaustion, ready to give up, when the crashing finally slowed. A wave picked me up, carrying me away from the breaking wall and towards the adjacent one. I beat my tail desperately to avoid colliding with it.

"Lysi?"

I couldn't sense her. Had she gotten carried on the same wave?

Casting my senses for her, I caught something enormous stirring below, coming towards me. More ice? Had it bounced off the bottom? This didn't make sense.

It was definitely ice. And it was coming towards me, fast.

My insides plummeted. It was the bottom of the breaking glacier. The iceberg's centre of gravity must have changed. It was flipping over.

I cast around desperately for an escape. It was no use. The ice rose towards me, an unstoppable wall.

The roaring current drowned my scream. I wanted to call to Lysi, ask her what to do, but my throat seized with terror.

I tried to race out of the way, but the wall slammed into me with a painful crash. The ice pushed me upwards so quickly my stomach swooped.

Cold wind hit my face as I broke the surface. The wall of ice was horizontal, and continuing to flip.

"Lysi!"

I was sliding, helpless, unable to grip anything. Ice and sky and water whirled.

Then I was sliding off the other side, still grasping for anything I could hold onto. I sucked in a breath before being plunged back into the water.

I pushed away hard, putting distance between myself and the iceberg. It continued to roll, sending currents and whirlpools that tried to suck me back towards it.

I used my webbed hands to push harder, diving towards blackness. I had to go deeper, further than before, down to safety. I passed the point of comfort, the depth pressing my eyes and ears, and still, I kept swimming.

The world became pitch black. The waves still tossed me left and right.

I reached the floor and stopped myself with my hands. I planted my fingers in the sand.

Far above, the enormous glacier continued to move, swapping its crystal blue bottom with its weather-beaten top. Shards of ice twice the size of me rained down in a thunderous storm. But they stopped, floating, before they hit me. I was safe down here.

I cast my senses around. The only sign of life was those tiny glowing creatures.

"Lysi?"

The sound drifted into the void. I waited. An endless moment passed that might have been a minute or an hour. My pulse rattled in my eardrums.

The emptiness of the water hit me more than ever. All I sensed were moving currents and vast walls of ice, trapping me there with growing dread.

Should I try to find Lysi, or continue on? What would she do? I decided she would definitely try to find me. Then I doubted myself. Maybe she assumed I had swum to safety, or kept moving in the direction we'd been headed.

I waited in the intense pressure and darkness. Slowly, the chaos overhead subsided.

"Lysi?" I said again, if just to hear a voice.

Nothing. I turned, casting my senses carefully in each direction.

She probably wouldn't have swum as deep as this—below the twilight layer. She would've been able to handle the current more easily.

I began to rise. Then I remembered Lysi telling me to go slowly when rising from depths like this, because depressurising quickly was painful.

I moved westward, rising gradually. No signs of life.

A knot of terror swelled in my heart, making it hard to think. No, Lysi would be all right. She'd always survived on her own, so this would be no different. I just had to find her.

By the time I made it to the surface and found myself still completely alone, I really began to panic. I considered doubling back. Could we have gotten that far from each other? Had she been flipped to the opposite side of the broken glacier, separated from me by a giant wall of ice? Or had she been crushed beneath the falling shards?

I shook my head, refusing to believe that.

"She's fine," I whispered. Lysi was a more agile and experienced swimmer than me. If I'd gotten away from the iceberg, so would she.

Even once I calmed the fear of what happened to Lysi, the idea of continuing alone was terrifying. I barely knew how to be a mermaid, never mind trying to survive the most extreme conditions as one.

Movement stirred ahead. My heart leapt. I jetted towards it—and stopped, cursing. It was a school of fish.

I chewed my lip, then made a decision. I would keep going. The school, at least, had a much larger presence than I did. If Lysi was nearby, there was a good chance she would feel the activity.

I approached the school from the side and made a wide arc like Lysi had taught me. I picked up my pace, expelling some breath so I created a vortex of bubbles that acted like a wall around the fish. They bunched tighter until they were a giant, swirling, silvery baitball.

I crossed my arms and admired my work, wishing Lysi could see my accomplishment. I glanced around.

Come on, Lysi. Where are you?

Lysi and I had barely eaten since being ejected from the Atlantic, and I was so far past the point of hunger that I was trembling. Or maybe it was from panic.

I watched the silvery swirl, debating whether I'd be able to hold down a meal. Then, in the distance, something else moved. I turned, concentrating on where it had come from. It was the right size to be a mermaid.

"Yes," I breathed.

My heart pounded. I thought I felt an aura but couldn't be sure. It could be a dolphin, for all I knew. Why was this so hard to sense? I wondered if transformed mermen and mermaids ever had control of their senses to the same extent as merpeople who were born with them, or if I was doomed to be subpar.

Whatever it was moved towards me. As it drew closer, I sensed a presence too complex to be an animal. It had to be a mermaid.

"Lysi?"

"Hello?" came the reply, and the male voice proved it was definitely not her. "Did you call me Lysi?"

Crap. I froze, considering whether to flee.

"Hello?" he said again.

Unless I was mistaken, this guy's aura was kind enough. Plus, he was alone. Maybe he could help me.

"All right, I can't tell if you're there or if I'm hallucinating again," he said. "I did eat some anemones that might have been a bit off. So if you're a mermaid, I'm going to need you to say words."

As his shape materialised, I wasn't sure how I possibly mistook him for Lysi. He was a bony, lanky merman about my age, with the hairstyle of someone who'd stuck a fork in an electrical outlet. He wore a backpack that had a stone blade sticking out the top.

"Have you seen a blonde mermaid?" I said, throwing caution aside.

"Wow, you really are looking for Lysi," he said.

"Yes, I lost—wait, what?"

"You know Lysi."

"*You* know Lysi?" I squeaked.

We stared at each other. He turned to my scattering baitball.

"Nice job. I felt it from a league away and thought it must be the work of a pod. Did you do this by yourself?"

I kept staring at him. "Sorry, but who are—?"

He slapped his forehead. "Of course! You're Meela!"

"How—?"

His gaze fell to my tail. "That hypocrite!"

I looked down at my tail as well, too confused to respond.

He extended a webbed hand. I took it and was met with an enthusiastic handshake. I wondered if merpeople shook hands or if he was doing the human-like thing for my benefit.

"Pleased to meet you. Name's Spio."

CHAPTER FOURTEEN - Lysi
Northern Detachment

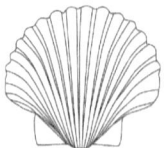

I opened my eyes to a blue-white haze. It brought to mind the blind eye I'd once seen on a dolphin.

Oh, no. Had I gone blind?

I turned my head and pain stabbed my spine. I groaned weakly.

Beside me, the haze gave way to clear water. So the blindness was just a glacier in front of my face. I would have been relieved, if not for the pain.

I tried to raise a hand to touch the glacier and found I couldn't. My arms were pinned across my stomach.

How had I ended up like this? I tried to remember what I'd been doing. My brain felt murky, slow to react to what was surely an unusual—maybe dangerous—situation.

Something hard pressed into me on all sides. Pain throbbed in my shoulder blades. I couldn't feel my tail at all.

I was pinned between two chunks of ice. They'd been thrust against each other, with me in the middle.

I had a fleeting surge of gratitude that these chunks weren't big enough to crush me to death. Then the gratitude vanished, because I couldn't tell if they were big enough to have paralyzed me.

But how …?

The breaking glacier came back to me. An icy feeling plunged into my gut. Where was Meela?

I opened my mouth to call to her. A sharp pain stabbed my lungs, and no sound came. I watched the bubble leave my mouth and float downwards.

I frowned. *Downwards?*

My heart jumped. I was pinned upside down.

I cast my senses and felt only ice. The sliver of open water beside me revealed nothing. I tried to wiggle and a jolt of pain shot down my spine. I moaned. Was it broken?

Doing my best to ignore the stabs of pain all over, I kept wiggling, trying to free myself. I was not going to drown here. I'd been through too much to die pinned helplessly between two pieces of ice.

A long time passed before I could make any progress. My chest and stomach felt less constricted, and I was able to move my arms enough to uncross them. My exertion must have created enough body heat to melt the ice.

But I still couldn't feel my tail.

What would happen if I was paralyzed? How far could I get using my hands?

No, I told myself. *Don't think like that. You're fine.*

I pressed my hands against the ice, trying to push it away. Nothing moved.

You won't be swimming at all if you don't get to the surface soon, said a voice in my head.

I let out a whimper of frustration.

"Well, well," said a merman beside me. "You've gotten yourself into a situation, haven't you?"

My lips prickled as my teeth lengthened. I hissed defensively before I could stop myself.

"Easy," said the merman. He was upside down—or rather, right side up.

His eyes raked over the ice, over my trapped body, and settled on my face. He was fit, youthful, all sharp angles and overworked muscles.

More mermen drifted shortly behind him. I couldn't count how many.

"I'm Thetis," he said. "We're part of King Adaro's northern detachment."

Any panic I should have felt at being discovered by Adaro's army was nowhere to be found. I needed to get out of here, and they could help me. The pain in my lungs told me I should have breached a long time ago.

"Want to help me out?" My voice was weak, as though the ice had squeezed the substance out of it.

"Of course." Thetis turned and shouted, "When I give the word, push."

A flurry of activity picked up as countless mermen positioned themselves around me.

"Ready?" shouted Thetis. "Go!"

The ice groaned and vibrated, sending pain down my body. I helped push, probably to minimal effect.

The pressure eased. A slow wave tickled my skin. The icebergs were moving apart.

I tumbled out without warning, flipping over. Pain shot through my tail as blood flowed back into it. It felt numb, swollen. But it had feeling, which meant I wasn't paralyzed.

I let myself float suspended, too exhausted to move. Air would come in a moment. I needed the shooting pains to ease off my tail before I tried to do anything.

"Thank you," I croaked.

"Of course," said Thetis.

Everyone was staring, dead quiet. Taking in the size of the army, my immediate danger dawned on me. I had to get away from these guys before they recognised me.

"I should keep going," I said.

I made to swim to the surface to catch a long-overdue breath. My tail barely functioned. I flushed at how laboured my swimming was.

A hand closed over my arm.

"Ouch!"

Despite my cry of pain at his firm grip, Thetis didn't let go.

"Wait a moment," he said, voice low.

My skin prickled. I didn't like the sneer curling his lips.

"Let go of me."

"No," he said calmly. "I never said you could leave, Lysithea."

CHAPTER FIFTEEN - Ben
Military Tech

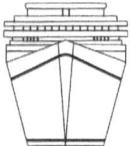

"What happened to your vacation?" said Officer Miller, watching Reeves bound through the tall grass at him.

Reeves leapt onto the trail and picked up a jog, keeping pace with Miller.

"The Caribbean is all booked up."

"The entire Caribbean?"

"Sir, I have information about the serpent you'll find interesting."

Miller glanced sideways with an air of exasperation. His mustache twitched. Then he returned his attention to the trail and grunted, which Reeves took to mean he should continue.

"I did some research, sir, and the legend spans several cultures. There's the Midgard Serpent in Norse mythology, and the leviathan from the Old Testament, of course. The indigenous peoples—" he tripped over a stone and caught himself "—of the Pacific Northwest have Sisiutl. Dharmic religions have Naga, and—"

"What's your point, Reeves?"

"This serpent is all over human history, but given the merman's pattern of attacks, I think we should look at one in particular."

Miller was silent. Their footsteps drummed through the silent morning air as they continued along the dirt trail, approaching the coastline.

"The Pacific Northwest, sir. I think we should find out more about Sisiutl. Maybe they have information on how this merman king got it in the first place. If you look back at the satellite images, the earliest indication shows up near Eriana Kwai about three weeks ago—"

"Near who?"

"Eriana Kwai. That island in the Gulf."

"Oh. Right."

"I think we should go there. Ask them about the serpent. I think the merman was targeting them."

The trail turned. They emerged from the meadow and continued on a low clifftop along the jagged coast. The scent of wildflowers faded on the wind, replaced by seaweed and brine.

"Reeves, I don't think those people will be happy to see us. We haven't exactly been helping—"

"There's something else, sir."

He heard the desperation in his own tone. Miller looked at him.

"The University of British Columbia has a primary document from Eriana Kwai. They must have bought it from the island ages ago. I'm not sure. But it mentions a serpent."

"What is it, a book?"

"Parchment. It was transcribed. I think it was an oral legend."

"So it's a story."

"Sir, you've seen the serpent with your own eyes. You know it's not a story."

The trail narrowed, and Reeves fell into step behind the large teardrop of sweat on the back of Miller's shirt. They jogged in silence, following the winding clifftop. Far below, the sea glistened, peaceful and unassuming. Waves purred against the rocky beach.

"Does the legend tell anything about an attack plan?" said Miller.

"Plan? No, sir. It talks about—"

"All right, look." He stopped and turned, forcing Reeves to an abrupt halt. "I appreciate the research you've done here, but save your breath. We've already decided we're going to nuke it."

"Nuke—what? No!"

"You're choosing to believe a legend over science. You want something this big gone, use a nuke. That's a fact."

"We can't blow up the ocean!"

Miller turned and resumed jogging. Reeves followed after a stunned silence.

The officer concentrated on navigating the narrow path for a moment before saying, "You seem opposed to retaliating against the mermaids—even before the whole thing with Perseus happened. Not a good quality in my number one man. Something going on with you?"

Reeves' stomach flipped. It was lucky Miller's back was to him, because he was sure his face betrayed him in that moment.

"No, sir. It's just—I don't know if nukes will work."

"Of course they'll work!"

"Sir, would you have believed a few weeks ago that this serpent could have existed?"

Miller said nothing.

"Me neither, sir, which is why I think we should be careful of what we assume about it."

"We need to get rid of this thing—"

"The legend says it's completely indestructible."

Miller hesitated. "Well, the legend was written before we had modern technology."

"I saw it chew up seventeen supercavitating torpedoes like a bowl of cereal!"

"Look, we're tracking the serpent on the most high-res satellites we have access to. Every time it surfaces, we plot it. It won't be long before we close in."

"That's great, but—"

"The problem is that we don't yet know its pattern. We don't know where it's *going* to be, so we don't know who to evacuate or where to send the helicopters. We're at an estimated thirty thousand deaths, Reeves. That's thirty thousand too many. So unless you know where it's going to attack next—"

"The serpent's power is passed by blood, sir."

Reeves' breath was shallow as he waited for the officer's reaction. This was the Holy Grail, as far as he was concerned. He had shared the key to the most powerful force in the world.

If Miller would trust him, everything would be fixed. He would have his respect back from Miller, his peers. From himself. More importantly—something he would never admit aloud—he would finally be able to ease his conscience. No more innocent mermaids would be killed by his country. He might, finally, feel like he'd made up for what his team did—what *he* did—to the one who saved him.

If Miller decided not to act on this knowledge, Reeves wasn't sure what else he could do.

Miller slowed his pace. After a moment during which he seemed to struggle for words, he said, "What the hell does that mean, *passed by blood?* We drink the serpent's blood like vampires?"

"It means if we kill the merman, we become master of the serpent."

Miller stopped so abruptly that Reeves ran into him.

The officer turned, heaving. "What?"

"We have to kill the merman."

"And if we kill him—"

"We control the serpent."

They stood panting, Miller more elevated on the narrow trail. Behind him, the tree line started, and Reeves could see mist reaching out from the dark woods in a way that reminded him of spirits.

"Jesus," said Miller. "You sure?"

"It's what the legend says."

"What about the other legends? That Asgard snake or whatever."

"None of them say anything about controlling it. Eriana legend is the only one that talks about transferring power."

Officer Miller ran a hand over his bushy mustache, contemplating in silence. Reeves studied his face, wishing he would think aloud.

Come on, he thought. *Don't make a nuclear war out of this. We're better than that.*

"I mean, think of what this could …" Miller swore under his breath. "The tech we've got is one thing, but to have the power of the leviathan under the American flag?"

Reeves waited, hardly breathing.

Abruptly, Miller pushed past him and started jogging back the way they'd come.

"I'm calling the Secretary of State. See what we can do to locate the merman."

Reeves stayed frozen. Was Miller agreeing to give it a shot? Would they actually try to target the merman instead?

He ran to catch up. "Where would you like me, sir?"

"Call UBC and get that document pulled. We don't want knowledge of this getting out."

Call UBC? What was he, an office assistant?

"I can, sir, but they're under the Canadian government so we can't really force them—"

"Ask anyway. Be polite about it. Say 'please' and 'sorry'."

"Don't you think if we tell them to classify a document that'll invite them to look at it more closely?"

Miller seemed to consider this for half a second. "Say you're part of a preservation initiative for Eriana Kwai. Tell them you want to buy it from them. They can name a price. Anything."

"I—yes, sir."

He wasn't trained for this kind of negotiating, but he would have to try—even if it did mean letting another nation in on the secret.

They ran back along the shore in silence. Reeves' chest lightened with relief at having changed Miller's mind. He looked out at the glistening sea, thinking of the gleam that had come on like a light in the man's eyes.

Were others similarly entranced by the possibility of controlling the serpent? It was hard to believe they and the merman could be the only ones who knew about the legend.

The victory faded as quickly as it had come, shadowed by a sense of foreboding. How many would soon know about the leviathan—and how many would be racing to gain control of it?

CHAPTER SIXTEEN - Meela
Eriana's Gift

I pointed southwards, and then back to Spio, trying to make sense of this. Though I'd never met him, I felt a wave of relief on Lysi's behalf that he was alive and unharmed.

"What are you doing way out here?"

"The Arctic isn't part of any kingdom, so it's a good place to hide," he said.

I glanced around at the barren iceberg hell that had just tried to kill me. The baitball had scattered, plunging us back into isolation.

"I guess. If you can stand it."

"Stand it!" said Spio. "Good one."

I raised an eyebrow.

He pointed at his tail. "Stand it?"

When I still didn't respond, he said, "It's not that bad, being a nomad. It's given me the chance to think about the universe and existence and life and everything."

We nodded wisely.

Spio motioned to my crossbow. "Is that all you have with you?"

"I'm pretty good with it."

He jabbed a thumb at his backpack. "I got a few weapons, kelp pus, and a couple of emergency buoys in here, if you need anything."

Kelp pus and buoys? I wondered what use those would be, but didn't feel like betraying how little I knew, so I just said, "Thanks."

We fell silent for a moment, looking at each other.

Spio swam past me. "So, you think she went this way?"

I followed. I supposed this meant Spio and I would stick together, now, and I was grateful for the company.

"I don't know. This is the direction we were headed when I lost her."

"She can't have gone too far. What happened?"

I explained how we were separated by the breaking glacier.

"Do you think Lysi would have continued to the Pacific?" I said. "Or do you think she would have gone back the other way to look for me?"

Spio considered. "She would do whatever she thinks you would do."

I groaned. "I'm trying to do whatever she would do!"

"I believe that is what's called Capelin's Conundrum."

I'd never heard of such a thing, but I took his word for it. We wove through the ice floes, Spio in the lead like he knew exactly where we were going.

"How long have you been up here?" I said.

"I can't keep track because of the sun. Hey, have you seen any belugas?"

"Sorry."

"Guess not," said Spio thoughtfully. "Well, I managed to train an attack pod."

"Really?"

"Yeah. The command is—" He hesitated, then said, "Better not, in case they're nearby."

I glanced around, half expecting to find a swarm of them coming after us.

"I ran out of bait," said Spio, "so they left me behind yesterday."

"Oh."

We swam for a long time in silence. I wanted to punch the stupid icebergs everywhere. Every time I felt movement, it turned out to be shifting ice.

"How far could she have gone?" I said, trying to sound casual.

Spio didn't answer. After a while, he said, "You dudes didn't decide on an emergency meeting spot? Any kind of plan in case you got separated?"

"No," I said defensively. "We've always been able to ..."

I looked away.

"To find each other?" said Spio, giving me a *that's cute* sort of grin.

It was true. Even as kids, we'd known where to meet. It was always the same beach, at the same tide pool, the time agreed upon by the tides and—

I expelled a large bubble. "Oh!"

I looked to the surface. A thick layer of ice was stopping us from breaching, but there was a crack in it a short ways ahead.

Maybe she had left me a sign, like she used to do with rock towers. If she dove, she would be able to find shells and rocks and all kinds of things to work with.

Spio followed me to the crack without question. I paused before breaching, feeling for movement or any sort of presence. When I was reasonably sure there were no bears, I poked my head out and looked around eagerly.

My heart sank. I'd been so sure I would find a rock tower, covered in webs of frost, pointing me in the right direction. But the area was as white and deserted as everything else.

Spio surfaced next to me.

"We can leave a sign for her," I said, voice carrying across the emptiness. "If we dive, I can get some rocks."

"What about this?" Spio pointed at the thin layer of powdery snow.

There was a shallow groove, barely visible, with a crook at the end. An arrow.

"I think maybe we're going the right way," he said.

I stared at it. He was right. This groove was from a finger. It hadn't formed naturally. Affection swelled in my heart for Lysi, and how clever and resourceful she was—followed by a wave of relief. If we swam quickly, maybe we could catch up.

We swam in the direction the arrow pointed.

"Why were you and Lysi in the Atlantic, anyway?" said Spio.

"She wanted to convince Medusa to help end the war."

Spio opened his mouth, but nothing came out, so he closed it.

"Medusa refused to help," I said. "But the trek wasn't a total waste."

Given that Spio was Lysi's closest friend, I decided to relay everything the queen had told us about Adaro.

"So he never did find his father?" said Spio. "Dang. I'd feel bad for the guy if he wasn't such a jerk."

I said nothing. It was hard to imagine any universe in which I could feel sorry for Adaro.

We found another air hole and surfaced. There was no arrow—but it hadn't been long, so maybe Lysi hadn't breached here. We kept going.

"Now you're going to find him, right?" said Spio. "You're going to get him when he can't fight back?"

I hesitated. Our plan was to go back to Kori Maru, first. But did we need to? The Reinas had been no help to us, anyway.

We'd spent enough time waiting. It was time to take action.

"Yes," I said firmly.

Spio raised his webbed fists in victory. "Any idea where he goes?"

"All we have to go on is his pattern of attacks, which isn't even much of a pattern."

As we swam side-by-side, I drew an invisible outline of the Pacific Ocean with my fingers and did my best to explain where Adaro had targeted so far.

"Interesting," said Spio. "Have you heard of the Bermuda Triangle?"

"Yeah, of course. Why?"

"It would appear there's some kind of similar triangle of death in the Pacific Ocean. Except this one ends in people being eaten by a giant serpent."

"I wouldn't call it a triangle."

We found another gap ahead and surfaced. There was another arrow. Spio made me high-five him. We adjusted our course and continued.

"Once we find him, I think we should get him with a wooden stake," said Spio. "Or fire. I don't know. What's the most creative way you've seen a human die?"

I grinned. Finally, someone to share my dark daydreams with.

Before I could put my gruesome ideas into words, something large hit my senses from ahead. Spio and I stopped. It couldn't be Lysi; it was much too big.

Several possibilities flashed across my mind, from a ship, to an army, to a massive school of sardines. Then it occurred to me that it was a singular presence.

"Spio, is that a whale?"

He nodded. "Don't worry. You'll be safe with me beside you. Not like if you were by yourself. It's mating season, which means the males can't tell the difference between you and a female whale."

I cast him a look of horror.

"Nobody told you?" he said. "Yeah, you need to be careful this time of year. If one comes after you, best thing to do is play dead."

When I kept staring, he said, "I'm kidding, Meela."

I smiled in spite of myself.

"Come on," he said. "Let's dive. We still don't want to cross paths with it."

I followed him deeper so we could pass it at a distance.

The whale drifted over us slowly, the current pulsing with every beat of his tail. I frowned, noticing an irregular rhythm.

"Spio, feel that?"

"What about it?"

"The way he's moving. His stroke is all off. I think he's hurt."

Spio followed my gaze into the distance, where the whale laboured along out of sight.

After a moment, he said, "Yeah. I think you're right."

My insides melted a little. "Can we help him?"

"Uh ..."

"Please?"

Part of him must have wanted to, because he didn't immediately say no.

I started in that direction.

"Fine," he said, "but if he gets all crazy and stuff, we'll have to turn tail."

It took us a few minutes to get to the whale, an adult orca. It was easy to see what was wrong. His entire body was wrapped in an enormous fishing net, white buoys hanging off him from nose to tail.

His dorsal fin was as tall as me, his overwhelming size rendering me light-headed. But he was thin, listless. He eyed us as we approached, and we stopped.

"Will he attack?" I said.

"I don't know," said Spio.

I followed for a moment. The orca's attention stayed on me, its aura blanketing the current, not unlike those I felt in merpeople. Spio hung back.

"You really should be careful, buddy. Orcas aren't exactly friendly to merpeople."

"Believe me, I've had plenty of bad experiences with them."

The nightmare of the Massacre was still fresh in my memory, when Adaro's army had used orcas to try and capsize our ship.

I swam alongside the animal at eye level, ready to zip away if his mood changed. His flesh was puckered near his face where the ropes cut deeply. My heart ached to see it.

"All right, boy," I said in my most soothing tone. "I'm going to help you."

The orca looked right at me. The small, black eye was so expressive it was as though he was trying to communicate with me. When I focused on his aura, I felt pain and resignation.

"Pass me that blade of yours, Spio."

My tone was so final that he didn't argue.

Spio moved closer to pass me the blade, and the whale tensed. Its eye shifted back.

"Stop," I said quickly.

Spio obeyed, but the whale didn't relax.

"Back up."

Only when Spio had returned to his original distance did the whale's eye return to me.

"Stay there," I said, and swam out to Spio to grab the blade.

Slowly, I returned to the whale's immense tail, which was the size of a kitchen table. I followed the languid up-and-down motion for a moment before reaching gingerly for the net.

The whale didn't protest.

I began slicing the ropes, careful not to pull.

The whale stopped moving. I paused, ready to flee, but felt no aggression. He drifted upwards until he brushed the surface. The distant hiss of his spout sounded as he took a breath.

I kept slicing while the whale lingered, resting limply while drawing long breaths. He cast the occasional leery glance back to Spio, as though to make sure he wasn't going to swim closer.

"There's one explanation for this," said Spio. "You have secret whale whispering powers and should be captured and studied."

"He's like this because he's injured."

"I'm pretty sure injured whales are even more crazy than ordinary ones."

"He knows I'm trying to help."

"No, he clearly likes you better than me. Have you considered donating your body to science?"

"Spio, there's nothing special about me. I'm just ..."

I lifted a shoulder. What was I? Patient? Gentle? Compassionate? I'd proven to be anything but those things these past weeks.

Still, Eriana came to mind. My own ancestor had been known as a charmer of animals. She had a way of communicating with them, a gift unparalleled by anyone. That was what led her to control the leviathan. Empathy for all living things was her greatest strength.

Maybe I had that part of Eriana in me.

I kept sawing the ropes until the tail was free, working quickly while trying not to pull and cause the orca more pain.

The whale drifted up and down with the waves, so limp he might have been dead.

"Nearly there, baby."

I moved to his face. Between his jaws, each tooth was the size of my thumb. The ropes here were worse, embedded in his nose. It would be painful to pull away—but worse to leave it.

I focused on cutting the ropes until the moment came.

The whale seemed to know freedom was close, because he began swimming again, slowly but with more confidence.

I sped up, cutting quickly. And then the only thing left to do was pull the rope away from his nose.

I steeled myself, both hands wrapped around the rope. I shot forwards.

The rope caught a little as it pulled from the whale's flesh. He groaned and wriggled away.

The entire fishing net, all tangles and white buoys, hung like a corpse from my fists. The whale was free.

With a burst of agility, he whirled to face me. I winced. A flash of panic crossed my mind as I wondered if the jaws were about to open.

For a long moment, the whale and I were nose-to-nose. I stayed perfectly still, pulse pounding, terrified that the slightest movement would cause him to snap.

Gently, he closed the distance between us. I blinked as our faces touched.

Then he turned, and his large, glassy eye stared at me, unblinking.

Finally, the orca turned away. He flipped his enormous tail fin with enough force that the current thrust me backwards. I let out a breath, stunned and relieved and elated all at once. The orca shot away from us, faster, faster, until his black body faded to blue. I kept watching long after he disappeared.

Spio came to meet me, picking up the trailing end of the net. "That was so cool," he breathed. "What do we do with this?"

I tore my eyes from the empty water. "Right. We can't leave it to float around for something else to get tangled in. Let's find the nearest shore and put it on the beach. Hopefully someone will pick it up."

Lugging the net with us, we continued on the path Lysi was hopefully travelling—but now we also had to find a place to dump this gargantuan piece of litter.

After mere minutes, the net grew painful in my fists. My pity for the whale increased.

"What's wrong?" said Spio.

I flexed my cramped fingers. "I see things like this, and I understand why Adaro wants humans out of the sea."

Spio was silent for a long time. Then he said, "I could be in the wrong wake here, but I don't think Adaro's reason for blitzing humans is to save animals from fishing nets."

Maybe that was true, but it still bothered me. Was Adaro right about humans? Were we—they—no better than he thought?

"You know," said Spio, "you're different than you let on."

"What do you mean?"

"Your aura was all—I don't know, sharky—when we met. It's better now. More like what I imagined you'd be like."

I avoided his eyes. Not for the first time, I had the feeling I'd been letting Lysi down.

"Getting that close to an injured killer whale was probably a stupid thing to do," I said.

"You'd be surprised how often the stupid thing is the right thing," said Spio.

Not long after, I began to wilt with exhaustion. It must have been night time. For all I knew, we'd swum until dawn, no thanks to the sun rotating around us in a slow-motion taunt.

Everything around me seemed to have a silvery glow. How long had I been awake? How long could someone stay awake before losing sanity?

"Next break in the ice," said Spio. "Let's take a nap. You're about to pass out on me."

I had no energy to argue.

We found a break in the ice, but tremors in the waves told me there was a huge something already up there. I squinted at the green underside as though to see through.

"With numbers like that, I have two guesses," said Spio. "It's either walruses, or a cruise ship let off and there are tourists having a fiesta on the ice."

Deciding to place my bet on the walruses, I poked my head up.

Dozens of enormous, chocolate-brown lumps of blubber were resting atop the ice on all sides, grunting so loudly it was as if they were all shouting at each other. I'd thought walruses would be cute, but up close, that was a stretch. Odour aside, they were lumpy, wrinkled, and scabby-looking, with thick white whiskers coming out of greasy muzzles. But their collective aura was content, so I decided they weren't bad. I began to pull myself up.

"Whoa, buddy!" said Spio, appearing beside me and grabbing my arm. "You can't just go up to a walrus."

I looked at the nearest one. He was so blubbery, it looked like if I slapped him on the back his fat would ripple as fluidly as if I dropped a stone in a pond. I squinted at Spio, wondering if he was joking.

"Walruses are jerks, Meela."

"They are?"

"You think those lung-poppers are for decoration?"

I supposed their tusks were easily as long as my arm.

I slumped. "So - tired."

"I know. We'll find something soon. A little—"

He looked down, staring at the surface.

"What?" I said.

Without a word, he submerged. I glanced longingly at the occupied ice around me, and followed.

"Crap," said Spio.

"What is it?"

"We've got a situation thirty-seven here. Military line."

I followed his gaze into the distance. An army of mermen—a hundred, at least—stirred faintly.

My blood ran cold. "Adaro's?"

"It's most likely."

"Which way do we go?"

Spio checked each direction before saying, "There. We should be able to go around."

We continued northeast, picking up our pace. The net weighed more painfully than ever. I hoped Spio knew what he was doing. I tried to feel the current, to pick out an identity and determine if this actually was Adaro's army, or something else.

I stopped. "Wait."

Spio turned, mouth open to argue. Then his expression slackened, and he spun back towards the army.

He felt it too. Lysi. Her presence was on the current.

My excitement turned to horror.

"Spio, who is she with?"

He grimaced. "I hate to say it, buddy, but it doesn't feel like our friend is in particularly good company."

"They captured her? What are they planning to do with her?"

We needed to save her. She was alive—but for how long? Could we smuggle her away?

Spio looked down at the net in our hands, and then into the distance, and then back to me. A smile spread across his face.

And then he said something I was sure instilled fear in the hearts of merpeople everywhere.

"I have a plan."

CHAPTER SEVENTEEN - Lysi
Murder in the Diomedes

I hadn't seen this level of security since the trained great white shark on the southern battlefront. I felt an odd surge of pride that six mermen felt they needed to go to this extreme to keep me tame.

They had broken away from the other soldiers to bring me to the Bering. I was suspended between them by rope, bound at the wrists, neck, and waist.

"I'll send the message when we get there," said Thetis.

"Why should you get the reward?" said Nestor.

"Because I found her!"

"You did not. You just happened to be closest," said a stout one, whose name sounded like *Gurr.*

I studied my captors, taking inventory of weapons and weaknesses. The plump one seemed the weak link—but he was between Thetis and some bearded guy who was roughly the size and shape of a beluga.

I'd found my longblade. Well, that cod named Nestor had. He carried it like he'd discovered treasure, swinging it around to taunt me.

"If we find the other one," said Thetis, "you can have the reward for her."

Nestor snorted. "What, the rest of us have to share a reward, while you get the full amount for this broad?"

"Hey!" I tried to smack Nestor in the head, but Thetis jerked me away. He carried a mace with spikes on the end that I wondered if he'd chiselled himself. I'd never seen one made with such care. My skin tingled from the points slicing through the water.

"Wanna tell us where your girl is, Lysithea?" said Nestor, flashing yellow fangs.

"I don't know where she is." It was the truth, however terrifying.

"Come on. We'll let you swim without the ropes."

"You think I'm going to believe that?"

"All right, how's this?" said Beluga. "Tell us where she is, or we don't let you breach next time."

"I don't know where she is! You think I was hanging out between those icebergs because I felt like it? We lost each other when the glacier broke."

They all glared at me. After a pause, they resumed arguing over how to divide my bounty and whether they would find Meela.

When Thetis and Beluga began shouting at each other, I seized the opportunity and made an abrupt dive, twisting so the ropes tangled together.

The shouting grew louder. "Don't let her go!" said Gurr stupidly.

In the ensuing chaos, I felt two of the ropes slacken.

But the other ropes tightened. They stopped me easily.

I hadn't really expected it to work; I was too overpowered. The huge knot that had formed in the ropes was a small consolation, though. It took some effort for them to untie.

"Would you cooperate for once in your life?" said Nestor, fighting with the ropes. "You anarchy warriors are half this kingdom's problem."

"It's not anarchy I want."

Nestor gave the others a maddening grin. "What they all say, isn't it?"

They laughed.

"We've got enemies to fight," said Thetis, "yet you warriors are doing everything you can to divide and weaken us."

"Enemies? We wouldn't have enemies if it weren't for Adaro!"

Nestor gave me a condescending look. "I'm just saying, we've got enough problems at the luna bin without you anarchy warriors causing problems at home, too."

Luna bin? Anarchy warriors? Did these terms come from Adaro himself, or was this some new slang I hadn't heard before?

"It's a selfish battle you're fighting," said Thetis. "He's your king, and you need to accept that."

"He's not my king. I'd rather die than serve him."

"Looks like you get to choose your fate, then."

When we next breached, I swiped a finger through the snow again to point Meela in the direction of our current. Once more, I managed to keep the action subtle enough that no one noticed.

After travelling another quarter-tide that felt like a year, my captors began arguing about whether to detour to find food or keep taking this current. I silently hoped for the detour. My stomach was painfully empty.

"We need to veer further east, anyway."

"No, we don't."

"We do. The acoustic channel is east."

"That one goes to the luna bin, you cod."

"I thought that's where the king was headed."

"No, he's headed towards their queen. She's in high security. West."

I looked up at the word *queen*, hoping someone would elaborate.

No one did, so I said, "Is that where I'm going? High security?"

"No, darling," said Thetis. "You're inked for execution."

Somehow, the threat incited no reaction in me. Maybe because I'd suspected as much for a while.

"So what did those prisoners do to avoid being executed?" I said.

"They have valuable information to give His Majesty. You, on the other hand, are no more than a glorified anarchy warrior."

Yes, a queen would have key information to give. It sickened me to think what Adaro might be doing to extract such information.

"So what's the *luna bin*? Do you get the word from *moon*?"

They exchanged a look that told me I was right. They were talking about the Moonless City.

"Queen Evagore's alive, then," I said. "Interesting."

Thetis tensed. "We didn't say—"

"Nice work, fishface," said Nestor.

"Not much she can do with that, anyway, guys," said Beluga.

Frustratingly, he was right. The rest of them appraised the ropes binding me to them and relaxed.

Evagore was alive. She was somewhere in a high security prison, being pried for information.

I considered what kind of information that might be. Insight into her kingdom? It must have been something vital. Adaro wouldn't keep opposition alive unless he got something out of it.

"I'm starving," said Beluga, scanning the ice. "Can we veer closer to land?"

I tried to imagine where they would keep high-security prisoners. It would have to be somewhere remote, off-limits to civilians and humans.

Abandoning pretense, I said, "Where is the high security prison? Can't be anywhere near Utopia."

"Like we're telling you," said Nestor. "Even if you are about to be executed."

I considered whether it would be worth sweet-talking the information out of him—but I couldn't bring myself to charm these idiots.

We made a sudden stop.

An enormous fishing net blocked our path, suspended from the ice floes and fluttering in the current.

"Dinner!" said Gurr.

This confused me, because the net was empty. Then they all turned to me.

I was the only mermaid—the one with the allure. I could catch them the easy meal.

"No," I said.

Thetis cracked me on the head with the butt of his mace. "We're hungry. Get us those fishermen and we'll consider letting you have a bite."

I opened my mouth to argue. All of them glared at me, shifting their weapons. I huffed.

"You'll have to untie my hands."

They traded uneasy looks. Hunger must have won out, because Thetis finally loosened the rope from my hands. He added an extra loop around my neck to be sure.

How was I going to get out of this? I'd never lured a human with the intent to kill. I didn't want to start now. I wondered if I'd be able to let these people escape and make it seem accidental.

I swam between Nestor and Thetis, refusing to make eye contact with any of them.

The fishermen were inexperienced. I could feel them stomping around loud enough to scare off every fish within a league. Also the ice was barely a hand thick and dangerously cracked. One wrong step and they would fall through. And what were they doing so close to a merman army with everything going on? Something was off.

Surfacing carefully to make sure no one was poised up there with a weapon, I prepared to turn on the charm—and stopped.

It wasn't fishermen. It was Meela, peeking out from behind a mound of snow.

I nearly shouted in relief.

She waved me over. I hesitated, still processing what was happening. Had she set up the net? Or had she found it here and climbed up? What the heck was her plan?

Meela gestured again, more urgently. I pointed to the ropes around my neck and tried to indicate that they were tied around my waist, too. She nodded in acknowledgement, but kept beckoning me over.

I supposed that even if she helped me sever the ropes, the guys would notice the slackening and come investigate before I could be cut free.

She must have had a plan. Or was this another reckless moment of hers?

I met her wide, green eyes.

She wouldn't endanger me. I had to trust her.

I hoisted myself onto the ice, doing my best to use the same careful pace I would use in luring a human. As far as the guys below were concerned, I was still hunting their dinner.

"Catch," whispered Meela, her voice a breath on the wind.

She threw something to me. It was a bag, jammed full of something soft.

What the—?

The stench hit me and I wrinkled my nose. The bag was full of blood and guts. It had begun to freeze, turning thick and slushy. Where did she get this from? What was I supposed to do with it?

Meela mimed shooting a crossbow at me.

Comprehension dawning, I curled my lips in a smirk. Her answering smile was the most wonderful thing I'd seen in days.

Giving her a grim salute, I upended the bag and let out my most blood-curdling scream. The bag's contents spread across the ice, most of it freezing instantly but some trickling into the cracks.

I imagined the guys below panicking, thinking I'd been shot. If they felt threatened by iron, they wouldn't surface right away—if at all. It gave me a precious fragment of time.

Meela slid a blade across the ice. I picked it up and began sawing the ropes.

"Hurry," she whispered.

After a tense moment that felt like ages, the ropes gave way. I'd just begun hacking at the one around my waist when a shout rang from the gap in the ice behind me.

"She's alive! Quick, grab on."

I whipped around. Beluga's fat head had popped out of the water. He extended a hand to me. For a moment I almost felt sorry for tricking them. Then I remembered he was trying to save me so he could collect his bounty.

The bag of guts caught his attention; he stared at it in bewilderment. I tried to angle myself to block his view of Meela, but it was too late. He had seen her.

Thetis popped up next to him. His jaw fell open in a mirror of his comrade.

"Pull her in!" he shouted, ducking back into the water.

The ropes jerked. I slid rapidly towards the gap, smearing blood in a bright trail across the ice.

I screamed, clawing uselessly at the bald surface. But the ropes cinched like a noose, and I had nothing to hold onto.

There was a sharp exhale, and one of the ropes snapped loose.

Meela was suddenly in front of me. Her fingers closed around my wrists, pulling me in one direction while the remaining ropes pulled in the other.

Another rope slackened. What was going on? Did she have her crossbow?

No, both hands were pulling me. So how—?

I looked over my shoulder and gasped. There sat my best friend, two unconscious mermen at his tail and a rock the size of a small child in his hands.

"That's what I call two birds with one stone," he said. "Or maybe it's two cods with one boulder in this c—"

The ropes yanked hard. I slid from Meela's grip, and she screamed. I caught a glimpse of Spio's surprised face before plunging into the water.

A pair of arms dragged me under as soon as I hit the surface. I thrashed. The ropes tightened so painfully, I wondered if I wouldn't be split in two.

Two splashes came overhead.

"Let's *rock*!" shouted Spio.

He heaved the stone, bludgeoning someone in the back of the head.

I caught a glimpse of Meela's crossbow swinging by my ear.

Thetis seized my wrist. I aimed a punch at him, but the ends of the ropes tangled around my arms and blocked the swing.

In a blink, Thetis' arm locked around my throat and he pressed something sharp to my temple.

"Stop!" he said, deafening in my ear.

Meela and Spio turned their attention to Nestor, weapons raised.

"It would seem you've hit *rock bottom*," said Spio.

Nestor seemed to realise his comrades had been rendered unconscious, because he turned and fled.

"I said, stop!" shouted Thetis.

Meela either didn't hear or did not care. She caught up to Nestor in three strokes and descended on him like an eagle with talons outstretched. Nestor roared as she wrapped an arm around his throat, locking him between her bicep and forearm. With her other hand, she raised my black longblade to his chin.

She lifted her gaze and perhaps caught sight of the blade pressed to my head, because her jaw fell slack.

She regained her composure quickly. "Let Lysi go or your friend is dead, mister."

"Mister?" said Nestor. He tried to turn his head, but Meela pushed the blade harder into his skin.

"She was in the Battle for Eriana Kwai," said Spio. "She's spent too much time around humans."

A muscle in Meela's jaw twitched.

"Ha," said Thetis at my ear. "You're the Eriana girl, aren't you?"

"And?" she said.

"Thetis, just let her go," said Nestor in a strangled voice.

Thetis tightened his hold on me. "We've got orders."

"I don't care. I'm not dying today."

Thetis pressed his blade harder against my temple, the point sharp and stinging. I didn't know it had broken through the thin flesh until I saw the ribbon of blood waving like seaweed in the water.

We were at an impasse, Meela's arm around Nestor's throat and Thetis' arm around mine.

Spio looked back and forth between us, calculating.

"Nestor, we can turn them both over," said Thetis.

"Hey," said Spio. "What about me?"

We all looked at him.

"I tried just as hard to get the king to snuff it, you know," said Spio. "I deserve to have a price on my head, too."

Seizing the opportunity, I reached up and grabbed Thetis' hair. With a roar, I pulled him over my shoulder and twisted out of his grip. Before he could retaliate, I punched him in the face. A cloud of blood burst from his nose.

Three more quick punches and he went limp.

I disentangled myself from the ropes. *Finally.* My skin burned where the ropes had been rubbing all day. When I looked up, Meela and Spio were staring.

Nestor made a choking sound. Meela eased off the blade, which she'd been driving into his chin.

"All right!" he blurted. "Go. I won't say a thing."

I must have been a terrifying sight. The pressure in my eyes and the ache from my fangs cutting into my lips reached a peak. I was stained hair to tail in blood, most of it not mine.

It dawned on me where the bag of guts had come from. Of course. I should have known Spio was behind that ridiculous plan.

"I have a family," said Nestor. "Please. I'll stay quiet."

I tried to decide if he was a liar, a coward, or if he was possibly on our side.

Meela and Spio looked to me.

"We need information," I said, voice flat. "What do you know about Adaro?"

Nestor swallowed. His chin was bleeding. "He's been attacking human settlements along the coast."

"We know. Do better."

"Wh-what do you want to know?"

"Where would someone go if they wanted to find him?"

"He's c-coming this way. He's hitting the Atlantic next."

"Right now?" said Meela. "So he's taken everywhere else?"

"Y-yes. He's coming."

If Nestor was telling the truth, this was our chance.

How long did we have until king tide? It must have been a few days away, at most—and then we had about a day to work with until he transitioned back to merman.

We had to time it right.

I didn't like this. We still needed to recruit help. We couldn't take down Adaro on our own, even if we did know where to find him.

"He just hit that big city in Canada," said Nestor, the panic in his voice rising at our silence. "You know it?"

"Shut up," said Meela, keeping the blade to the merman's chin. "You say he's passing through here?"

"He told the northern detachments to meet him at Steller Point."

"Where's that?"

"The Aleutians. Sort of. A little northeast. It's on some current—I can't remember its name—"

"All right, stop," said Meela. "Let me think."

A red gleam appeared in her eye. I knew what she was thinking. But it was too risky to tail him until he transitioned. He could easily set the serpent on us before we got anywhere near.

"Mee—"

"Where were you taking Lysi?" she said to Nestor.

He spluttered.

Meela pressed the blade upwards, drawing more blood. "There's a price on her head, is there not? On both of us?"

"You're wanted for treason!"

"So you're supposed to take us to Adaro?"

"Yes."

"Why didn't you just kill Lysi, if she's a traitor to the crown?"

"The king wants to question her on the rebel group."

I didn't like the look in Meela's eye, or the feel of her racing pulse. What was she thinking about so hard? Was she worried they were closing in on Nilus? Or was she planning something?

Before I could voice my concerns, she said, "Take me to him."

"No!" I said.

"Uh," said Spio.

"The timing is right. He wants information, so he won't kill me. If I can get close enough to him at the right moment, I can finish this."

"But Mee—"

She addressed Nestor. "I have the information he wants. Take me to Adaro and I'll let you live."

"Done," said Nestor.

I grabbed Meela's arm. "Mee, think. Even if he doesn't kill you right away, you're still in danger."

"Not if I time it right. I'll make sure I get to him as the tide is pulling."

Spio looked between us, evidently unsure what the best option was.

"Lysi, this is how I can get close enough to kill him," said Meela. "It's worth it."

I tried to understand her desperation. This was her chance to end the life that had caused her so much suffering. I thought of her people, and Nilus, and the stress of the Massacre. It was a tempting plan. But that didn't mean it was smart, or safe.

"Take us both, then," I said to Nestor.

"Am I chopped sardines over here?" said Spio. "Make it three."

Nestor made a gagging sound. Meela relaxed her hold, not looking at all sorry that she kept managing to choke him.

"When you've finished deciding how noble you all are," said Nestor, "I'd like to breach."

Meela glared at me, and then at Spio. "Fine. All of us."

Spio nodded once, jaw set.

"All right," I said, turning to Nestor. "Take us to Adaro."

CHAPTER EIGHTEEN - Meela
Back in the Bering

While I tied Nestor around the neck and wrists, Lysi and Spio wrapped our unconscious victims snugly in the fishing net and left them to drift.

My insides fluttered at our good luck. Finally, we had an inside source to take us to Adaro. Yes, there were risks if we got close to the king. At the same time, he had not ordered Lysi dead. He'd wanted her alive so he could question her, which meant what I knew about Kori Maru and the serpent would be my protection. Not that I would tell him about either.

"If you try anything, you'll get your ass kicked by all three of us," I said, pressing the blade against Nestor's throat for emphasis.

He gave a pathetic squeak.

I returned the black longblade to Lysi, and we each took an end of rope.

"Lead the way, Nestor," said Lysi.

With a sour glance at this reversal of fortune, he led us south.

Now, to figure out the timing. We had to get to Adaro before it was too late—but we couldn't be early, because every moment we were near him while he was a merman, we would be in danger. We had to get this right.

"Thanks for saving me," said Lysi.

"Yeah," I said distractedly. "Hey, what day is it?"

"I don't know."

"What do you mean, you don't know? Can't you track the tides and moon?"

"It's harder up north."

I huffed.

"Well don't get mad about it," she said. "When we're farther south I'll be able to see the moon phase."

When I said nothing, she added, "I don't see you offering insight over there."

I glared. I was perfectly aware of my ineptitude as a mermaid without her reminding me.

"Why do you need the moon phase?" said Nestor.

"Shut up," I snapped.

Would Adaro's transition happen the moment king tide started, or would it happen at the apex of the tide's pull? I guessed the latter, but what if I was wrong? We would have to tail him in secret as soon as we found him, to be sure we didn't arrive too late.

I was dimly aware of Lysi and Spio talking. I caught the words "attack belugas" and "baitball" and "whale whisperer". I ignored them, thinking through various scenarios.

We travelled across the North Pole with Nestor in tow, taking shifts when we needed sleep. He rarely spoke, and only once made a feeble escape attempt while Lysi was on watch. I woke up to find Lysi clubbing him on the head and telling him not to be such a cod. We tied his ropes tighter.

When we got to the Bering Strait, no one was there to block our passage—much to Nestor's dismay—as the army was under orders to meet Adaro at Steller Point. We travelled beneath the ice and entered the Bering Sea. The trip south was as stormy as it had been on the way up, the waves overhead white and choppy.

I thought about what I would do first once I had control of the serpent. More enticingly, what would I do once the war was over? The possibilities were endless. With Eriana's spirit bound to mine, I would reach a near-goddess status.

I could command her to stay near Eriana Kwai, or at least return to my first home often, to keep my people safe. I would be a true warrior of Eriana Kwai—more of a warrior than anyone else had been on any Massacre.

Then, once my time in this world was up, I could pass the honour to my children—assuming I had any. Did I want to? I hadn't thought much about it. But if I wanted to keep the Host of Eriana alive and under the control of a descendant, I would have to pass it down my bloodline.

A goddess. The very thought sent a thrill up my spine.

Soon, I would be more powerful than Medusa. Was any woman in history more powerful than her?

This was how legends were formed. I would carry on the story of Eriana as no one else could. I would be Metlaa Gaela, descendant of Eriana, master of the leviathan.

"If you're hoping to stay hidden, we should stop here," said Nestor.

The water was clear of ice, the landscape reminding me more of the Gulf of Alaska. The floor sloped towards two volcanic islands that sat close together, an unfathomably deep trench some distance ahead. We must have been back in the Aleutian Islands.

I searched for the serpent's massive presence but felt nothing. No matter. We would find her soon. I flexed my fingers, then raised and lowered my arms a little, imagining how it was going to feel to control the serpent. How had Dani done it, before she died? Was it thoughts or actions that controlled Eriana?

"Where do we go?" said Lysi.

"If you don't mind land, there are caves along the beach," said Nestor. "We can wait there until he comes."

"As long as we don't have to take out any Kodiak bears," said Spio.

I let them discuss it. It occurred to me that I hadn't spoken once since that morning, but I had no words to offer. The prospect of finally killing Adaro, of inheriting Eriana's most powerful secret, drove me into a silence too precious to share.

I trailed behind the three of them as they started towards the beach.

Abruptly, Lysi's scream cut through my thoughts like a knife.

I snapped my head up, looking for the danger, and not until a wisp of blood appeared in the water did I notice something protruding from Spio's neck.

A bubble left his mouth. Lysi dashed forwards and grabbed his shoulders.

Coldness spread through my body. I watched blankly as everything slowed down.

Spio's mouth opened and closed. Lysi screamed for him to keep his eyes open.

My jaw opened in dim surprise. Where had that weapon come from?

I belatedly turned to Nestor and caught the cruel smile curling up his face. I was the only one still holding his ropes.

"Lysi," I said, voice hollow and distant. "Get away—"

Something whooshed through the water behind me, and Lysi's screams were cut short.

My body went numb.

I met Lysi's gaze—those vibrant, unimaginably beautiful sapphire eyes. Their precise shape and colour had never left my memory as long as I'd known her. They were the first thing I'd fallen in love with, all those years ago on the beach. They were the first thing to appear in my mind whenever I thought of her, and the shade of blue that had haunted my dreams over the years we spent apart.

Those eyes were wide with fear.

Her mouth was open. Those soft lips, and those teeth like pearls—her smile had been the second thing I'd fallen in love with. Back on the Bloodhound, floating in the middle of violent waves and wind, that was the smile that gave me hope. Those were the lips I thought I'd never be able to kiss.

A bubble escaped those lips as Lysi gave a soft, "Oh."

She looked down at her chest. Something protruded from it—right over her heart.

Her heart: the part of her I'd fallen so deeply, so permanently in love with.

I wanted to scream, but no sound would come.

Her eyes rolled back. For a moment, she just hung in place.

"Lysi!"

The entire world ground to a stop. This wasn't happening. It had to be a nightmare. The world could not dispose of something so pure.

I started forwards, but something closed tight around my arm. I spun around, fists swinging—

"You make it so simple, Meela."

I froze. A small sound caught in my throat, like a gasp for air that didn't exist.

I had to be imagining that face. He couldn't be here. I hadn't felt the serpent. We were supposed to be hunting him, not the other way around.

But there he was, reptilian face close to mine, a snarl revealing his pointed teeth. That black crown topped his head, seeming to grow from matted hair that was just as dark, and framed his face like a lion's mane.

A roar burst from deep in my chest, so loud and furious I wasn't sure it even came from me. Nothing seemed connected. My senses, my body, the screams coming from my mouth, all of it was a part of something scattered, a universe I was not a part of.

My reactions were too slow. Adaro's arm came up, a stone mace in his hand.

He swung it at my head. My teeth cut into my lip as I threw one last punch.

There was a sickening crack as the mace hit my skull.

CHAPTER NINETEEN - Ben
Sworn Oath

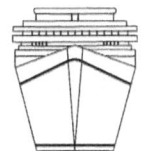

"We're calling it sonic charges."

Reeves stuffed his hands in his pockets, hoping the plan wasn't as ominous as it sounded. Miller's voice was muffled by the activity in the warehouse, full of gear, artillery, parts, and a dozen trainees. A high, rhythmic whirr sounded somewhere near the amphibian plane as the mechanics worked.

"You know how those environmentalist types have been saying ship noise is harmful to marine animals and all that crap?"

"Yeah," said Reeves, frowning.

"Well, this gave us an idea for two potential paths to victory. First, we can take out the merman and all the other sea demons with a high-powered blast of sound. Burst their eardrums, drive them insane, whatever it is the noise does. Second, maybe that serpent's indestructible, but that's not to say we can't incapacitate it. You get a high-intensity, low-frequency noise, and even a blue whale would rather beach itself than endure it."

Reeves stared, not knowing what to say. He was saved by a faint buzzing sound. Miller took his phone from his pocket and looked at the screen. He typed something and put it back.

"I gotta go. Sensors picking up seismic activity. Might be related. Don't know what they want me to do about it. A tremor's a tremor. Not like we haven't been expecting the Big One to—"

"Sir, what about everything we talked about?"

Miller leaned back, giving Reeves a once-over with narrowed eyes. Reeves ran a hand over his mouth, aware of how his face had tightened in horror.

Lowering his voice, he said, "How control is passed, sir. Targeting the merman?"

"I've spoken to the Secretary of State about this. We have official orders to go forward."

"Did you tell him everything I told you?"

"Of course I did. But we discussed it in detail and we agree we can't get to the merman without being attacked by the serpent. We need something to incapacitate one or both of them."

A battle raged inside Reeves' head. Half of him wanted to shout at Officer Miller for ignoring the facts he'd pulled straight from the only historical document ever recorded on the serpent. The other half of him knew his place.

"Sir, the serpent is indestructible. This won't—"

"If the legend is true—" Miller paused, letting Reeves know that he did not, in fact, believe the legend was true.

"—we'll still get the merman with this. If power is passed as you say, then that's not a bad thing, is it?"

Miller clapped Reeves on the back, a grin on his face that plainly suggested Reeves needed to take a vacation for his mental health.

A group of trainees passed by, heading to dinner. They acknowledged Miller and Reeves on the way, forcing Reeves to keep his rising panic in check.

He waited until they left the warehouse before continuing.

"Can't you take out the merman with something that won't hurt or kill everything within a several-mile radius?"

Miller gave Reeves a long, searching look. "You're concerned about the environment?"

"Aren't you?"

"I'm more concerned about what'll happen to humanity if we don't stop this."

How could he convince Miller that mermaids could be talked to and negotiated with? These insane tactics could be avoided.

"Sir, we need to protect the innocent. The mermaids who are no more than victims of—"

He wished he hadn't said it as soon as the words were out.

Miller crossed his arms. "Protect?"

Reeves tried to think of a way to explain. He needed Miller to know some mermaids could be trusted—but his every instinct was telling him to zip it.

"Bagh," said Miller, not raising the volume of his voice.

Across the warehouse, a clanking noise stopped. Bagh appeared from behind an amphibian plane.

"Sir?"

"Bagh, tell Reeves what you told me the other day."

"About what, sir?"

"What you heard about Reeves' mission last year."

Bagh glanced between them, forehead wrinkled. "They passed a pod of mermaids, sir."

"And?"

Bagh looked down and mumbled something inaudible.

"What's that?"

"They opted not to attack, sir."

Miller turned back to Reeves. "You told your team to spare the mermaids. Tell me, does this sound like the kind of behaviour I'd expect from you, chief?"

Anger battled with the hot shame filling his gut. Who did Bagh think he was, telling Miller something like this?

"No, sir. I was trying to keep my team focused on the task at hand."

"I hope so. Because I would hate to have to relieve you of command."

There was a heavy silence. Reeves nodded stiffly. Miller pushed past him and walked away. Before leaving the warehouse, he turned.

"Go help the boys clear the beach. The tide is supposed to rise higher than usual tomorrow, and I don't want to lose anything."

The door slammed with echoing volume.

Reeves stood facing the friend who'd betrayed him. His heart hammered. Sweat dampened his palms.

Relieve you of command.

The words rang in his head. He would never let that happen. He would not let everything he had dedicated his entire life to be discarded so easily.

"Man, I didn't think—" said Bagh, but Reeves turned away.

Bagh grabbed his elbow. "Look, I'm sorry!"

"What did you hope to accomplish by telling him that? Trying to tattle on me like a little kid?"

"No! It was about the mermaids, not … I didn't think Miller would care."

"Of course he's going to care!"

Reeves tried to pull away but Bagh gripped his arm tighter.

"We're done, here," shouted Reeves. It was with enormous effort that he did not hit Bagh. An apology would not erase the fact that Bagh had treaded on his career—his life.

"I said I'm sorry!"

"I don't want to hear it!" The anger burst from him, ricocheting through the warehouse.

Bagh stepped back. Recovering, he set his jaw and nodded.

"Fine. See you around, chief."

"Yeah. Maybe."

Reeves stormed outside, fists clenched. He had not worked this hard to be demoted because of Bagh's careless words.

But what was he supposed to do? Just let these sonic charges happen? It was Operation Perseus all over again.

He stood at the edge of the beach, facing the water, and crossed his arms. The tide swished against the rocks. The glistening head of a seal poked out of the waves, bobbing slowly. This beach was so pure, so alive. What would happen to it in a few days' time?

The man he'd sworn to be would accept Officer Miller's decision. Reeves knew his order to spare the mermaids had been a betrayal—and that was why Miller had cared so deeply. As Team Chief, it was Reeves' duty to obey, to protect his country. He had to do whatever it took to stop this outside force from harming the American people. Sometimes, harsh actions had to be taken, and this was one of those times.

But he could also make a choice.

When he'd become a Navy SEAL, he'd sworn to never quit, to never drop out of a fight. This fight was no different—the one defending what he knew was right. He knew in his gut that mermaids had meaningful lives, families, and emotions not unlike his own. It wasn't their fault they were forced to serve this merman king. They were victims. They were innocent civilians worth fighting for.

Being a soldier was supposed to mean fighting for the value of life. Maybe that oath was not intended to include mermaids—but the technicality didn't matter to Reeves. He wanted to be the kind of man who valued and fought for all life equally. He had a choice to make, and looking out over the water, the scent of ocean air carrying on the breeze, he realised he had already made it.

CHAPTER TWENTY - Meela
The Effects of Iron

My first instinct upon opening my eyes was to gasp for air—but I couldn't. I was underwater. The next thing I realised was that I could not move my arms. I pulled and heard the creak of a rope.

The world was dim. I looked around to find the glimmering surface a long ways up.

I was tied to a boulder, lying face down on its rough surface as though waiting for a guillotine to drop. And I was not alone.

A merman floated beside me, staring through blood-red eyes.

Thetis, I thought, recalling his name.

How long had I been out? Had he been staring at me like this for hours? I averted my gaze.

A familiar black longblade rested against another rock. Behind it lay my crossbow and quiver, bolts scattered in the sand.

The events leading up to this situation came rushing back. *Lysi.*

"Oh, no, no, no …"

My heart seemed to collapse on itself, the agony too much to bear. I pulled hard against the rope.

Thetis moved his lips. Was he talking to me? I heard the sound, but the words and meaning were hollow, not reaching my brain.

Another merman appeared beside him. *Nestor.*

How were the two of them here, free and unharmed? What was going on?

But I knew. My chest constricted, and I wheezed as though punched in the ribs.

The enormous, all-consuming presence of the serpent lingered, wrapping around me like a cloak.

Adaro was close.

He should have been dead. Instead, he'd killed her. He'd killed both of them. What he was about to do to me, I didn't want to think. How had this gone so wrong? I'd been so sure of my plan.

A voice in my head roared, scolding me for thinking I could do this. *What plan?*

I hadn't listened to her. My whole life, she had been my guardian. My love for Lysi had brought my ship home from the Massacre. It had saved my life when she'd turned me into a mermaid. Love had always led me in the right direction—so why had I let myself become this monster? I'd done exactly what she had been warning against: I'd acted reckless, too blinded by vengeance to consider a better way.

Nestor trembled, his eyes darting nervously.

"He says to leave her here. He'll be by soon."

"What's keeping him?" said Thetis.

"The humans are flying overhead. They must have seen the serpent when he put it ashore. It's back under now, but they keep circling."

I strained against the rope, trying to either break it or wriggle free. They'd bound me so tightly, I couldn't feel my hands.

"So he's waiting them out?" said Thetis.

"Doesn't want to move until they're gone, in case they see."

They looked at me. A moment passed in which we all seemed to be waiting for another to speak.

Nestor swam back and forth, pacing. "I heard they dropped something on the Nereid Peaks."

Thetis tensed. "Did the prisoners get out?"

"Don't think so."

"Lucky. Don't know why he's keeping her alive. It's giving the luna bin hope."

Keeping who alive? Was he talking about me? But no—I had no idea what Thetis was referring to by *the luna bin.*

"If I had the serpent, I'd have done away with ..." With a start, he seemed to realise what he was saying and snapped his mouth closed. His greyish skin paled.

Nestor backed away from Thetis as if retreating from a hungry shark.

"I only meant—if I were king—not that I think—" said Thetis, but Nestor shook his head.

Their fear leeched onto me, my pulse accelerating. I didn't understand—why should I care about this merman speaking ill of Adaro? Then I became aware of the presence behind me. A dark, overpowering aura filled the water, blocking my ability to feel anything else.

I went instinctively still.

Adaro drifted into my line of sight, his focus on Thetis and Nestor.

Something about the black crown sent a chill through me. His red eyes popped against that reptilian skin. How had I possibly thought I could take him on? Even without the serpent, all the power I'd admired in Medusa was here in front of me—twice as large, a hundred times more terrible.

There was something else, too. Something that prickled my skin. Iron. Clutched in his fist was what looked like a broken, rusted pipe.

I glanced to the longblade on the floor, straining against my ropes with increasing desperation.

Adaro raised the iron rod to Thetis. Thetis flinched. But Adaro merely held it out to him, a calmness about his aura.

"Go on, then."

"Y-your Majesty?"

"You think you can make a better king than I."

"N-no, Your Majesty, of course—"

"But I just heard you, Thetis."

"I meant—"

"Go on," said Adaro. "I am making this simple for you."

Nestor watched, still and silent, trembling worse than ever. Thetis looked from the iron rod to Adaro, and then around as though to ask for help.

"I give you permission, Thetis. Kill me. Stab it through my heart."

Adaro kept the weapon at arm's length, unwavering. His aura was calm, yet Thetis and Nestor cowered as though staring into the cavernous jaws of the serpent.

I saw no way out of this for Thetis. In another universe, one where he had not tried to turn Lysi over to Adaro, and one where my every emotion was not focused on the fact that I would never see her again, I might have felt sorry for him.

I watched with detachment as, slowly, Thetis reached for the iron rod.

Nestor made no sound of surprise or protest. He was so still, I would have missed him if relying on feel.

Thetis' webbed fingers closed around the rod. His flesh hissed and sizzled. The smell hit me, bringing back the sensation of dread, of hopelessness, that had consumed me on the Massacre.

A large bubble left Thetis' mouth. I wondered what he was going to do. Surely he wouldn't do what Adaro said.

Maybe what came next was inevitable. He raised the weapon—and plunged the iron into his own heart. The sizzle was drowned by his scream. The pungent smell intensified. Blood leaked out around the pipe, clouding the water.

My heart leapt against my ribs as though trying to free itself from a mortal body. Adaro watched with indifference.

After a long, terrible moment, the life drained from Thetis' eyes. Adaro approached the body and pulled the weapon free. He pushed the dead merman aside.

I flinched as the water stirred, and out of the murky blue appeared the serpent. Her eyes were fixed on Thetis' body.

Everything darkened as her tremendous body curved around us. A silence descended so complete that a puff of air leaving her nostrils could be heard.

Gently, like a mother dog picking up her pup, her teeth closed over Thetis' tail fin and pulled him closer. She opened her mouth.

I wanted to close my eyes but couldn't.

With a movement too fast to see, the serpent's jaws snapped closed over Thetis' entire body. The pulse of water slammed into me, pushing me hard against the boulder.

Thetis was gone, and Nestor stared, open-mouthed, at the empty space. I was not aware that Adaro's attention had turned to me until he spoke.

"This was an admirable effort on your part, Meela."

Panic rose, but I met his gaze, determined not to look afraid.

"Do you know what my armies are doing this very moment?"

Keeping my voice even, I said, "They're invading the Atlantic."

Adaro tilted his head. He gave a peculiar smile. "Indeed. My last battle and then the oceans will be under the absolute crown, the way they were always meant to be. Medusa never understood what a true monarch should be."

"You mean killing everyone who isn't Utopia-born? Anyone who might not be prepared to die for you? You're afraid of your own kingdom. It's pathetic."

I almost added the things I knew of Medusa—but a voice in my head that sounded like Lysi's told me to be quiet.

Adaro snarled. The serpent coiled around the three of us, blocking the currents and casting us into isolation.

"As the absolute crown, I cannot have opposition."

He circled behind me. A faint sting across my neck told me the iron rod was dangerously close.

"Opposition includes, of course, any organised rebel groups. I will happily spare you, Meela, if you tell me where the rebel group is."

The sting spread across my shoulders, down my back.

I gritted my teeth. I thought of Nilus and Ephyra and all of my nieces. He would have to burn me to death before I turned anyone over to him.

"No."

The sting intensified, like someone held a lit match against my skin. I bit my lip, forcing myself not to cry out.

"Then I want to thank you for this opportunity. It will enlighten you as to what your people have been putting my army through all these years. And, I suppose, you might understand what you put Lysithea through, what with that terrible, unsightly burn on her flesh."

I thrashed, pulling the ropes until they groaned and threatened to snap.

"Think," said Adaro, mock pain in his voice. "Think of all the suffering your rash actions are causing. Lysithea, and that goon, and now all of your people. You can be sure, Meela, that my next stop with the Host of Eriana will be her home. She will destroy every part of your island until there is nothing left but rock."

My chest hurt so badly I could barely think. I couldn't tell if the pain was from devastation or lack of air.

I couldn't let him take everything and everyone away from me.

I wished desperately for him to transition into his human form. Why couldn't it happen now? Why couldn't the universe be on my side, just this once?

A thought ran through me like ice. What if Medusa had lied to us? What if her allegiance was with her son, and she'd purposely led us into this trap?

"My people beat you before," I said. "They'll do it again."

Pain exploded across my lower back. It penetrated my whole body, digging deeper. It burned my skin, my blood, my bones. I writhed, screaming, unable to control myself. A singular thought ran through my head, desperate and consuming: *Make it stop.*

How could anything hurt this badly? How had I not passed out?

Abruptly, Adaro released the pressure. I heaved, trying to gasp for air that wasn't there.

"That was before I understood my full power over the Host of Eriana." His voice came slow, distorted, as though from the other end of the ocean.

The press of the iron was gone, but the pain stayed. I bit my lip to stop from moaning.

All those times I'd slain a mermaid—every one of them who died on the Massacre—was this what they felt? Was I the cause of this unbearable pain in hundreds of mermaids? I thought back to the first mermaid I'd killed—Panopea, Lysi's cousin. I'd burned her face with an iron lantern. How could such a young child cause that amount of pain?

I thought of Lysi's scar, how my own father had given it to her that day he found us on the beach. My eyes filled with tears.

"You have one precious thing left, Meela, and that's your own life. You might as well tell me where the rebels are and save it."

"No!"

He was wrong. My unconditional love for Nilus had never faded during all the time he'd been ripped from me—and now that same love filled me for my nieces. They were a part of me, my blood, my heart. I would die before betraying them.

I screamed before it happened. The iron rod jabbed the same place on my lower back. A pain like nothing I'd felt exploded through me, worse than a broken bone, worse than the torn and bleeding tissue I'd experienced on the Massacre.

I only had to say that one name, as Deiopea had done. *Kori Maru.* Saying it would end all this pain. But I couldn't do it. For Nilus, for his family, and all of the Reinas. To say that name would be to put everyone there in danger. They were this war's glimmer of hope. They were our chance of winning freedom from King Adaro.

Thinking of them kept my heart beating and my jaw clenched tight. I ground my teeth until my ears rang, refusing to let a single word pass over my tongue. Through the endless pain, I thought of my parents and friends on Eriana Kwai, who had shown me love and compassion through the most difficult moments of my life. I thought of Lysi. I thought of the day we'd met, and the way our hands had lined up perfectly, like two halves of a broken stone. I remembered the shade of her eyes, the sound of her laugh, the smoothness of her skin, the purity of her heart, and the way I felt when it was the two of us together—like the world was perfect and peaceful.

Abruptly, Adaro stopped and whirled around. He squinted into the distance. Someone was coming.

A young merman jetted towards us at top speed. He skidded to a halt with a blast of bubbles that hit me in the face. He clutched his chest, mouth opening and closing.

"Your Majesty. It's Utopia."

Lying limp on the rock, I fought past the spots in my vision. I couldn't find the energy to lift my head. My whole body felt too heavy to move.

Needles tingled in my hands. I wiggled my fingers. Even in my stupor, I understood the sensation meant blood was flowing back into them. The ropes must have loosened a little in my struggle.

While Adaro was distracted, I worked my wrists. I was able to twist them better than before.

"Is it another explosive?" said Adaro.

"No. It's—" The merman choked on his words. He glanced around at the serpent.

"Speak!" roared Adaro.

"Y-your Majesty, it was an army. Mostly southern."

Adaro's temper rose, prickling the surrounding water. I worked my wrists faster, feeling the ropes strain and loosen. It took every bit of strength to keep moving, when my body wanted to collapse from exhaustion.

"They have overthrown the g-government," said the merman. "Nemertes is d-dead."

Southern army. Utopia. Nemertes dead. Did this mean what I thought?

I curled my fingers over the bottommost loop of rope on my right hand.

"W-we have summoned the nearest army, Your Majesty, and they will be coming from the Ice Channel—"

"Obviously! What about the south?"

Before the merman could answer, someone shouted in the distance. Then, several things happened at once. The merman turned to look. Adaro whirled back to me. A high-pitched squeaking filled the water—and I tugged loose my right hand.

My heart gave an enormous leap, pumping adrenaline through my veins. Adaro's crimson eyes widened. In his moment of surprise, I untangled my left wrist with shaking hands.

Adaro roared. He swung the iron rod at me, slicing the water so close that I felt a sting across my waist.

I tore free and lunged for the longblade on the floor. My fingers closed around the hilt and I flipped over, swinging with all the strength I had. Adaro sucked back—and then the current churned. The serpent was coming to help her master.

This was not the time to try and fight. Without a thought, I shot away as fast as I could.

The high-pitched chorus became louder—squealing, chirping, whistling, like a flock of birds.

Someone in its midst shouted again.

I had no time to think. I kept swimming, lungs aching for breath. I hadn't had enough of a head start on the serpent, and she was much too close. I would never be able to outstrip her. I dove and slid into a groove in the coral, sharing the space with a rockfish.

The current pulsed as the jaws snapped at my tail.

"Blubberforce!" shouted the voice. At least, that was what it sounded like.

I swung the longblade at the serpent. It ricocheted off her snout. She grabbed it, snapping it in two, and tossed the pieces aside.

"Blubberforce, attack!"

I finally placed the voice. But it couldn't be. Was I going mad?

The squealing and chattering grew so loud I had the urge to cover my ears.

The serpent snapped both heads around with a deep huff.

A rush of something blindingly white came towards us. They had long, lumpy, rotund bodies, squishy foreheads, tiny eyes, and mouths that seemed to curve in a smirk.

"Spio?!" I said, my voice a pitch to match the belugas.

The pod split, going wide around the serpent. Adaro, Nestor, and the messenger merman raised arms to fight but seemed unsure of where to swing.

Another voice rose over the din, familiar, feminine, blissful in my ears. "Mee, where are you?"

My heart swelled. Was this really happening? Pain and happiness and numb shock swamped me at once.

She pelted towards me, golden hair flowing among at least fifty white belugas. They engulfed the serpent like a large-scale swarm of bees. While not particularly quick swimmers, they were significantly smaller than the serpent and made tight turns and easy double-backs.

"Attack!" shouted Spio, raising his bag overhead.

Lysi found me in the coral and extended a hand. I seized it. She pulled me out.

"Lysi." Her name came as a sob.

She shoved me towards the open water. "Go!"

"Lysi, how—? Are you hurt?"

"I'm fine! Go."

Past her, the leviathan snapped at the belugas. They zipped around her enormous body, spinning and chirping like this was all a game. Spio swam with them, pulling chunks of bloody meat from his bag and tossing them into their mouths.

Lysi forced me the other way.

My back stung as the water rushed over it, bringing tears to my eyes. I didn't want to see what the wound looked like, picturing a black hole over my spine, torn at the edges—and then I had to stop thinking of it for fear of throwing up.

Adaro was trying to push his way out of the chaos. Spio threw dead fish at him so they bounced off his face. The belugas swarmed closer to catch the falling morsels.

"What about Spio?"

The serpent twisted and snapped, keeping Spio moving.

"He'll catch up," said Lysi. "Don't stop."

We kept swimming until the commotion faded behind us. The current still churned, but with the serpent thrashing so violently, I imagined such a scene would cause a stir in the water for leagues.

The floor rose, and we followed it to land where a cave opened, the surface pulsing with the tide. It was fully enclosed, the tiniest flecks of light peeking through the ceiling.

Lysi breached, panting. "Up here."

I didn't question her. We pulled ourselves from the water and further inside the dark cave. The clay was cool and smooth beneath my hands and tail. I couldn't keep my eyes off Lysi.

"I thought ... I saw you get hit in the chest—"

She shook her head. "Blow dart. It didn't go deep. It had a sedative. They wanted to knock us out for questioning."

I moved closer and reached out, tracing my fingertips over the place it had hit, searching for a wound. "How'd you get away?"

"Spio's attack belugas."

Tears flooded from my eyes. "I thought you were dead."

I kissed her, half crying, unable to believe she was there.

She pulled back, eyes raking over me. "Mee, are you all right?"

I wanted to nod, but I couldn't.

"You're in pain," she said, voice breaking. "What did he do to you?"

I closed my eyes. "I'm sorry. I should have listened to you."

Before she could say anything more, I turned around.

She let out a small scream. She seemed to try and speak, but instead dissolved into tears.

"Don't," I said. Her sadness was as bad as the pain.

"This is my fault—"

"How could it possibly be?"

"I failed you. It's my job to protect you."

I grabbed her wrists. "Lysi, it's not. I know I'm new to all of this, but you can't possibly think it's your responsibility to keep anything from happening to me."

She gazed down at the clay with puffy eyes. "I'm trying to understand everything Adaro has taken from you. I get it. I should have been more sensitive to that."

"That wouldn't have made a difference. This is my own doing. I haven't been thinking clearly."

Lysi drew a shaky breath and wiped an arm over her face. "I don't think anyone has. Adaro is bringing out the worst in all of us."

My face felt hot and swollen, temples throbbing in the early stages of a splitting headache. Neither of us could stop crying, the hitched sounds whispering against the cave walls.

"This is not the scene I hoped to pop in on." Spio hoisted himself onto the clay and shook his hair like a wet dog. "Either way, it's good to see both of you alive."

He tossed my crossbow and quiver onto the floor beside us. "I only managed to save one bolt. He's gone, though."

"Spio, do you have that kelp pus?" said Lysi thickly.

Spio's face fell. "Don't tell me that lumpsucker ..."

At Lysi's expression, he hastily opened his bag and pulled out a squishy canteen. She asked me to turn around.

I flinched as she smeared the paste over the wound, gritting my teeth.

"Damn," said Spio. "Was he trying to drill a hole right through you?"

"Spio!" said Lysi.

The paste had a cooling, soothing effect. Though it didn't mask the pain completely, it eased the persistent burning.

Once it was done, the three of us sat side-by-side and stared at the pulsing surface. I curled my tail up and wrapped my arms around it like I still had knees. If this was a weird thing to do, Lysi or Spio didn't show it.

"Why didn't he chase us?" said Lysi.

"He's going to Utopia," I said.

"How do you know?"

"The Reinas succeeded. The government's fallen."

Lysi and Spio exchanged a look of surprise.

"We have to follow him," I said.

When they gaped at me, I added, "We've got him. He's within reach. We can't lose track of him."

"Mee, let yourself rest."

"We don't have time. I—"

I winced as a wave of pain coursed through my body. The last time I'd been in agony like this was on the Massacre. It felt a lifetime ago.

Then, too, I'd been determined for revenge, hunting sea demons to avenge Nilus. Was I going to let hatred keep consuming me?

My heart gave a squeeze as I thought of Nilus, who would be in Utopia right now with the Reinas.

"We have to stop Adaro before he gets there. This is our last chance to kill him."

Kill. How many times had I said that word? How much more of my life would be dedicated to the act?

Medusa had said Adaro was out for revenge on humans because of his father. What had that reduced him to?

"He won't make it," said Lysi. "Feel the way the tide is pulling. It's almost here. It'll take longer than that to get to Utopia."

Indeed, all of the currents seemed to be shifting towards land—and there was an inexplicable pull building inside me. I recalled what Lysi had said about king tides and imagined the moon trying to pick me up, to pull me closer.

"All the more reason to follow him," I said, voice stronger. "Besides, his armies are on the way to help fight. This is it, Lysi. It's king tide, and we need to make sure we don't lose him."

But something was breaking inside me. Battle after battle, I kept joining the fight, an obedient warrior. I was raised to massacre—to act on hatred. But what had gotten us safely home from the Massacre? My feelings for Lysi had been the driving force, not my need for revenge. Then, when we'd returned home, my blood had been the way to free the serpent—the blood of Eriana, the goddess dedicated to protecting the flora and fauna of my island.

I understood what Lysi had been trying to tell me. I understood what Spio meant after our encounter with the whale.

I couldn't keep chasing revenge—not when compassion was so obviously my guide.

A deep, rhythmic thrumming sounded outside the cave. It grew louder, a mechanical groan pounding my eardrums.

It was the sound of a helicopter, large and low-flying.

"Do you think it's looking for the serpent?" said Spio.

"Yes, and Adaro knows it," I said. "He was keeping the serpent low in the water."

The sound grew louder until it was directly over our heads, and then faded into the distance.

"We need to guarantee lasting peace," I said. "Both underwater and with humans."

"But how?" said Lysi.

Like she'd been trying to tell me, this had to be about more than killing Adaro. We had to take care of the Pacific Kingdom, especially with the world fighting against it.

"We can't get rid of him and then leave the kingdom in anarchy. His armies will still be on the move, his civilians still living under his shadow. We need a new king or queen to take his place, someone the kingdom will follow and respect, and who's willing to negotiate peace with humans."

"What about Queen Medusa?" said Spio.

"No," said Lysi and I together.

Spio raised his hands in surrender.

"Evagore," said Lysi. "I agree with the Reinas. She's the rightful queen of the Pacific. Don't you think? She ruled long before Adaro came. She's the one we need on the throne."

I nodded slowly. "Ideally. But we don't know if she's even alive."

Lysi sat taller. "Oh, I haven't been able to tell you. She is. Nestor and Thetis were talking about her."

"She's back on the South Pacific throne?"

"No. Held captive somewhere. They wouldn't tell me where."

That was a start. Theoretically, we had a queen. We just had to find her. The prospect was daunting—but at least she was alive. Maybe the Reinas had an idea where she was now that they had overthrown Utopia.

"Right," I said. "A monarch is one thing, but we need to make sure Utopia holds an election to decide on the government. Everyone should be able to vote."

Lysi and Spio looked surprised.

Heat rushed into my face. "Oh. Is that not—? I'm sorry. I don't know how merpeople—"

"No, it's a great idea," said Lysi. "It's not something we've ever had."

"Think everyone will go for it?"

"Of course they will," said Spio.

A ray of hope passed between us. I felt calmer than I had in weeks. We had a plan. Now, could we find Evagore? Where would Adaro keep someone like her captive?

The water in the cave pulsed higher, trickling over the clay at our tails. The tide was pulling. We didn't have long.

"We should go, buddies, if we want to track him," said Spio.

No one moved. They both seemed to be waiting for me to go first. I wondered if they thought I was too weak to keep moving. The hole in my lower back seared, but my mind, for once, was clearer than ever.

I grabbed my crossbow and the single bolt. It would have to do.

Neither Lysi nor Spio had weapons.

"We'll steal some, first chance we get," said Lysi, reading my expression.

I took her hand. Her pulse beat a rhythm of fear—but there was something else in her aura. Excitement.

I gave her a tremulous smile.

We slid into the water and eased into the open, checking for signs of life and finding we were alone.

In the distance, headed towards Utopia, was the serpent's immense presence. Adaro kept her long body undulating at depth, hidden.

My stomach churned to think what would happen if that helicopter knew exactly where the serpent was.

CHAPTER TWENTY-ONE - Lysi
Plan in Flames

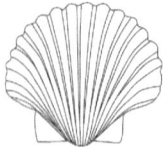

"Found one."

Spio returned with the end of a fishing net. It trailed so far into the distance that I lost track of it. He'd cut off most of the buoys so it bobbed below the surface.

We helped him reel it in. I tried not to let Meela catch me stealing glances at her. She acted as though she wasn't in pain, but I knew from experience how debilitating an iron burn was.

Meela growled. "Who do people think they are, leaving litter like this?"

"It was technically still in use," said Spio.

I cast my senses into the distance, searching for the other end. "Were they trying to catch every fish in the Pacific?"

"Possibly. I had to rescue a dolphin from it."

Meela pursed her lips.

Catching a flare of red in her eyes, I grabbed an end and started swimming. "You can wage war on fishing nets later. Come on."

We dragged it along. It weighed more than I'd anticipated.

My rescue in the Ice Channel had inspired us. Maybe there was nothing big enough to snag the serpent, but a trap of this size would at least slow her down.

"How do we make sure the serpent goes towards it?" I said, still unsure of the details of Spio's plan.

"Remember that time you acted as bait to lure the sharks away from the frenzy?"

I looked at him sharply. "What, you want me to be the bait that lures the serpent away from Adaro?"

"Bait?" said Meela, voice rising in pitch.

Spio gave her a thumbs-up. "Don't worry, buddy. She's done worse."

"Has she?"

"Well, no. But covering yourself in blood while you're beside a bunch of sharks in the middle of a feeding frenzy counts for something."

"Sure, but—"

I raised a hand, deciding Spio had a point. "I'd like to mention I've also avoided being eaten by the serpent twice."

Meela groaned. "So you think this is a good idea?"

A good idea? No. But it was an idea.

Before I could come up with a reassuring response, Spio said, "It's something we've had practice with."

Meela eyed him.

"So," said Spio, turning back to me, "while you keep after the snake monster to make sure we don't lose it, Meela and I set up the net. When it's go time, you get its attention,

I help steer it into the Ropey Trap of Terror, and Meela slips away to where Adaro's hiding."

He mimed shooting a crossbow.

Meela looked desperately between us. "Does anyone need to be bait, though?"

"You need the serpent out of your way," I said. "This will do it."

My courage was mostly feigned, fed by Spio's confidence in his plan, but Meela didn't need to know that.

She considered for a long moment. "Have you two always been this insane?"

"Yes," I said.

"Never," said Spio.

We continued in the serpent's wake, waiting for Adaro to veer towards land. He kept the serpent at the bottom. For easy breaching while dragging the heavy net, we stayed close to the surface. The pace was quick. We dropped further behind, the net making it hard to keep up.

I hadn't said it aloud, but I was terrified Adaro wouldn't transition. Maybe I'd counted the days wrong and had missed our chance, or king tide wouldn't happen for another tidecycle. Maybe he was already on land and had sent the serpent swimming by herself as a false trail. Too many things could go wrong.

As Utopia drew nearer, Meela kept touching her crossbow and remaining bolt, like she was afraid they would disappear. Twice, something dark eclipsed the daylight, and we looked up to see a helicopter zoom by.

The question that kept popping up was how we were going to find Evagore. I'd been so close to knowing where she was; if only I'd tried harder.

"I should have made Thetis and Nestor tell me where the high security prison is," I said.

"No, you shouldn't have," said Meela. "You were in no place to pry for information."

But the knowledge was right there, I thought. My insides roiled with frustration.

"The Reinas are in Utopia," she said. "Maybe they already figured out where she is. Maybe they already have her."

"I doubt it. The way they were talking, the high-security prison is an entirely different direction from Utopia."

"Which direction?"

I closed my eyes, trying to remember Thetis and Nestor's conversation. "They said it was on a different current."

Another dark shape passed overhead, low in the sky. We looked at each other, none of us voicing our fear. The floor had begun to grow shallow. Could they see the serpent from up there?

The rising floor also meant we were close to Utopia. What if we couldn't find Evagore before Adaro got there, or before the humans did something drastic?

Meela's aura was so taut I could have snapped it.

"Lysi, are you sure it's king tide?"

Swallowing back the fear that my senses and intuition were all wrong, I said, "Positive."

"This current's going the wrong way," said Spio. "If he was going to Utopia, he would have hopped streams back there."

He was right. A flutter of anticipation went down my spine. If Adaro wasn't going straight to Utopia, then he was going somewhere else, first—and what could be more pressing than what was happening in Utopia?

My ribcage seemed to compress. Whatever happened, we were about to confront Adaro for the last time.

Meela met my gaze. I could see in her eyes she wanted to say a thousand things but couldn't.

The helicopter passed overhead again, a mechanical thrum beyond the surface. For the amount of times it kept passing, I was sure—

A sudden pain ripped through my head, pressing from every direction. I cried out. My hands shot to my ears. Every cell in my body was vibrating. What was happening?

I couldn't see. My brain seemed to swell, pressing against my skull. My eardrums were going to burst.

My ears. The pain was coming from sound. A barge of sound, impossibly loud, was pulsing towards us. I couldn't tell which direction it came from. I couldn't think.

Meela and Spio were covering their ears, too, agony twisting their faces. The net floated away.

Spio caught my eye and jerked his elbow skywards. Moving in a fog, I followed him to the surface.

At once, the pain stopped. We bobbed in the waves, gasping for breath and staring at each other in stunned silence. The sound was still in the waves, buzzing over my skin like toxic jellyfish.

"What is it?" said Meela. My ears were still ringing. A moment passed before I understood what she'd said.

I shook my head. Spio, too, was uncharacteristically silent. I'd heard plenty of strange noises in my life—the distant rumble of earthquakes, shifting ice, huge creatures from the deep sea—but never had I experienced anything like this.

We turned in the direction we had last sensed the serpent. I could no longer feel her. The sound interfered too much.

By sight, she was invisible, hidden beneath the waves. But something else had broken the flat horizon, coming towards us.

"A ship," whispered Meela. "That's what's doing it."

"You think?" I said.

Was the noise intentional? Was this another attack by the humans?

I looked around. We were alone except for the ship and the helicopter.

The ship coasted towards us, hazy through the mist. It was enormous and blocky, like a tanker. For a long moment, we stared at it. I didn't know what to do. We could continue swimming with our heads above water—but then what?

No sooner had these thoughts crossed my mind when a black giant rose from the water and towered over the ship. I watched it happen as though in a dream. The serpent's massive jaws parted.

She had not yet struck when the ship crumbled from below. It was like the hull had popped, tipping the ship sideways. It shuddered. Then her upper head curved to meet the deck. Her body writhed, her jaws biting everything she could reach without restraint.

Meela cried out. "The crew!"

The painful vibrations against my skin stopped abruptly. Whatever had been making that sound, the serpent had destroyed it.

My relief was overshadowed when Meela dove. I shot after her.

"Mee, wait!"

A pungent smell hit me as I submerged, poisonous and chemical.

Spio was close behind. "Right. I guess we're moving towards the toxic pool of death, then."

From the ship, a thick, black cloud flooded towards us like lava. Meela stopped some distance away, looking on in horror.

Over and over, the serpent's fangs pierced the hull, tearing the frame. Oil and chemicals spilled from every hole. It flowed around the serpent, clouding the water and obscuring her black scales.

"We need to get out of here," said Spio. "Don't let that crap get on you."

The helicopter circled. It tried to hover over the sinking ship, but one of the serpent's heads followed it, and it was forced to keep moving to stay out of striking range.

It had found its target—but it couldn't drop anything now. Not over their own ship, with the crew still aboard.

"For someone who hates humans so much, he sure understands a lot about them," said Spio.

It was true. Adaro must have known the helicopter would stop pursuing him if he put the crew in danger.

Through all of this, it occurred to me Adaro could have been anywhere.

"We need to get around this," I said. "We're losing—"

A blast of heat hit my face. The chemicals had ignited.

Fire engulfed the ship. Shouts filled my ears from the deck.

The chemicals swelled towards us, reaching, billowing. I tasted poison on the water.

We had no option but to flee. Flames and toxins blocked every forward direction.

"If we go back far enough we can go around," said Spio.

I cast desperately for any sign of Adaro. We couldn't lose him now.

"What about the crew?" said Meela.

A cloud of smoke swelled into the sky. One of the enormous black heads rose through it, snapping at the helicopter. The people inside fired at it, bullets clanking off her scales.

"The helicopter will help them," I said. "There's nothing we can do."

To try helping would be a waste of time, not to mention dangerous. Besides, though I wouldn't admit it to Meela, I hardly cared about the wellbeing of those humans at the moment.

Globules formed in the oil, drifting in every direction. On the surface, the slick spread and bobbed on the water like a raft. The flames were ravenous.

Meela conceded, letting out a moan of despair.

We surfaced far from the disaster. The breath caught in my throat as I looked back at the black cloud in the distance. The enormous ship, half submerged, looked like a toy next to the spreading smoke. It billowed into the atmosphere, blacker than iron, so high my head spun to watch it.

Meela looked at us fiercely. "We need to find Evagore before it's too late."

I knotted my fingers in my hair. "I know! I'm trying to think of where the prison could be."

"What did Thetis and Nestor say, exactly?"

I screwed up my face, thinking hard. "I don't remember! The acoustic channel was east and the luna bin was west— or that was east and the king was going west—"

"Luna bin?" said Meela sharply.

"Yeah. Some witless nickname they came up with for the Moonless … What?"

Meela's mouth had fallen open.

"When Thetis and Nestor were waiting for Adaro to come, they said the humans dropped something over a prison. They said *luna bin*."

"They did?!"

"They were talking about the queen, then, weren't they?"

"Yes!"

Spio cleared his throat. "Not that I'm trying to discount your detective work, but that still doesn't tell us where the prison is."

"Hang on," said Meela. "They said where it was. Something Peaks."

Multicoloured flames licked the sky, trying to spread as far and wide as possible.

The serpent backed away, disappearing behind the wall of debris and smoke.

Not only had we lost Adaro, but we were also about to lose the serpent. We had to get around this mess and keep following.

The helicopter wove around the column of smoke, presumably finding a clear spot to rescue the crew.

"It was something like …" said Meela. "Ugh, I remember reading the word in one of Tanuu's textbooks, but I can't remember the details. It's from Ancient Greece."

"Again," said Spio, "nothing against your sleuthing skills, but basically everything this side of the waves is named for Greek history."

"Peaks …" I said, recalling something from when I was a kid. "There's a range east of Utopia. We passed through when we moved to Utopia from Eriana Kwai so I could start training."

"Are you talking about the Nereids?" said Spio.

"That's it!" shouted Meela so abruptly that I clutched my heart. "The Nereid Peaks!"

"That's the place they mentioned?" I said.

Meela nodded. "That's where our queen is."

We stared at each other, the beat of silence alive with adrenaline.

"You need to go there," said Meela.

"Now?" said Spio and I together.

Meela looked desperately towards the retreating serpent. "After you've made the decoy. Go as fast as you can and get Evagore."

"What about you?" I said.

"Once I have the serpent, I'll find the nearest ship and tell the Americans to meet us at Eriana Kwai."

"Once you—? Mee, you can't do that by yourself!"

I tried to process what she was saying. How was I supposed to let her throw herself into danger like that, swimming up to a ship full of humans?

"I'll have the serpent with me for protection," said Meela.

I cast her a look of horror.

Spio glanced between us, then said evasively, "In the way of bodyguards, the serpent's a pretty good one to have."

"It might be invincible, but Meela isn't."

"You have to trust her, buddy. From what I've seen, Meela can fend for herself as well as you can."

I opened my mouth, but no sound came.

"Lysi, please," said Meela. "We're out of time. Trust that I can do this."

I wanted to trust her. I knew how much this meant to her. But I was so afraid of losing her.

Meela pointed eastwards. "I think that's it. I think that's where he's going."

I tuned my senses beyond the wreckage. Past the serpent, undulating away from us at high speed, the floor rose.

There was a bump on the horizon, like a wart.

A wild mix of terror and elation and shock rose inside me. Had we found the place Adaro went to transition?

It pained me to know Meela was right. Every moment we waited before making a peace treaty, the more danger we were all in. We had to split up.

"Lysi, if you're going to be our bait, now's the time," said Spio, squinting in that direction.

Meela grabbed my hand. "Once you've diverted the serpent, keep going. I'll meet you at Eriana Kwai, okay? Tomorrow night."

I glanced to the sun, descending to the horizon. We could do this. By the time king tide receded, Adaro would be dead. Our new queen would be ready to take the throne, and peace would be restored to the Pacific.

I nodded. Then we were kissing, Meela's face between my hands, her fingers knotted in my hair. For a few, blissful seconds, I forgot the fear pressing in on us. I knew only the feel of her body.

Too soon, we broke apart. Neither of us said anything. I couldn't get the words out if I'd tried.

I wanted to refuse to leave her.

Instead, I swam after the serpent as fast as I could.

CHAPTER TWENTY-TWO - Meela
The Secret Island

Hot flames and that toxic sting crept towards us. In unison, Spio and I dove.

My senses were more honed than ever as we swam. Every ripple told me the exact state of the wreckage, where the serpent was, how fast the chemicals were spreading. I felt the iron in the ship, the overpowering aura of the serpent, and when I focused, even the carbon in the oil slicks.

I gritted my teeth against the fresh wave of pain in my lower back as the iron-tainted water washed over the burn.

We retrieved the net and pulled it away from the smouldering ship.

It was hard to stop myself worrying about Lysi.

"Listen, buddy," said Spio. "We'll only be able to keep the serpent chasing us for so long. Once Adaro commands her back, there'll be nothing we can do."

"I know."

"Don't overthink it. Do it quickly."

Did he know how nervous I was? Did he think I would hesitate at the final moment? I wasn't offended, because it was true: I was terrified. After spending so long waiting for this, I thought I would be less anxious. But the reality of how this could end pressed against my ribs. What if that was the last time I saw Lysi? I regretted not saying a better goodbye.

"Thanks for all your help, Spio."

We pulled the net along in silence. It was heavier now with just two of us pulling. But would it be heavy enough? It was our only chance at slowing down the serpent. If it didn't work, I didn't want to think what would happen to Lysi and Spio. And once the serpent turned and came back, would I have enough time to get out of there?

"Did Lysi ever tell you about the time she and I messed with a Kodiak bear?" said Spio.

I tried to say, "No," but the word got caught in my throat. I shook my head.

"He was as big as a whale, I swear. He was on the beach on one of the Aleutians, and he'd caught a deer and was getting ready to rip in."

We stopped at a boulder.

"I'd always wanted to try deer. We don't get to eat it much, obviously, but anyone who has says it's really good. And I'm all about expanding my palate."

We wrapped the end of the net around the boulder several times. Spio secured it with the most intense set of knots I'd ever seen.

"Well, Lysi lures it away from the dead deer with a couple of live salmon. While it's running after her, I pull myself up the beach and grab the deer."

We dragged the other end of the net over to a second boulder.

"The thing's faster than we anticipated. Lysi chucks the salmon and gets into the water before it catches her—but man, it's close. Then, of course, the bear turns and sees me with his deer."

We pulled it taut between the two rocks. I wanted to say something about creating the world's largest volleyball net, but Spio wouldn't know what I was talking about.

He surveyed our work with his hands on his hips. "It looks like that game humans like to play. You know?"

My lips pulled into an involuntary smile.

"Anyway," said Spio. "We were nearly eaten by the bear in the process. But you know what? That deer was the best thing I've ever eaten in my life."

We stared at each other for a minute. My heart beat frantically. Spio clapped me on the shoulder.

"You got this, whale whisperer."

Without waiting for a ceremonious goodbye, he took off. I stared after him until he became a pulse on the current. Then I dove.

I swam hard towards the island until a steep cliff rose in front of me. Atop the cliff, the floor sloped up to the beach.

I wedged into a crevice, reminding myself of the reef fish I'd seen the first time Lysi had shown me coral. I waited, perfectly still, letting my body sway with the surrounding weeds. I felt detached from my body, its movements oddly vacant and methodical. I forced myself to stay in that frame of mind, afraid I would panic if I contemplated what I was about to do.

The plants around me crackled gently. I focused on each note, the way I used to do with leaves moving in the breeze.

The earth gave a shudder. There was a pull in the tide. I pushed my hands against the rocks to hold myself in place.

I squinted upwards, every sense jostled by the rushing current.

Two small figures shot past—Lysi, long hair flying, and Spio, lean and lanky. The serpent followed them with its jaws open. A blast of bubbles shot from her nostrils, clear and blue but reminding me of a dragon breathing fire.

Her body, as thick as a ship, seemed to go on for ages. Darkness fell as she blocked the light.

I didn't dare move.

Finally, the second head passed.

I pulled myself from the crevice and shot upwards, taking care not to expose myself in the open. I couldn't let the serpent feel my presence or else their decoy would have been a waste.

I crested the cliff and followed the sloping floor to the beach, moving cautiously over the sand. When I could climb no further, I let the top of my face break the surface.

A shipwreck crumbled on the beach, rusted over and broken into shards. Its size and ghostly presence paralyzed me.

Keeping my body below the surface, I scanned the mess of driftwood and seaweed strewn across the beach. Adaro was nowhere to be seen.

I chewed my lip. What if he had pulled himself into the forest?

No. For someone who hated land as much as Adaro did, he would have stuck close to the shoreline. Besides, the island could have bears, like Spio had talked about, or even people. It would be dangerous to wander, especially in a weakened condition. He had to be nearby.

Below the surface, a burst of energy ricocheted through the water and shot up my tail. Had the serpent collided with the net? The activity hit my senses with such force I wondered if we had underestimated her size. She could snap the rope or easily move the boulders. Still, she would have to untangle herself.

I ran a reassuring hand over the crossbow at my back and pulled myself from the water. My tail scraped over the rocks, the sound rising above the hissing waves.

Far behind me, flames roared around the sinking ship. The helicopter thrummed as it rescued the crew trapped aboard. I crawled across the shore, stopping periodically to listen for sounds over the distant explosions like a cautious deer in the woods.

Daylight peeked through the shipwreck where rust had eaten into the hull. The sting of iron blew towards me on the wind. Though the ship was upright, it sagged heavily in the middle as if a fire or explosion had brought its life to an end.

A fierce ache in my lower back made me think of Lysi's scar. It must have hurt every time she was near iron, yet she hadn't once mentioned the pain during the time we spent at Kori Maru. My heart squeezed for her.

I was close enough now to see inside the broken hull. The breath caught in my chest. A man was lying inside, crumpled, as if he had been washed ashore.

I smelled the earth and sweat of human presence. His chest rose and fell with quick, raspy breaths. His skin was milky beneath black hair, his legs twisted, devoid of muscle, lying on the rocks at unnatural angles. He must have used his arms—which were smaller than a merman's but still showed considerable strength—to drag himself from the water. Grimy blankets and canvas littered the rocks around him.

If not for the black crown over that long, matted hair, I would not have believed it was him.

I reached for my crossbow. The stock clicked beneath my grip—and Adaro's eyes snapped to my face, wide and terrified. They were blue.

Then, just as quickly, his expression melted into something else. It was almost a smile.

"I suppose your girlfriend was a decoy."

His voice was the same: slow and deep.

I raised the crossbow.

Before my finger touched the trigger, Adaro dove sideways behind a piece of hull. I jerked my hand away, cursing. The burst of agility surprised me.

Adaro's paralyzed legs dragged behind him, scraping over the rocks and debris.

"Hiding from a fight, Your Majesty?" I said coldly.

I should have reacted more quickly—but with a single bolt, I couldn't afford errors.

"Do not lie to yourself, Meela," he said from behind his barricade. "You are not so heartless as this."

Though he was hidden, the sight of him lingered in my mind's eye. Could I kill someone so defenseless?

"You gave me no choice," I said, more to reassure myself.

"Everything is a choice."

I resisted the urge to look back to the water, afraid the serpent was approaching. But I refused to take my eyes off my target. For all I knew, Adaro had a weapon and was preparing to throw or shoot something at me.

I dragged myself further up the beach. As long as he was out of range, I could do nothing. I had to get a better angle.

"Would you really kill the man responsible for your happiness?" he said.

I kept advancing. "Happiness? You've given my people starvation, grief, poverty—"

"I am not referring to your people. I am referring to you."

His words slid past me as I braced to shoot. I would have to move quickly—to roll into firing range, aim, and release the bolt before he could escape.

I heard a clatter of rocks and flattened onto my stomach. Nothing happened.

Finger braced over the trigger, I craned to see further into the hull. Adaro was pulling himself deeper into its shadows where there were fewer holes in the sides.

I could do it from this distance, but I would need perfect aim.

"Coward," I said. "Is the great King Adaro afraid to face me?"

Anger flashed across his face. For an instant, I thought I saw crimson in his blue eyes.

Was he still merman enough to kill me, or was he human enough that he needed iron to do it? I couldn't be certain.

I raised the crossbow to my line of sight, aiming carefully.

"You will regret that," said Adaro.

He hunched over, accentuating how vulnerable he was inside the massive hull. My gaze fell to his legs, all bones and twisted at odd angles on the rocks.

My targets had always been sea demons. All of them would have killed me if I had not killed them.

But this was a man.

All the lives I'd taken over the last months—and here I was pointing my crossbow, for the first time ever, at a human being.

"I have shaped your life, Meela," said Adaro, lip curled to bare flat, human teeth. "From your father, to your battles, to Lysithea."

I rolled my eyes. "Yes, you've made my life miserable. Well done."

"Ten years ago, I was visiting Eriana Kwai with a few experts. I had already spent years searching for the serpent."

I narrowed my eyes, but let him continue.

"We spent several days searching for a passage beneath the island, to no success. It was obvious the serpent was hidden somewhere on the island itself, and only a human could get to it.

"While we were there, I noticed a young girl coming to the beach every day."

My stomach churned. I kept the crossbow on him, but my hands were paralyzed.

"The girl did not venture close enough to the water to catch, but I watched her. She returned every day, searching for something—someone.

One day during our search, I noticed another little girl, a mermaid of the same age. She was exploring out of bounds, poking around this human-infested island. How curious, I thought, that these two girls come here every day but do not see each other. They are separated by the surface, yet they are so close they could touch."

A voice in my head was yelling at me to shoot, to kill him now before he called the serpent back, but I couldn't. I had to hear what he was telling me.

"I had watched you save starfish and nurse drowning insects back to health, Meela. So, acting on a hunch, I arranged to have the young mermaid caught in a net and tossed ashore for you to find. Sure enough, you freed her. You became friends, like I intended.

"But then that brat, Panopea, got in the way. She came to me with news that she was learning to speak Eriana from her cousin, who learned it from a human. When I discovered what was happening, it was too late. She had made an attempt to kill you and blamed the runt—and all my work to solidify your friendship was ruined. I killed Panopea and arranged it to look like a suicide. She was scarred and bloodied half to death, anyway, after you had finished with her."

Tears blurred my eyes so Adaro became a pale blob against the dark backdrop. Was my entire life a setup? Even the first mermaid I'd ever killed—or thought I'd killed—was another of Adaro's victims.

"My plan to use your new best friend to make you hand over the Host met its demise. So I thought. Ten years later, I could not believe it. My young friends had reunited—and their bond was better than I could have imagined. They were in *love*. I was able to use Lysithea to manipulate you, after all. You got me the Host at the threat of her life."

I gritted my teeth, blinking back tears. All these years, I had assumed fate had brought Lysi and me together. But everything, from the day I'd met Lysi to the day I'd woken the leviathan, had been a part of Adaro's plan.

What about the rest of my life? My father and Nilus? How different would everything be had they not been forced on Massacres?

"But you didn't know I would be on the Massacre." My words came out strangled through gritted teeth. "You didn't know my people would retaliate so hard. You didn't know I would be here, a mermaid, and that I would be the one to kill you in the end. My Massacre training put me here with a crossbow. You're the reason I spent years learning to shoot it."

My own words gave me strength. He could try to make me another victim, but I would fight to my death to avoid that. This was still my life, and starting with the crossbow in my hands, I could control how it played out.

Something like fear flickered across Adaro's face—but then a blast of air sounded outside the hull. Adaro sneered. She was coming.

"As amusing as it has been to contrive your love story," said Adaro, "the time has come for it to end. I hope you said a proper goodb—"

"Love? You're cowering inside a shipwreck, hiding from everyone. You built your life and your kingdom on hatred. Don't pretend you understand love."

He failed to take it into account, again and again. It was the most important part of life, as Lysi had said. Here was the girl in front of him, who had become a mermaid and gotten to this island because of it. Here was the girl willing to sacrifice her own life for those she loved, and with those she loved ready to do the same. As I would always be there for Lysi, she would always be there for me.

That was a kind of love Adaro had never understood. He'd never learned to trust anyone. Did he even trust himself? How could he, if he hated himself so deeply?

"The great King Adaro," I said, "too weak, desperate, and scared to tell anyone what he is. This is how you'll be remembered. Your Majesty."

Inexplicably, pity seeped through my veins. I felt sorry for the crippled man in front of me. Since birth, he'd learned through rejection and cruelty that he could not trust humans. He'd grown up to hate a significant part of himself and the world he lived in—and he let that hatred become his downfall. He would never experience self-acceptance or peace.

A high wave splashed over the hull, drenching us both. I felt the serpent's presence, angry and drawing nearer.

It was time to end all the horrors Adaro had brought to this earth.

And for once, instead of being driven by anger, I felt calm. This was the only way forwards. It was almost tragic to think Adaro had spent his entire life suffering in hatred.

Adaro snarled. He raised a muscular arm, calling the serpent.

A wave slammed into me at her arrival. I held my ground, letting the deluge wash back down the rocks.

After years of practice, aligning my aim felt natural. I held the crossbow firmly, not taking my eye off my target.

Adaro grabbed at whatever he could reach to pull himself further into the hull.

The sky darkened as the serpent raised a massive head. There was a wet, cracking sound of her jaws opening. The back of my neck prickled.

Adaro was scrambling away, but not fast enough. Bile crept up my throat at the thought of shooting this man in the back.

I exhaled. "For Eriana Kwai."

For the protection of everyone back home, for Lysi, for merpeople—and for myself—I pulled the trigger.

A hot breath of air washed over me. I dove sideways, catching a fleeting glimpse of the bolt leaving my crossbow.

The serpent's snout slammed into the rocks where I'd been and snapped closed over nothing.

The bolt plunged into Adaro's ribcage.

The serpent drew back to lunge again. The remains of the fishing net fell from her jaws, scattering over the beach.

Adaro fell, bolt protruding from his side. Crimson blood oozed from the wound. But he was still alive.

"No," I whispered.

I needed something to act as a second bolt. A rock, or a branch.

The serpent was too quick. The other set of jaws opened overhead with a wet crackle. The beach darkened further. I rolled to the side, but I was helpless out of water. A tooth caught my arm, knocking me flat. I dropped the crossbow.

The serpent's breath engulfed me. My fingers found a sharp rock.

I lunged for the crossbow, stretching, reaching. I slammed the rock against the shaft. It was too short and fat, but there was no time.

I aimed at Adaro's crumpled body, teeth gritted. My makeshift ammo wasn't going to leave the weapon properly.

A drip of hot saliva hit my shoulder. I squeezed my eyes shut and pulled the trigger a second time. The crossbow vibrated as the sinew snapped.

I waited for the pain of those fangs sinking into me, thinking of Lysi.

CHAPTER TWENTY-THREE - Lysi
The Liberation of Utopia

The Nereid Peaks cascaded into the distance, each underwater mountain higher than the last. I stopped to get a feel of the landscape. The prison could have been anywhere in these peaks and valleys. It would take days to scour the whole range.

Maybe the mountains broke the surface to form islands. It would be a good place to keep a lot of merpeople. Was I looking for a good place, though? Or was I looking for something miserable? The vista of coral felt too close to paradise for it to be a prison.

No matter what happens, keep going.

Spio's words looped in my mind with every stroke. I'd done what he said, expecting him to catch up. But I kept going, and going, and the sun changed positions, and still I swam alone. I forced myself to keep a quick pace, fighting the urge to turn around and search for him.

Panicking would do me no good. I had to keep going. If I didn't find Queen Evagore, how were we supposed to make a peace treaty with the humans? We needed a reformed kingdom, and for that, we needed our queen.

I'd shouted to Spio as he turned in the opposite direction of where we were supposed to be headed. "Where are you going?"

"To get proof!" he'd shouted back.

Proof. That would imply Meela had succeeded in killing Adaro. I needed to trust that she had. I needed to be convincing when I told the guards Adaro was dead.

I couldn't help thinking that if Adaro was alive, it meant one thing for Meela—in which case I would have nothing left to lose. So I would believe with all my heart that Adaro was dead. If that was a lie, I would deal with the consequence when it came.

This place was a medley of wildlife. Given that this mountain range was in the middle of nowhere, it must have been untouched by both humans and merpeople; the plants and fish grew to enormous proportions.

Keeping a fast pace, I dove and skimmed the ocean floor, trying not to think of the others. Then everything became cold and dark. I jerked to a stop, looking around, an unsettled feeling washing over me. The landscape was strangely naked. The coral was gone. Entire chunks of rock were missing, as though they had been blasted away.

Meela said the humans had dropped something over the prison. Was this the result of an explosive?

The desolate hush sent a chill down my spine. I had to be close.

I'd spent the journey both wishing I had an army behind me and feeling grateful I was alone; I would be less of a threat to whomever guarded this place. Now, I wished for at least a friend.

I would have to play the role of a messenger from Utopia, here to deliver news of Adaro's death. Revealing I was there for Queen Evagore might put her life in danger. The guards could bar my entry and kill her. I would have to tell them their order was to free all Nereid prisoners.

I chewed my lip. Was this a dumb plan? After spending so long avoiding Adaro's armies, even fleeing them, it was hard to convince myself to simply swim up to his prison guards. Plus, what if they recognised me as a traitor to the crown, as Thetis and Nestor had? Even if they didn't, what were the chances they would believe me?

Maybe I should try to sneak in.

The idea was comforting. But this prison was supposed to be high security. I doubted I'd be able to get in, set free their most valuable prisoner, and make it out alive.

I was so immersed in coming up with a plan that I nearly missed it when something odd hit my senses from below. I could feel a vast opening in the earth, yet there was only rock and sand.

I plunged into the darker depths.

There was a presence on the current, but I couldn't tell where it came from. It seemed to be beneath the rock. Was it inside the peak? I felt the auras of what must have been a hundred merpeople.

This had to be it. I hovered, casting for signs of a break in the floor. How was I supposed to get to them?

I wondered if I should wait for Spio and whatever proof he was getting. Whether I tried to sneak in or pretended to be a messenger, I wanted his help.

Under a nearby boulder was a gap just big enough to fit. I would wait there until Spio arrived.

I'd barely pulled myself inside when something tightened over my hair and yanked me out.

"Ouch!"

I found myself face-to-face with the point of a stone blade. Behind it was a merman, teeth bared.

"Trespasser," he said. "Who are you?"

"I'm from Utopia! I was sent to deliver news," I blurted, then grimaced. *Guess we're going with the first plan.*

He leaned back, studying me. "You were?"

"Yes. The government—"

"Why were you trying to hide?"

I opened my mouth, struggling for an explanation.

Behind the merman, a female voice said, "Who is it?"

"Someone from Utopia."

"Utopia?"

"Says she's here to deliver news."

"What news?"

"That's what I'm trying to find out!"

I winced at his firm grip on my hair.

"Where's Guenevere?" said the mermaid.

She whirled around and disappeared.

"Come on," said the merman, following her. He gave me little choice, pulling me along by the hair.

I stayed quiet, deciding compliance would be my best course of action.

"Get me Guenevere," shouted the mermaid.

We crested the top of a hill and I let out a soft, "Oh."

I found myself facing an army of at least a hundred mermaids and mermen. They held their weapons up, ready to defend—what, exactly? Behind them was more rock and patches of dead coral.

A murmur passed through the crowd. A brunette with a stone mace came forwards. My gaze landed on the rubies in her braid—she was their commander.

"What is it?" she said.

"Found this one hiding," said the merman. "Says she was sent to us from Utopia."

They all looked at me expectantly.

Spio or not, I had to persist.

"The government's fallen, Commander. King Adaro is dead. You are to abandon your post and release your prisoners."

Tension swept through the crowd. A whisper seemed to pass over them, though none moved their lips.

"This is treason," said Guenevere. "This is exactly the lie His Majesty warned us about."

I cast my senses through the guards, finding contempt. "What lie?"

"That His Majesty is dead. What proof do you have? None have come close to defeating him or the serpent."

Hurry up, Spio.

"The serpent is no longer under his control," I said. "It's in the hands of the revolutionaries."

Guenevere snarled. "You're lying."

I knew this would happen. Adaro would have warned his armies against news of an assassination. He had been bitten by this lie when Spio, Nilus, and I had taken part in the attempt on his life. He would have taken precautions since then. More than proof, we needed Meela here with the serpent. My fear over her fate was betraying me. I shouldn't have listened to her. I should have insisted we stay together.

"Surely you've heard of the coup in Utopia," I said.

The guards exchanged glances.

"We heard rumours," said Guenevere.

Interesting. Was this why they were so keen to listen to someone who said she had news from Utopia? They could easily have turned me away. Instead, I was here in front of them.

"The rumours are true," I said, summoning confidence. "I'm here to tell you that the Pacific Kingdom is no longer under Adaro."

Everyone was silent—listening to me. The grip on my hair loosened, but the merman didn't let go.

"It was a revolution. There's going to be an election. *We* decide who's in government."

The guards shifted, unease rippling through them.

I understood their dilemma. If I was lying about Adaro's death, and if they abandoned their post to join me, they would become traitors to the crown. As someone who once served under Adaro out of the same fear, I empathised.

I was about to speak honestly about this when a clamour drifted down the current.

Everyone turned towards the roar of voices coming this way, the noise echoing in the mountain range, slow and distorted. I strained my ears to figure out what was happening.

This couldn't be Spio, could it?

"Who are you with?" Guenevere said to me, a fierce look on her face.

Everyone raised their weapons. The grip on my hair tightened painfully.

"No one!" I said. "I came alone."

Guenevere scowled, but said nothing. We waited. I wished I had something, anything, to defend myself.

Then a horde of merpeople came into view, and my jaw fell open. It was a wall of Utopians, led by Dione, Ephyra, and the others I remembered from Kori Maru. They dragged with them a line of four mermaids and three mermen, gagged and connected by rope. I recognised the hostages from demonstrations and ceremonies during training. These were the faces of Adaro's government—most of it. Nemertes was missing.

My heart raced. This was the result of the coup. They'd rallied all these civilians. They'd found out where Evagore was, and they were here to get her.

The roar became clearer. They were chanting.

"Not my king! Not my war! Not my king! Not my war!"

Invisible ropes around my chest seemed to loosen. We had more allies than I'd dreamed.

Dione's voice rose above the masses as they advanced. "Adaro's government is no more! We are here from both the South Pacific and Utopia, and we ask you to release your prisoners, and join our new kingdom."

Guenevere raised her mace. Around me, the guards tensed, ready for a fight.

I cursed inwardly. If I'd had another moment, I was sure I could have convinced them to drop arms.

"If you surrender, we will welcome you as allies," said Dione, unfazed. "We will join together and fight the tyrant Adaro."

"What are you on about?" said Guenevere. "First you say Adaro's dead, and now you're here to fight him?"

The crowd drew to a stop in front of us.

"Dead?" said Dione. "We never said he is dead."

Ephyra spotted me and said, "Oh!"

Dione's gaze snapped to me. Her expression changed to one of bewilderment.

"What are you—?"

"He is," I said. "I've just come from him."

Gathered in a valley between two peaks, the mounts on all sides acted as a sound funnel. My voice carried with unusual clarity.

A hush fell. Then, excitement and fear flew through the crowd at these words.

"Dead. He's dead. The king is dead!"

"How?" whispered Dione.

"King tide," I said. "We followed him. Meela killed him. We need to meet her—"

"She did? Where is she?" said Dione, peering through the guards.

"And where is the serpent?" said the white-blonde mermaid from Kori Maru.

"Traitors, turn away from this place or we will be forced to fight," shouted Guenevere.

The guards raised their weapons higher. The merman gripping my hair let go so he could face his opponents.

"Look at the numbers before you," said Dione. "We are peacefully asking you to surrender and join us, along with the prisoners you keep."

At the mention of the prisoners, Guenevere's eyes reddened.

We hung suspended, two armies facing each other— Dione's several times larger, Guenevere's better armed.

Those behind Dione examined the mountainside the guards protected, possibly seeking out an entrance.

Though they were my allies, I wished I could have done this alone. I worried what plans Dione had for Queen Evagore.

"Dione," I said, hesitating. She needed to know how vital it was to get the queen to Eriana Kwai—but I was still reluctant to mention Evagore outright in case the guards did something drastic.

A guard behind Guenevere spoke. "Are all of you a part of this movement?"

I followed his eyes across the Utopian army. The leaders floating on either side of Dione had been chosen wisely. I'd been worried Utopians wouldn't follow Dione if she went storming into Utopia with a group of South Pacifics. But she'd selected a balance of north and south, mermaids and mermen, young and old, to join her. The message was clear: this was a revolution for everyone.

"We are," said Dione.

Guenevere hissed. "Don't believe them. He's not dead."

"Even if he's not—" said the merman.

"You swore to protect this kingdom! After everything His Majesty has done for you—"

"Done for me?" He shook his head. "So he didn't take away my wife, my children. What about everyone else? My neighbour's family disappeared. All of them."

Guenevere leaned back, regarding him like he was a tumour.

"I've known it for ages," he said. "That is not the kind of kingdom I want to live in."

Motivated by his own words, he dropped his longblade. We all watched it sink. It hit the rocks soundlessly.

"If you join them, you fight against all of us," said Guenevere.

"If the king's still alive, I'll face the consequences. But this—" The merman pointed to the Utopian army. "—is proof enough for me that I've been fighting on the wrong side."

He swam to them. My heart lifted.

There was a heavy silence. I turned my gaze subtly to the dropped longblade. Something beside it caught my attention. A gap in the rocks. It was wide enough for a merman to squeeze through. The way the water rushed in and out told me it stretched a long ways. It was a tunnel.

Dione spoke in clear, ringing tones. "If anyone else wishes to help us bring a new kingdom to the Pacific—"

"Remember your oath," shouted Guenevere. "Traitors, turn around if you do not wish to fight."

I glanced again at the longblade, dreading what might come. How quickly could I grab it if a fight broke out?

There was a period in which no one moved. Then somebody in the crowd of prison guards let loose a roar, and everything happened at once. My body changed instinctively; I felt my teeth descend as the guards spilled over the rocky landscape, weapons up. The two sides met in a clash that filled the water with sand.

Whether anyone else had intended to switch sides, we never found out.

CHAPTER TWENTY-FOUR - Meela
Daughter of Eriana

The pain didn't come. The serpent's breath continued to bathe me, warm and sticky.

I opened my eyes, trembling, and saw fangs the length of my arms hovering above me.

The serpent had stopped with her jaws open over my head.

In the silence, the purring waves returned to my attention. The groan of the distant helicopter pulsed in my ears.

Through the serpent's fangs, I could see Adaro lying on the rocky beach inside the broken hull. Blood pooled from both the bolt and the rock embedded in his ribs. His eyes were wide. He was perfectly still.

The sky lightened as the serpent's heads arched away from me, bobbing in the air and hissing—perhaps tasting Adaro's blood on the wind.

A presence consumed me, as though my body gained a second soul. I gasped, feeling her in my mind and spirit, a goddess greater than myself.

"Eriana," I whispered.

Her reply came to the front of my mind, the thoughts forming as though my own.

Daughter. It is a relief to share a mind with someone pure.

Slowly, heart pounding, I turned my back to the island and Adaro. From the frothy waves, two massive heads stared down at me. In those deep blue pupils, glassy and vertical, I saw no threat. She gazed expectantly at me. The vastness of the ocean lay beneath her expression, filled with millennia of wisdom.

Is the serpent mine? I thought, heart beating faster yet.

Yes, daughter.

My throat constricted. I was grateful to have no need to speak aloud, because I would not have managed it.

Help me, I thought. *Our island has been at war, and now the rest of the world is, too. I need to stop it.*

A forked tongue emerged from each head, tasting the air. Behind her, the ship fire consumed ocean and sky, multicoloured flames and black smoke billowing. The sun was on its descent to the horizon.

If you are concerned about war, we can force others to leave our island alone. With the leviathan Sisiutl as your guardian, you will never be defeated.

I don't want to use aggression. I want peace.

The sea gurgled as the ship took its last breaths. There must have been at least one crew member left to rescue, because the helicopter still hovered, dodging flames and smoke.

As long as the leviathan exists, there will always be those seeking to control it, said Eriana. *You will never have peace as long as others see potential to control the world's most powerful weapon.*

I shook my head. *It is the most powerful force, then? Nothing can defeat it?*

Nothing in this world is stronger than Sisiutl.

I considered what this meant. If nothing could defeat the serpent by strength, did that mean I had to defeat it by wit or logic?

Where did the serpent come from? I thought. *Help me understand.*

Sisiutl was born from the volcano that created our island. She swam free for millennia, fearing nothing and driven by hunger.

Skaaw Beach came to mind—the black swells of lava rock that marked Eriana Kwai's most remarkable section of shoreline.

I've been told the legend of how you came to control the serpent, I thought. *Now your soul is bound to her body. If I kill the leviathan, you'll be free, right?*

Yes. I will ascend to the stars and will protect our island as the Gaela intended. It pains me to know the suffering my children have endured in my absence.

But how do I kill it?

Fae could kill other fae, Lysi had said. What about a creature who had no equal?

For a moment, no further thoughts came to me. I scanned the sparkling waves, feeling like the world met my senses with new clarity.

Then Eriana said, *Nothing can destroy the leviathan. With the presence of two heads, there is also nothing the leviathan cannot destroy.*

I considered her words. *The leviathan can destroy anything in the world?*

Yes, daughter.

My gaze drifted to the burning ship. It disappeared beneath the surface, leaving behind a smouldering chemical slick and scattered debris. The helicopter rose and came towards us. They must have rescued the last of the crew—or had given them up for dead—and were now free to drop explosives on the serpent without worrying about endangering human lives.

We had to get away from here.

In my most private thoughts I'd wondered how it would feel to command the serpent, and whether I would know what to do when she came to me.

Now I understood. She was a part of me. There was no command to give.

Let's fix this, I thought.

The serpent submerged. A wave crashed over her, and she became no more than a black shape in the water.

Reluctantly, I took a last look at Adaro. I didn't care to ever see him again—even if he was dead—but I wanted to be sure.

He lay in the hull where I'd shot him, blood pooling under his twisted limbs. It had splattered over the rocks and was still oozing from his ribs. One side of his face was crushed against the ground. His eyes were open but I could see, even from here, that they had grown glassy and vacant.

Only the black crown remained unspoiled. It had not moved, rooted in its nest of black hair.

I left my crossbow on the beach.

I dragged myself to the water, following Eriana. We passed beneath the helicopter on its way to the island. It was looking for her.

Though I knew I was safe, I fought the instinct to flee from the serpent. Every encounter with her since the moment she'd woken had involved her trying to eat me. To swim as equals—as her master, even—was hard to comprehend.

When we drew near enough to the sinking ship that the chemicals burned my nose and skin, I let Eriana continue on. My stomach flipped at the feel of the massive structure sinking to the vast depths.

The wall of smoke blocked our view of the helicopter. I heard it circling back. They knew the serpent was here—but they didn't know exactly where.

The serpent moved gracefully around the ship, spiralling through the inky water. She opened both mouths and began to swallow the chemicals and flames. The waste disappeared inside her massive body until only the ship itself remained, rapidly disappearing into the void.

The sky was dark with smoke, but the flames had gone. A few pockets of oil remained. Eriana had swallowed most of it, but there was no time to get the rest. We needed to leave before we were seen.

I commanded Eriana to dive to the bottom.

You wish to find humans, she said.

Yes. We have something to discuss.

Eriana fell silent for a moment. She swam at my pace, far below.

Follow me, she said. *I will take you to a ship.*

CHAPTER TWENTY-FIVE - Lysi
Nereid Secrets

Several others lunged for the longblade on the floor in a scuffle. I squeezed through the crowd and shot towards the gap in the rocks, determined to finish this before lives could be lost.

"Don't let them get to Evagore," shouted Guenevere.

I cursed. They knew, then, why we were here.

The tunnel was short and pitch black. I followed it into a massive cavern, too big to feel how far it reached. Above the surface, the smooth walls converged in a dome. A hole at the apex let in a beam of daylight. The only other light was a soft blue glow cast by tiny bioluminescent creatures. They brightened at the wave of activity.

Where were the prison cells? This would take searching.

Dione's army and the Nereid guards swarmed in behind me. Based on numbers, Dione and her army would get to Evagore before I did. I had to find Dione.

A merman blasted up to me, sending a whirl of bubbles in my face.

"Where's Meela?"

I dropped my fists. "Nilus!"

His eyes were wide, aura clouded in panic. "Why isn't she with you?"

"She's taking the serpent to find humans," I said, stomach knotting.

"Serpent? How—she killed him?"

"Yes." I hesitated. She had to have done it. It was the only outcome I would accept. I repeated it more firmly. "Yes. She did. We split up so—"

Fingers closed around my tail. I screeched, whirling. My fist made contact with the mermaid's temple at the same moment as Nilus punched her in the stomach. She toppled away, dazed. Nilus pulled me closer to the rock wall.

"Where is she now?"

"East. She told me to meet her at Eriana Kwai."

"Eriana Kwai," he breathed.

"I have to bring the queen—"

He was gone.

I had half a mind to call after him, to tell him not to try and chase her, but I had more pressing matters. Dione was shoving through the crowd a short distance away, scanning the cavern. I raced over and grabbed her arm.

"We have to meet Meela at Eriana Kwai with Queen Evagore."

She looked at me sharply. "The queen needs to secure her throne in Utopia."

"I know, but first we need to make a peace pact with humans."

From the black tunnel, her army continued flooding into the cavern. The Nereid guards fought to stop them, but they were outnumbered. Weapons and fists collided everywhere I looked.

"Queen Evagore has spent years imprisoned," said Dione. "She will not be in a state to go make bargains with humans."

"Dione, the humans are stalking the serpent, waiting for the moment to drop an explosive. They've already tried some kind of sound explosion below the surface. If we don't negotiate something as soon as—"

Two bodies somersaulted into us in a storm of bubbles. One hooked an arm around the other's neck. They stopped brawling. It was Galene, holding a guard in a chokehold.

"Lysithea's right, Dione."

Dione looked affronted. "If you understood the state of the Pacific Kingdom as I do, then you would know Her Majesty needs to go directly to Utopia."

"I understand plenty, which is why I know the bigger risk is from above. We need to take the humans seriously."

Dione scowled. "I trust Her Majesty will do what she must to restore peace. This is her decision, not yours. Excuse me."

Before I could say more, she left, continuing to search the cavern.

I turned to Galene. What did this mean? Maybe Dione hadn't agreed, but she hadn't disagreed, either. A decision this big was up to the queen.

Galene grimaced. "I'm here if you need me, sugarkelp."

She took off, dragging her victim with her. A corral was forming in the centre of the room. Dione's army surrounded a group of disarmed Nereid guards. Though this hadn't gone according to plan, I was grateful to have Utopia as my ally. Our bigger numbers were proving favourable.

I cast my senses around the cavern, wondering where all the cells were. Maybe there were tunnels or secret passages leading to the inmates.

A faint presence overhead caught my attention. Something in the way the current broke as it swirled around the dome was suspicious. It would make sense to put the cells near the surface, wouldn't it?

I was about to rise when someone slammed into me, knocking me so hard that spots erupted in my vision.

I righted myself, teeth bared. For a moment, I saw no one. Then fingers closed around my upper arm. Too close, I felt the rush of a swinging mace. I caught a glimpse of brunette hair—and a merman jetted out of nowhere and tackled her. They rolled away. Their struggle stopped with the merman locking an arm around the mermaid's neck and snatching her weapon.

"Thanks," I said, the word escaping as a bubble.

"Let go of me," shouted Guenevere, voice strained as the merman squeezed her throat.

I did a double-take of my saviour. I'd seen him before—fought him, let him escape. He'd been on the South Pacific battlefront and a reluctant part of Adaro's guard.

"Anthias?"

"Hi!"

"You made it back!"

Guenevere thrashed beneath his arm, roaring. He squeezed tighter.

"Sort of. I was in the Aleutian Trench. I got to Utopia as everyone was leaving after the coup."

"The Aleutian Trench? I thought a soldier like you would get sent back to the battlefront."

Anthias' forehead wrinkled. "Battlef—Lysi, I abandoned my post protecting the king."

I grimaced. *Right. Treason.*

"I'm sorry."

"Don't be. I was hiding with a former human and his wife and kids. They were supposed to be sent down to the labour camp. Anyway, you here for the queen?"

At the word *queen*, Guenevere struggled harder in Anthias' grip.

"Which cell is she in?" I asked her, pointing to the dome's perimeter.

In answer, she blew in my face.

"All right," I said, "Anthias, help me search ..."

My chest tightened. A feeling like homesickness overcame me. Deeper than homesickness, this was an overwhelming ache.

I whirled, heart pounding. They were here, both of them. The cavern was too dark to distinguish faces. Everyone's auras blended together.

They must have come with the coup at Utopia. Unless—

"Oh, no," I whispered. Were they in one of the prison cells? Because of me?

A group sped over to us. It was Galene and the three young mermen from Kori Maru.

"There's gorgeousness that needs rescuing," said Creon. "You look like you've got a plan."

I looked around, mind hazy. I couldn't think of anything but that feeling squeezing my heart. If I felt them, that meant they must have felt me. Were they out here searching for me, or were they stuck somewhere waiting to be rescued?

I shook my head and, with great effort, pulled my attention back. I had to stay focused. This was too important.

"A plan," I said, taking in what had suddenly become my team. "Right. I think there are cells near the surface. One of them should have the queen."

They all looked up.

"She's definitely here?" said Creon.

I looked at Guenevere's fierce, desperate face.

"Positive. Spread out—"

Dione rushed to a stop beside us. "What are you all doing?"

"We're helping Lysithea find Evagore," said Creon. "She's in one of the cells up top."

Dione glared at me.

I scanned the cavern. My pulse had reached a peak, pounding in my ears. They were so close. Where were they?

Dione addressed the others. "Spread out. Trace the walls. Anthias, bring that one over here with the rest."

"Yes, ma'am," said Anthias.

I grabbed his arm. "Wait. Keep her with us. I want her to tell us where Evagore is."

Anthias glanced between me and Dione.

"I'm not telling you anything," said Guenevere, her voice strained under Anthias' arm.

"See?" said Dione. "Now put her—"

"Force it out of her," I said. "We're wasting time. Creon, take your friends over there and search the far wall."

"Do not tell my soldiers what to—" said Dione.

"Aye aye!" said Creon, speeding off.

Dione looked at me furiously. I shrugged and hurried away. I smelled blood. We had to get out of here before anyone was killed—if it hadn't happened already.

I hit the wall two-handed and pushed along it, feeling for anything odd in the stone.

Around the cavern, the army was slowly disarming the guards and pushing them inwards, circling them like a baitball.

Ephyra flashed by. She was searching the crowd instead of fighting. I wondered if Nilus had told her he was going to find Meela, or if he'd left without saying goodbye.

Such a jumble of activity met my senses that it was hard to feel for any halls leading to the prison cells. I kept sliding my hands along the stone.

But there was that presence squeezing my heart. Instinct told me to search for them, more strongly than the logic telling me to find Queen Evagore.

Stay focused, I told myself. *You can find them later.*

"Lysi."

My chest constricted. That voice. I hadn't heard it in so, so long.

I turned, and there she was, blurry through the whirl of activity. She stared at me with an expression of mingled shock and elation.

"Mom!"

The word came as a sob. I shot towards her and threw myself into her arms before she could say anything more. I buried my face in her hair—the exact shade as mine.

I wanted to say so many things, but no words would come.

"Hi, babygirl."

The sound of her voice reduced me to tears.

A second pair of arms wrapped around me, large and strong. I turned around to hug my father.

For several years that felt like a lifetime, I'd been a soldier, a warrior, a fugitive. Beneath all of that, I'd forgotten what it was like to be a kid. I wasn't old enough for any of this. At eighteen, I'd fought more battles than anyone should have ever had to face. In my parents' embrace, my body seemed to shrink into a kid's again.

"What are you doing here?" said my mother.

I pulled away fractionally. "Same thing as Dione and all of you."

"Dione?" said my father.

"The leader of the South Pacific group."

"The lead—you know her?"

I nodded.

My mother smoothed back my hair, studying my face with a pinched brow. "You're wanted for treason. We nearly died of shock when we heard."

"They didn't question you about me?"

"They tried. We've been living in hiding in the kelp forest behind Clymene's place. You remember her?"

I opened and closed my mouth. My parents had been in hiding, after all. Of course they had. It was their only option. They would have been tortured or killed the moment I'd failed to assassinate the king.

"When I sensed you, I thought you were imprisoned here," I said thickly. "Because of me."

"You never need to worry about us, babygirl," said my father. "We've been safe and hidden. When we heard the news, we were more worried about you."

I'd known my decisions would have wide impact, yet, somehow, all of this—my parents in hiding, their friend

Clymene risking her freedom and possibly her family's—made everything more real. Everyone I loved was in danger. Everyone they associated with was at risk. I had to keep them all safe. The way to do that was to make sure Adaro and his kingdom broke beyond repair.

"We only came out of hiding yesterday," said my mother. "We had to go to Utopia to see the rumour for ourselves. Can you believe all of this?"

The sounds of the fight pounded in my ears. There was too much to tell my parents, and no time. I hadn't seen them since training. The entire world had changed since then. They didn't even know about Meela, or the serpent, or why I was wanted for treason.

"We heard from your brother," said my father. "He's on his way home."

I squeaked. "Really?"

My eyes burned with emotion. For years, I had stopped myself hoping that someday my family might be reunited. The prospect seemed too impossible.

"They were met by Medusa's army," said my mother. "They surrendered."

My brother was alive. I was so absorbed in the idea of seeing him again that her words nearly passed by me.

"Wait, Medusa decided to fight?"

My mother's eyebrows shot up.

"I'll explain later," I said, looking around for the others.

Anthias, Galene, Creon and his friends were still skimming the walls in their search.

"How long has she been on the move?" I said.

"A few days," said my father. "A lot of Adaro's armies have surrendered under her."

So Medusa had listened to Meela and me. She was fighting back.

"But how did she get to the South Pacific so fast? When we talked to her …" I counted backwards on my fingers, trying to figure out how she travelled the length of the Atlantic so quickly.

"Talked to her?" shouted my father. "What do you mean—?"

"Never mind. Are you sure she's in the South Pacific? Where did you hear this?"

"Her army came through the canal," said my mother. "Adaro wasn't expecting her to hit his armies from the middle, so his defenses were weak."

"The canal? You mean the Panama Canal?"

My mother nodded. "She negotiated with the humans. They allowed her passage."

I let out a bark of laughter. Adaro would be fuming to know she'd beat him because of an alliance with humans.

"Lysi!" Creon waved me over.

I glanced from the crowd to my parents, desperately wanting to spend more time with them. I wanted to tell them everything—and especially about Meela. I wanted to know what they had been doing, and exactly what my brother had said. But this was not the time.

"I have to go."

They nodded.

My mother motioned to the corral of guards forming in the middle. "Us, too."

The fight was still going, the taste of blood in the water. I hoped we hadn't lost lives. We had higher numbers, but the guards were armed and able to fend off several at once.

My father pulled me into another hug and whispered, "We're proud of you, babygirl."

I bit the inside of my cheek so I wouldn't start sobbing again.

They let me go, just like that. They trusted that I'd survived this long, and that I would continue to do the right thing.

I thought of Meela, wherever she was. She, too, had proven her abilities countless times. She'd made it this far. It was my turn to stop worrying. If I truly loved her, I had to trust her. I had to let her live, and make her own choices, and learn from her mistakes.

I darted over to Creon. "What'd you find?"

Before he could say anything, I heard a hoarse voice. "What's happening?" it said.

I snapped my attention to the wall. The voice had come from beyond the rock.

I tuned out the chaos, and a gap revealed itself in the wall. It was narrow, no more than a hand's width, too dark to see through. I pressed my palm to it, feeling what was on the other side.

The way the water swirled told me the cell was circular, with smooth walls and no room for comfort. A lone merman was inside. He was weak, his aura pale.

"The others are checking for more gaps in the wall," said Creon. "We must be getting close because that commander mermaid is getting desperate."

"Well done," I said. "Can we get him out of here?"

Creon and I felt around the gap. A boulder blocked the cell entrance. It was wide, roughly rectangular. We pushed, but it didn't budge. We would need a team to move this.

"We'll come back," I whispered, throat tightening with guilt. The truth was, Evagore was our priority. We had no time to free the prisoners one-by-one.

"No!" said the merman inside. "Get me out of here. Please."

I backed away, deflating. We had to stay focused. I motioned for Creon to follow.

The merman rushed at the gap. He pressed his face against it, shouting after us. "Wait! I can help if you let me out!"

A few lengths ahead, Anthias dragged Guenevere around the cavern, still keeping her in a headlock.

"Are we close?" he said, to no response.

The other young mermen had crossed the dome to search the far wall. Dione and Galene had disappeared somewhere ahead. We needed more help.

There was a flash of darkness and a huge splash. Something erupted at the surface. Screams broke out. Everyone scattered. I instinctively threw my arms over my head, my mind leaping from human explosives, to the dome caving in, to a crashing meteor.

There was a mass scramble to get away from the object, and—

"Cannonbaaall!"

A lanky merman uncurled himself from the eruption of bubbles. His hair was wilder than ever, like he'd escaped a windstorm.

"Spio?!"

I looked from him to the top of the dome, where the sliver of daylight had grown wider. Pieces crumbled from the edges and rained down on us.

Spio turned at the sound of my voice, face brightening, and said, "Proof."

In his hand was a black, opaque crown. Locks of black hair clung to it, severed at the ends. I gaped. I'd spent my life looking at that crown—and not once had I seen it detached from its owner's head.

My throat constricted. Of everything this orphaned crown represented, one victory rose above all: Meela had succeeded. She was alive, and she had the serpent under her control.

"Now we have what we need to rally everyone," said Spio slowly, misreading my expression as confusion.

"Brilliant," I said, voice strangled.

He shoved the crown into his bag and glanced around. "I thought the plan was to talk to them quietly."

"Everyone from Kori Maru and Utopia showed up."

Spio nodded, taking in the carnage with an air of mild interest. "Huh."

"We're trying to find Evagore. There are prison cells in the walls."

"Challenge accepted."

He took off.

I cast my senses around the cavern to check on the others. They were still running fingers along the walls, feeling for gaps.

A mermaid called out from the next cell.

"My name is Medea," she said. "Please, I am not a criminal. I was South Pacific government. I never did wrong."

"I believe you. We're going to get you out of here soon. Do you know where the queen is?"

She hesitated. "No. But I can help you search."

Guilt pressed on me again. I had to leave her. Time was too tight.

If I knew anything about Adaro, none of these prisoners were here because they were dangerous criminals. They were all innocent, stuck here for being enemies of the crown.

"I'm sorry," I said. I continued to the next cell, ignoring her pleas.

In the centre, the fight was subsiding. The guards were clustered tightly together, surrounded by the army and as helpless as a baitball. Their weapons were ours.

Spio appeared next to me with what must have been the largest mace he could find. The end looked like a barrel.

He motioned across the way. "I think they found something interesting."

Dione, Galene, Creon, and the others from Kori Maru were gathered by the wall.

I ground my teeth. Why hadn't they called me over?

Dione, I thought. *That's why.*

Spio and I rushed over to join them.

"What do you want?" said the prisoner faintly from the back of the cell—a female.

"We are here to help," said Dione. "What's your name?"

When the occupant didn't respond, Creon said, "You can trust us."

More silence.

"Queen Evagore?" said Dione to the gap in the wall.

"Why do you need her?" repeated the prisoner.

The group of us traded uncertain glances. Was it her? Maybe she was sceptical about what would happen if she revealed her identity. Then again, maybe she was another mermaid who suspected that saying she was the queen would grant her freedom.

"I think it is her," said Dione to her council. "I know her aura."

"Well, are we getting her out, or what?" said Spio, moving closer to the boulder.

"Of course," said Dione, snapping. "I'm formulating a plan."

"Run it by me," said Spio. "I'll tell you if it sucks or not."

She glared at him.

"Come on," I said. "Let's start pushing."

"No!" said Guenevere, renewing her struggle in Anthias' grip. "Stop them! Someone!"

But none of her guards were free to help her.

Energised by her panic, the group of us moved in to push the boulder. I found a spot between the wall and Galene. We pushed and pulled, using the wall and floor for leverage.

"Find a rhythm," said Creon. "Heave! Heave! Heave!"

It worked. A gap opened into the cell.

Closest to it, I slid an arm through and reached for the mermaid. "Grab my hand."

She stirred at the back of the cave.

Please be Evagore. Please let the queen be alive and well.

If this was her, the true queen of the Pacific, our plan would be in motion. The Pacific Kingdom could start anew. What would it be like to live under a monarch not driven by hatred or fear of humans? Would our world become as rich and as free as the one Meela and I had seen in the Atlantic?

The boulder gave a loud rumble.

"It's slipping!" said Anthias.

Before I grasped what was happening, the rock smashed against me. I cried out, pinned to the wall, the air shoved from my lungs.

All of them began to shout at once.

"Grab it! Pull it back!"

The crushing feeling grew more painful as my ribcage compressed. I whimpered. It felt as though my bones were about to shatter.

I'd been too focused on getting to the prisoner. I'd caught no warning signs from the slipping boulder.

I groaned, trying to wriggle free. I couldn't die like this—not when, for the first time ever, I'd felt hope for a life free from King Adaro.

Creon tried to shout everyone back into the rhythm. There was too much panic.

Then Anthias and Spio appeared above and below me, wedging themselves between wall and boulder.

"We've got you, Lysi," said Spio, his words calm and reassuring. "Everyone, heave!"

They picked up Creon's rhythm. I shoved against the wall, trying to help.

Guenevere's sour face appeared through the group. She rubbed her throat. Anthias had let her go to help free me.

Our gazes met. Contemplation passed behind her eyes. Whatever action she took next would define her and the world she would live in.

She looked to my friends, and then to me. She made her decision. She extended her hands and slammed into the boulder next to Galene, helping them push.

Together, they eased the boulder away.

The moment the crushing weight was off my chest, instinct told me to rise for air. I ignored it and reached for the prisoner.

She took my hand.

I pulled her from the cell, dragging her frail, wilted form as lightly as if she were a string of kelp.

Everyone grew still as we squeezed into the open. She was a southern mermaid.

My friends let the boulder go. It slammed back into the wall with an echoing *boom*.

The noise and current ricocheted through the cavern. We hovered, staring, until it faded. Creon and the others straightened like soldiers at attention.

Dione broke the pressing silence.

"Your Majesty."

CHAPTER TWENTY-SIX - Meela
A Resounding Hush

I couldn't explain why I trusted Eriana to guide me towards a mysterious ship when the creature had spent so long trying to kill me.

But now, she was a part of me, an extension of my mind and body. As definitively as I could trust my survival instincts, I could trust her to keep me safe.

With senses more powerful than my own, she found a ship floating a few leagues away and led me towards it.

We encountered nothing along the way—presumably because any creature that felt us coming fled as fast as possible.

The closer we drew to the ship, the more nervous I became. I contemplated what I would say. How was I supposed to convince these people to listen to me?

I considered my options. As a mermaid, I could lure them. I could threaten them with the serpent. But I didn't want to use force. They had to agree to peace on their own volition.

We stopped at the ship's bow. The materials stung my skin and coated my tongue in something thick and bitter. The sight of its broad hull, so unnatural among the blues and greens, sent a chill through me.

Abruptly, pain stabbed through my body. Every cell vibrated. I moaned, raising my hands to my ears. It was that noise again. But how? The serpent had destroyed the ship.

Hadn't she? I couldn't think, couldn't remember. That terrible pain filled my head, paralysing me. I grew dizzy from the pressure of it against my ears.

Eriana shook her head, releasing blasts of air from her nostrils in agitation.

I barely heard her speaking to me.

It is from inside the ship. Should I break it?

No, I thought. *Don't attack. Let me talk to them.*

I summoned her closer. Her eyes narrowed and her head lowered, reminding me of a cowering dog. I climbed onto one of her great heads. Shielding myself with the mane of horns, I asked her to rise from the water.

We broke the surface and a different explosion of sound met my ears. It took me a moment to understand what was happening. They were firing machine guns at us. Bullets ricocheted off the serpent's scales. She didn't offer so much as a groan of protest, and soon, the bullets stopped.

My ears rang in the silence.

"I am not here to hurt you," I said in English, uncomfortably aware of my accent. "Please, lower your weapons so we can speak."

My words were met with silence. I leaned around the mane of horns enough to see their faces. A crew of about twenty Americans stood on the deck, aiming at the serpent. They were faint with terror, several of them visibly trembling.

"I am Metlaa Gaela, Daughter of Kasai. I come from Eriana Kwai, and so does this serpent."

The crew followed my voice and caught sight of me atop the serpent. I must have appeared small and insignificant compared to her. They glanced to each other, still looking frightened.

"I'm here on behalf of merpeople. We wish to negotiate with you to end this war. Please, turn off that noise."

A man with a neck as wide as his head stepped forwards. "We thought the serpent was commanded by the merman king."

"The king is dead. The serpent is under my control, now."

The crew tensed. There was a groan of fingers tightening over triggers.

"She will not harm you."

"And if we kill you?" said the wide-necked man.

Eriana gave a low hiss. *Careful, daughter. These soldiers do not know control is passed by blood.*

"Then the serpent will avenge her master," I said, lying easily.

There was a beat of silence. I felt Eriana's pain, her second head still beneath the surface where the noise blasted.

I said again, more firmly, "Please stop that noise."

"Are you surrendering?" said wide-neck man.

"No. I'm negotiating a cease-fire."

Once, I would have considered this guy intimidating, but now that I'd spent time in the presence of mermen, he seemed laughably small.

"Why the sudden change?" he said.

"This war was King Adaro's. I used to be human, and more than anyone, my people understand what pain this war has caused. With cooperation, we can stop this."

The man raised his eyebrows. "What are your terms?"

"I only want peace—starting with ending that noise."

I forced my anger down, not wanting to transition into demon mode. I wanted them to feel like they were talking to a human. My tail was masked behind Eriana's mane of horns, and I had the impression they'd relaxed a little since I'd begun talking.

The crew stared, seeming to weigh the threat of the serpent against my request.

The back of my neck prickled at Eriana's continued discomfort. Any living thing for leagues around was suffering, and we all knew it.

The wide-necked man turned and strode into the helm. He was gone a long time. Nobody spoke. Finally, Eriana let out a groan of relief. A moment later, the man returned with a phone.

"I've told the others to pause the sonic charges. Now start talking."

Others? How many places was this happening? My mind jumped to Lysi. I gritted my teeth.

The man held out the phone as though expecting me to come aboard.

"Um," I said, scanning the machine guns aimed in my direction and wondering if the bullets were iron. "Pass it to the serpent, please."

Eriana raised her other head beside the ship. The nearest soldiers scrambled back as seawater cascaded onto the deck.

The man obliged after a moment's hesitance, dropping the phone onto Eriana's tongue. She brought it to me. I picked up the phone gingerly, trying not to get water on it. I had the urge to laugh. What was wrong with me?

A call was connected, the timer on the screen counting up. I raised the phone to my ear.

"Hello?"

"Officer Miller here," said the other end brusquely. "I understand you are holding my ship hostage."

"My name is Metlaa Gaela. I am a mermaid and a former human from Eriana Kwai. King Adaro is dead. I have possession of the serpent, and I intend to make peace between us."

He was silent, then said in a constricted voice, "That is quite a remarkable achievement, Metlaa Gaela."

"Um. Thank you."

"Are you prepared to have all merpeople cease their attacks on human ships and beaches?"

"Yes. The king's armies no longer serve him."

"I see," said Officer Miller. "Interesting."

"We have a new queen. She would like to meet you and sign a peace treaty."

It wasn't an outright lie, but my stomach twisted all the same. The plan had better follow through on Lysi's end.

"A treaty? Metlaa Gaela, are you aware the last peace treaty we signed with merpeople was broken? Are you aware we lost lives in the Aleutian Islands?"

"Those actions were King Adaro's. You have my word that merpeople will stop invading beaches and sinking ships under our new queen."

"What's the word of a girl from Eriana Kwai?"

I flushed at his taunt. "What would you know of Eriana Kwai? You left us to die."

"The struggles of one small island aren't—"

"I am offering to end this war," I said, not wanting to hear his pitiful excuses. "Given that I have the serpent under my control, I recommend you accept."

Officer Miller sighed. "That's exactly the problem. You're on one of my most valuable ships with twenty American soldiers aboard, and you have the power to destroy it in seconds. You'll understand why this conversation feels like a hostage situation."

I closed my eyes, summoning calmness. "I do not intend to harm your crew, Officer Miller. If you agree to meet, you can discuss your terms with the new queen of the Pacific."

He paused. I wished I could see his face, read his aura.

"I see," he finally said. "And then what happens with the serpent?"

"I will destroy it."

"Destroy?" His tone was harsh, clipped.

"Yes. Once we come to an agreement, the serpent will cease to exist."

"But it's the only one of its kind!"

I didn't respond.

"Metlaa Gaela," he said, a note of false warmth in his voice, "it would be a shame to lose something as incredible as the leviathan. What can we offer you in exchange for it?"

"I will not let her become a weapon."

"We're prepared to offer you anything. Any amount of money."

"The serpent is not my bargain."

"Consider—"

"No. I have seen what she is capable of."

So have they—and that is why they want me, said Eriana.

"A peace treaty. That is my request," I said.

"And if we don't agree?" said Officer Miller.

I hesitated. "Then I suppose you will keep dropping iron bombs in the water, and issuing these sonic attacks, and doing everything you can to destroy all life in the Pacific Ocean. But you should know that I have spent my life training for war and fighting in battles more terrible than you know. And if you keep fighting, I will fight back."

There was a long silence.

"All right," said Officer Miller. "I need to contact the right people. Can you meet me in Anchorage?"

"No. I want you to come to Eriana Kwai." I looked towards the setting sun, weighing how long it would take me to get there. "Tomorrow. Sundown."

Another pause. "I can make that work."

"You won't drop anything into the ocean? You won't issue any more assaults, noise or otherwise?"

"Not between now and then."

I chewed my lip. If he was being honest, at least I'd be able to get to Eriana Kwai without helicopters or ships waiting.

"I'm passing you back to your crew," I said. "See you tomorrow."

Without waiting for an answer, I tossed the phone back to the crew on deck.

Eriana and I disappeared beneath the surface before they caught it.

CHAPTER TWENTY-SEVEN - Ben
Grouse and Cormorant

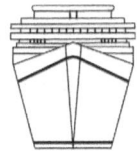

Reeves screeched into the airfield and leapt from his truck, leaving the keys in the ignition. Their fastest jet waited on the asphalt, a DH-70R Grouse. It was already running, the engine bellowing its war cry. He smelled the fuel, pungent and toxic on the fresh Alaskan air.

Officer Miller was striding towards it. Reeves sprinted to catch up.

"What do you want?" said Miller.

"Anderson told me my team's dispatching—"

"Yes. Her team, not yours."

"Yes, sir. But she said the mermaids want a peace treaty."

"They do."

"And you're sending special ops?"

Miller stopped at the jet. He faced Reeves with crossed arms, as though bouncing the Grouse's entrance.

"A mermaid has control of the serpent now. She killed the merman king."

Killed? The merman king was dead? Reeves hardly dared to believe it.

"Who's this mermaid, sir?"

"Don't know. Some girl. Used to be from Eriana Kwai."

"A girl? What, like a kid?"

"She sounded like a teenager. Who cares? She's a mermaid now."

Reeves rubbed a hand over his eyes, making sense of this. A mermaid, a former human, killed the merman king, and now she wanted a peace treaty.

"Incredible," he whispered.

And yet, special ops was going. Why?

"So you're going to sign the treaty?"

Miller placed a hand on the railing. "We need that serpent. There's only one way to get it."

"Wait—you're going to kill the mermaid?"

"She won't give it to us. Says she's going to destroy it."

Anderson and her team arrived. Reeves kept his glare on Miller as they climbed into the Grouse.

"Isn't that a good thing if this mermaid wants to destroy it, not use it?" said Reeves.

"You want to destroy the most powerful weapon in the world?" said Miller.

"Sir, think about what it would mean to have power over it. You'll spend your life with a target on your head, because once word gets out that it's passed by blood—"

"This isn't your decision to make."

"You're going to kill a teenage girl!"

"She's a mermaid, Reeves. There's a difference."

"There's not!"

The words burst from Reeves' mouth with such volume that Anderson leaned out the jet door to check on them.

For a long moment, he and Miller stared at each other.

Miller's lip curled. "And you wonder why you were demoted."

"Sir—"

"Go home." Miller pointed eastwards, as though indicating all the way back to mainland USA. "I don't want to see your face here again."

Reeves trembled from anger. He clamped his jaw shut, afraid of what might come out if he opened it again.

He watched the officer climb into the jet. Anderson cast him a look of mingled apology and exasperation before the door slammed.

Reeves backed away as the ground crew jumped into action around him.

He couldn't let this happen. Miller's words about the mermaid being a former human settled uneasily over him. It drove home exactly what Reeves had been struggling to comprehend all along. The value of a mermaid's life was no less than the value of a human's. They were at war like nations around the world had been throughout history—and like all of those wars, there were innocent civilians to protect on both sides.

He had to get to Eriana Kwai before Miller did.

There wasn't a proper airport, however. Miller and the team must have been going to Seattle first. Would they take one of the big choppers from there? Would they pick up the President, or Secretary of State, or anyone else arriving from the White House? Dammit, why was he so out of the loop?

The only way Reeves could get to Eriana Kwai first was if he went straight there in a helicopter.

He scanned the airfield desperately. How far was Eriana Kwai? 750 miles? He'd never be able to get there in something standard. He needed something long-range.

Then his eyes landed on her, waiting on the flightline in all her glory: the LM-80 Cormorant.

Reeves shifted his weight from foot to foot.

Miller hadn't officially relieved him of command. He'd only yelled at him a bit.

He'd surely be sent home for real after this—but he could deal with those repercussions and overly supportive but secretly disappointed parents later.

Right now, he needed access to that helicopter.

He pulled out his phone. It rang twice.

"Bagh. I need a favour."

CHAPTER TWENTY-EIGHT - Lysi
Queen Evagore

The queen who had been missing for so long was here in front of me. Dione and her council, Anthias, Spio, and I remained motionless, staring at her.

We'd spent so long searching, and still, I could not get over the disbelief at having found her. In the back of my mind I supposed I had never expected it to happen.

Or maybe I couldn't yet process the idea of living under any power other than Adaro.

"Is he really dead?" Queen Evagore whispered.

I nodded.

A shudder swept over her frail body. She gazed across the dark cavern towards the crowd. Surrounded and overpowered by the Utopian army, the Nereid guards' defiance had faded. They were silent, their fear heavy in the water.

The dreadlocked merman from Kori Maru came forwards with a bag in his hands. He opened it and produced a pale blue crown. It was smooth and opaque, with a single prong at the front.

Dione took it delicately into her hands as if holding a newborn baby.

"The Pacific is yours once more, Your Majesty," she murmured, and passed Queen Evagore the crown.

I studied the queen, understanding what Dione had meant when she said Evagore would be in no condition to make negotiations. I'd worked her up to be bigger in my mind, longer, with the aura of a deity. I'd half expected her to burst out of here with all the power and glamour of Medusa, ready to rebuild the kingdom.

But she was a normal mermaid. Beneath her withered appearance she was small, even young. Evidence of torture was burned across her stomach and back. Would she want to be queen after all she'd been through? Would she be able to sway the masses—or, more pressingly, negotiate with humans?

All I could think was that we needed to get her to Eriana Kwai, and fast. How much time did I have? Through the hole in the ceiling, I couldn't see where the sun was.

With trembling hands, Queen Evagore took the crown from Dione. She didn't put it on. She held it, staring down at the pale blue point. The emotions that surged from her caused a lump to rise in my throat.

There was a scuffle in the crowd. A few guards tried to break away from where our army had them corralled.

I heard a few thumps of a weapon against a body, and the scuffle died.

"Please don't," said Guenevere. "You can take Evagore if she's who you came for, but don't hurt my guards."

She hovered away from the rest of us. No one tried to restrain her.

"We won't," I said, and then louder so everyone could hear. "We don't want to hurt you. That's not what we're here for."

Queen Evagore's eyes flickered to me. They were soft, kind, and heavy with exhaustion. She said nothing, so I continued.

"Adaro is dead, and his government has fallen. It's time to restore the Pacific Kingdom to what it once was. Under Queen Evagore—"

"The king is not dead!" shouted a merman from the crowd.

"If you don't believe me," I said over top of him, "I ask that you consider the word of this soldier, who has proof in his hands!" I beckoned to Spio in what I hoped was an impressive, sweeping gesture.

Spio blinked at me from where he floated. His hair was singed and blackened from the ship fire, the barrel-sized mace dangling at his side. He scratched his nose.

"Spio," I whispered, "the crown."

"Right."

An unbearable silence fell as Spio struggled to pull the crown out of his bag. It caught several times on the straps before he managed to yank it free.

He held it high over his head. The single beam of light poured from the ceiling and illuminated its opaque black points. The severed locks of hair fluttered around it. The crowd broke out in whispers.

"The serpent is under the control of Queen Evagore's allies," I said.

"Control?" said Dione, temper flaring. "*Meela* controls the serpent? How?"

"She's using it to approach the humans," I said, evading the question. "We're asking them to meet Queen Evagore at Eriana Kwai to make a peace treaty."

I looked meaningfully at the queen, hoping she would agree to this without question.

She frowned. "When you refer to a serpent, are you talking about the Host of Eriana? He unearthed it?"

"Yes."

Evagore dropped her gaze. I caught a quickening in her pulse.

"How do you know about the serpent?" said Spio.

Her aura flickered with shame. She traced a finger over the cracked skin on her arm. "The legend of the Host of Eriana was passed down my family."

I glanced to the iron burns wrapped around her midsection. Was this the information Adaro had been trying to pry from her this whole time?

Guenevere narrowed her eyes. "Is it true that Medusa already overpowered his armies?"

I nodded. "She's pushing back in every direction."

Across the cavern, the army and guards fell into absolute silence.

"Why should we accept this southern mermaid as our new queen?" said Guenevere.

"Commander, remember his warning. We swore an oath," shouted a mermaid from the crowd.

Guenevere ran a hand over the rubies in her braid and straightened, seemingly bolstered by the feel of them.

"Adaro's reign has ended. Utopia and the South Pacific are resisting. His army is surrendering under Medusa's power, and the serpent is allied with those in front of us. We must consider the future of our kingdom."

"We don't intend to force a leader upon anyone," I said. "We'll hold an election. Everyone gets a vote."

I felt horribly unqualified to be saying such things, but someone had to. Why not me? Why not someone who'd been working towards a new kingdom as tirelessly as I had?

Dione cast me a look of mingled surprise and anger.

But Queen Evagore said, "Everyone votes. You all have the right to decide what kind of kingdom you wish to live in."

"And what will you have to offer?" said Guenevere.

Everyone turned to Queen Evagore. She looked too tired to hold herself upright, much less defend her position as queen.

Finally, she lifted the crown. The instant it was placed over her pale, limp hair, she became radiant. The crown's weight drew her body longer, prouder. Her shoulders squared. Her tired eyes brightened.

"My kingdom is built upon freedom," she said, voice soft and clear. "You are free to live as you wish, to choose your future, to express your voice. We live without prejudice. You will not be sent to a war in which the gruesomeness of the battle is determined by your gender. You will not be put to death because of your affiliation with humans. Your loved ones will not be sent to suffer and perish in a labour camp."

The words seemed to suck the air from my lungs.

"The labour camp," I whispered. How many were still trapped there?

"We will free them next," whispered Dione.

"What about everyone in these cells?" said Creon. "We need to free them, too."

"Do we?" said the dreadlocked merman. "What if they're here because they're criminals?"

"They're here because Adaro deemed them too important to send to the camp," said Guenevere.

Queen Evagore nodded gravely. "We have much to fix."

My eyes roamed desperately over the walls full of cells. So many urgencies competed for our attention. Every moment we spent here, merpeople could be dying in the camps. Every moment, they were working closer towards unleashing a fatal storm on the Pacific coast.

And Meela. She was at risk waiting for us to get to Eriana Kwai with the queen.

How were we supposed to do all of this at once?

The crowd was murmuring, getting louder.

It was not a noise of protest.

My heart pounded. The darkness itself seemed to lift.

"Free the labour camp," a merman shouted.

His words were met with cheers. The mood seeped through the crowd like a burst of oxygen.

Queen Evagore nodded. "Dione, please assemble a team to go to the labour camp, and another to stay here and help free the prisoners."

"Yes, Your Majesty."

The queen's energy was rising. It would likely be brief, considering her condition, but her willingness to lead inspired hope in me.

"Your Majesty," I said. "We've arranged to meet the humans at Eriana Kwai so we can come to an agreement."

She studied me. I prepared to launch into an explanation of everything the humans had been doing, all the assaults we had faced and the threat of more damage—but she nodded.

"When?"

"We have to go now," I said, breathless. "I'll take you."

Dione was watching us. Queen Evagore met her eye, and something passed between them.

"I require Dione and a few of my council to accompany us."

"Yes, Your Majesty," I said.

It was reasonable. We could use a guard on the way there, and afterwards, they could take her back to Utopia.

Spio swam up behind me.

"Well, off to the labour camp," he said, like he was telling me he was going for a jaunt to catch dinner.

"Wait, what? I didn't mean you—"

"You're right, buddy. We need to get to the labour camp before any more damage is done. For all we know, we're hours away from that seismic crapstorm King Asshat wanted."

"But Spio—"

"Besides, apparently Amathia is there. I have a maiden in misery to save."

The thought of Spio travelling all the way there with this army, of fighting through more guards in the ocean's most painful depths, constricted my throat.

He clapped me on the shoulder. "Lysi, it's been weird. It was good to share it all with you. Next time I see you, it'll be a new world."

I had to trust his judgment. I had to let him do this. Maybe I would get to meet Amathia next time I saw him.

But one last hug. I threw myself at him.

Around us, the crowd took up the chant—more voices than ever joining in.

"Not my king! Not my war!"

When Spio and I broke apart, we shared a smile—the first real smile in what might have been a lifetime.

Victory pulsated through the cavern. I felt it in every part of me. Utopia was united, and we had the allegiance of the Nereid guards. Across the world, Medusa was taking down Adaro's remaining armies. There would be no more labour camps, no more wars.

Spio was right—we were entering a new world. At long last, the sun had set on Adaro's kingdom.

CHAPTER TWENTY-NINE - Meela
The Gaela's Intention

Maybe Eriana's homesickness amplified my own, because when my island materialised before us, the emotions crashing through me were too much to bear. Every time I breached and saw those familiar mountains, trees, and beaches, I ached.

I was returning home with Eriana in my possession—a true descendant, heir to the most powerful creature in the world. I'd never felt so proud to be a part of this island.

We arrived at the Welcome Centre, the port that had been unused my whole life. I made Eriana stay below surface while I waited half-submerged, feeling protected by the layer of water.

The totem poles scowled down at us, weathered and faded yet more alive than ever. I studied Sisiutl, wondering who had carved that totem, and whether the artist had known the real one rested so close by.

Had the beach always been so peaceful, or did my new senses make it this way? Waves purred against the rocks, seagulls chattered to each other, and the nearby forest whispered in the breeze. The smell of the woods summoned countless memories of running through those towering trees. Warmth spread through me, along with a new feeling of acceptance. I loved and cherished those memories, and at the same time, I cherished the ones I had yet to make. In a life that changed so rapidly as mine, I resolved to accept each day, and never to ache for the past again. My memories on Eriana Kwai were a beautiful part of me, but that era was now over. My future would be one of bright coral and kelp forests.

Something to look forward to, I thought, as the sun touched the horizon.

Someone is coming.

I frowned. She was referring to the sea, not the sky. A moment later, I felt the ripples at my tail.

Who?

I closed my eyes, trying to form a deeper connection with Eriana, to feel what she felt.

"Nilus?" I said aloud, my heart swelling.

The moment my brother surfaced beside me, we threw our arms around each other in a bone-crushing hug.

"You're okay!" he said.

"Why are you here? Where's Lysi?"

"I met her at the Nereids. She said you killed—well, I guess you succeeded."

Words failed him as he looked back to where the serpent lay submerged. Then he looked past me, taking in where he was. His mouth hung open as he scanned the totems, the Welcome Center, beach, forests, and cliffs.

"Welcome home, brother," I said.

If I were able to go back in time, to tell my past self that someday Nilus and I would return home together, in this state, under these conditions, I never would have believed it.

"Gaawhist," he said. *Home, sweet home.*

The thrum of a helicopter met my ears. I lifted my gaze to see a dark shape break through the grey clouds.

Right on time, I thought.

"Nilus, I need you to hide below the surface, all right? I want them to see only me."

He hesitated. "Okay. I'm here if you need anything."

We shared a smile, and he ducked down.

The helicopter circled over the empty gravel lot, seeming to decide where to land. Finally, it sank. A hurricane blew at me from its massive rotor, pushing the waves back.

I expected a group of official men in suits. I'd pictured the face of the President of the United States.

Instead, a single figure stepped out, sweaty and wide-eyed. He looked to be in his twenties. I hadn't pictured Officer Miller so young. Based on his voice, I'd guessed him to be much older, maybe with a mustache.

Tentatively, I asked Eriana to raise her head so he would see us.

He balked when he saw the serpent, apparently frozen in fear. Then he squared his shoulders and ran towards us.

"Officer Miller?" I said, sitting taller.

The young man tore his eyes from the serpent and found me in the waves. He stopped, keeping several strides between us.

"No," he said. He seemed uncertain whether or not he should look directly at me; his eyes kept skittering over the waves to my left. "I'm Ben Reeves. Officer Miller will be here any minute. I came to warn you. You have to stay away from them. They know."

"What do you mean, *they know*?"

A second helicopter thrummed in the distance.

Ben paled. He whirled to examine the sky. The helicopter descended rapidly, this one darker and larger.

When he spun back around, his forehead glistened with fresh sweat. "I mean they're going to kill you!"

"But—they can't know. How did they find out?"

"It's my fault. I told Miller. I thought it would make them go after the king instead of you. I mean—not you specifically, but—" He gestured broadly at the ocean.

The helicopter circled the lot, taking a wider swing than Ben had.

"Go!" said Ben.

I hesitated. Something needled at me, but before I could wonder, Eriana said, *She is coming.*

I faced the water, picking up her urgency.

"What's wrong?" said Ben.

Nilus surfaced. "Meela—"

The next wave slapped the shore, and when it retreated, a mermaid was there on the rocks. The sinking sun glinted off her crown, which sat atop ropes of hair that hung heavy without the tide to lift them. Her orange-brown eyes glimmered. She spoke in a powerful voice that carried across the shore.

"Metlaa Gaela. I have come to collect what is mine."

Medusa reached behind her to pull a bow from across her shoulders. She did not notch the arrow—but held it in her other hand, ready.

"I'm not going to pass control," I said, knowing that even if I wanted to, I wouldn't be able to without sacrificing my life.

"Do not back out on your word! You promised me the serpent in exchange for my help."

"You refused our offer."

Medusa's eyes reddened. "My armies have stopped Adaro's across the globe. Without me, the war against Adaro's regime would have been hopeless. I am the rightful master of the serpent."

Eriana gave a low hiss.

"You're not," I said, feeling my own eyes redden. "I'm her descendant. This island is my home. Its legends are a part of me. I have the right to decide."

Ben looked between us in alarm. It occurred to me that he had no idea what we were saying.

Medusa's fingers, which gripped her bow and arrow more tightly, became webbed.

"I will have control, Metlaa Gaela. So unless you know a way that does not require blood, you leave me no choice."

Before I could react, shouts carried on the wind. I snapped my head around to see people—my people—rushing towards us. They must have heard the helicopters.

My heart ached. Were my parents among them? Annith, Tanuu, and Blacktail?

Medusa raised her bow. The arrow was notched, its deadly tip pointing at me. "Metlaa Gaela, consider the arrangement you requested in the Atlantic. This is your final chance to give me what is mine."

My ears pounded. The helicopter hovered lower, scalping back the shoreline. Eriana followed it with both heads. She could easily strike at my command—like a frog catching a fly.

A whizzing sound echoed in the air. My body reacted before my mind processed what happened, and suddenly I was in demon mode, lying flat in the sand, pulse racing. Had they just—?

Rat-tat-tat!

Sand and rock exploded across the beach. Eriana leant over Nilus, Ben, Medusa, and me, protecting us from the shower of bullets. A torrent of seawater rained on us from her head and horns.

The helicopter buzzed lower, groaning in a rhythm as the pilot tried to swerve into position.

Eriana's second head rose to meet it, like a plume of smoke rising from a volcano.

"No!" I shouted.

Daughter, they are trying to kill you.

I don't care. You're not murdering anyone under my command.

And still my people sprinted closer. They shouted, waving at the helicopter. I couldn't be sure if two figures at the front were my parents. I couldn't be sure if the one next to them was Annith.

It was hard to breathe or focus.

From above, a male voice boomed over a speaker. "Everyone keep back! You are entering the line of fire!"

The time was now. Too many forces were after the serpent. Too many of my loved ones were in danger. If all had gone according to plan with Lysi, Queen Evagore would be on her way.

I needed to end this.

At my thought, Eriana lowered an enormous head towards me. Several people screamed as her jaws snapped closed over my body. Inside her mouth, she held me safely behind her pointed teeth.

Pitch darkness and her hot breath engulfed me. My stomach swooped as she lowered her head into the water.

Take us away from here.

We rushed forwards, the feeling in my stomach the only indication that we were moving.

Time passed in black, empty minutes before Eriana slowed. She opened her jaws, and seawater flooded in. I swam between her long fangs and back into the world.

Black lava rock spread below me, rising to the land in gradual swells. We had stopped at Skaaw Beach. The section of shoreline had formed when lava oozed through the earth a million years ago and rapidly cooled. Tides and earthquakes had since shaped the lava into sporadic patterns, full of holes and cracks.

I pulled myself from the waves and up onto the dry lava rock, glancing around.

You are safe here, said Eriana.

I faced her. Wind blew locks of hair around my face. Waves pushed my tail back and forth.

For a moment, I held the serpent's gaze, level with those deep blue pupils that seemed to hold the entirety of the ocean. What a beautiful, magnificent animal. The thought of what I had to do next brought tears to my eyes.

In the distance, the helicopter thrummed. Eriana and I turned to watch its fast approach, a black hornet in the deepening sky. She tasted the air.

They would never surrender.

I considered how powerful I could be if I kept the serpent in my control. A treaty was one way to keep peace, yes, but signatures on a page were no guarantee.

But it was too dangerous. In the wrong hands, Eriana was apocalyptic. And, while she could protect me, someone desperate enough could fire an iron bolt through my chest and plunge the world into a worse state of war than ever.

Besides, there was Eriana, my people's goddess, the soul and protector of our island, to consider. She was trapped inside this creature. I owed it to her to free her.

The serpent had served her purpose. She'd been the force that brought these leaders together. Without her, Medusa would not have come to claim her. The Americans would not be here to fight for her. Evagore would not be on her way here with Lysi.

The serpent had been vital to ending this war. But now she had to go.

I knew what I had to do. It was like Lysi had said about the law of fae. Fae could kill other fae. Maybe nothing could kill the leviathan—but the leviathan could also destroy anything.

My heart pounded as though it were my own life I was about to end. I wondered if the serpent could sense what was coming. Maybe it was her fear I felt, fluttering in my own chest. Or maybe she accepted death as readily as she had done anything in her time on earth.

Goodbye, Eriana.

She looked at me with both heads, the power of the oceans in those blue pupils. I saw knowledge of everything that had happened in the world since the day she was born.

Perhaps that birthplace was in the volcano whose lava still spilled across the beach beneath me, cooled and hardened and chiselled over time.

The two enormous heads faced each other, not a trace of protest in her thoughts. My mind was blank, peaceful.

Eriana obeyed the command as willingly as any other.

The heads recoiled. The jaws opened. Seawater and saliva dripped from those long fangs.

They lashed at each other, colliding with the sound of a thunderclap.

Gashes opened beneath her scales. A molten red torrent flooded onto the beach.

The moment it splashed onto the rocks, it blackened and thickened. It oozed over the land and into the water, slowing, pulsing like a dying heartbeat.

The serpent lashed again. The lava gurgled and spat as a fresh layer poured over top of the cooling one. The moment the waves touched it, it blackened and hardened, forming a new blanket of ripples and divots.

She continued to strike, opening gashes. The lava spewed widely, painting Skaaw Beach with the story of Sisiutl's demise.

As I watched her energy drain and felt it weaken in my body, I thought the story was beautiful, in a way. From the same place this creature had been born, here she would meet her end. Her remains would be forever imprinted on the shores of Eriana Kwai.

At last, when it seemed there must be no blood left in her great body, she surrendered.

I gave a shuddering gasp as the presence left me, as though she had taken all the breath from my lungs before departing the earth.

Slowly, with the awe-inspiring grace of a toppling sequoia tree, she fell. One head hit the beach with a shattering rumble. The hardening lava hissed and gurgled, absorbing its mass. The other head splashed into the water, her body laid out like a bridge between two places. The subsequent tidal wave curled over the beach, cooling whatever lava was still flowing. A spray of mist erupted high into the air.

As Eriana's soul departed its Host, my mind was cocooned in silence.

CHAPTER THIRTY - Meela
The Pacific Kingdom

I was left panting, alone on the lava rock, more exposed than I could ever recall feeling. Eriana's disappearance from my body drove a sharp ache through my chest.

Overcome with loss, I wanted nothing more than to follow her into the sky. How could I possibly continue living without her?

I shook my head. My emotions were not making sense. Eriana had been part of me, but she was not my mother, or father, or brother. She was not Lysi. We had spent mere hours together.

This was how it had to be. Eriana was free to ascend to the stars—and her children, her island, her legacy, were free to live as the Gaela intended.

You're better off without her, I thought. But the answering silence felt strange and lonesome.

A sound in the water made me gasp, and I spun around, heart still pounding a hummingbird's rhythm.

Medusa rose from the waves, rage flaring behind eyes of deepest red.

"I had to," I said. My voice was weak, like I'd just fought a hundred Massacres. I would not have the strength to fight her if she decided to attack.

She looked past me. A rumble carried on the wind. Voices, footsteps. My people were sprinting towards us.

Medusa said nothing. I couldn't be sure what she was thinking. Was she angry? Did she understand, or did she think I'd made a huge mistake?

They stopped at the edge of the fresh layer of lava, black and bubbling between us.

Ben emerged from the crowd as the whirr of the second helicopter closed in overhead. I tensed, ready to dive, but it landed on the bank. An entire team waited in the open door, armed and wearing protective vests.

Two men leapt out as the rotor slowed. They ran towards us, hopping clumsily over logs and rocks on their way down the beach. One was dressed sharply in a suit; the other, a mustached man, in military uniform.

They had their eyes on the massive leviathan, lying motionless behind me, streams of cooling lava everywhere. Then the mustached man saw me.

"Do you have any idea what you've done, demon?" he shouted. He strode towards me, but Ben lunged into his path and grabbed him.

Several of my people stepped forwards, putting another barrier between me and the men.

Everyone I loved—everything I loved about the island—was there. My parents, Annith, Tanuu, Blacktail, Fern, Blondie, and Anyo stood nearest me. They looked back at me, and I held each of their gazes in turn, trying to convey all the love and gratitude swelling in my chest. They were forever my allies, in battle and in life, and that meant more to me than they would ever know. Behind them were my classmates, teachers, neighbours—everyone I'd grown up with and fought for on the Massacre. They faced the men from the helicopter with their chins high.

"If you are any indication of what the serpent's presence will do to our world, then we are better off without it," said my father.

"You declare war on merpeople, you declare war on all of us," said Anyo.

The suited man raised his hands. "I don't intend to declare war on anyone, here."

His tone was calm, drawling, his accent distinctly American.

"Then stay away from my daughter," said my father. The men regarded him with open shock. "She was born and raised on this island. Don't tell me her life is worth less than a human's."

Ben and the mustached man looked into each other's faces. Too many emotions flew around for me to catch what passed between them.

"Officer Miller here tells me that this mermaid—I mean, your daughter—said the merman king is dead," said the suited man. "With him gone, and now the serpent, we'd like to know what this means for the American peop—"

He faltered, attention caught by something out in the waves. The crowd turned to see Lysi surface with two other mermaids. I was so overcome with relief that it took me a moment to see that the mermaid between her and Dione was wearing a crown.

Lysi had done it. She'd found Queen Evagore. Most importantly, she was safe.

Queen Medusa stretched taller, like these new arrivals were the most interesting yet. She and Evagore locked eyes and gave slight nods of recognition.

"Gentlemen," I said, gesturing, "I'd like to introduce Queen Medusa of the Atlantic, and Queen Evagore of the Pacific."

The suited man glanced to each mermaid at the shoreline, and back to me, and then to the surf. His eyes moved rapidly, as if he was afraid to hold any of our gazes for long, lest we lure him.

"Right," he said, smoothing his tie. "James York. I'm here on behalf of the United States Department of Homeland Security, and I'd like to know what the hell is going on. Are the American people in danger?"

"They are not, sir," said Evagore. "I am here to offer humans free movement across the seas again."

"Free movement? On what terms?"

"You agree not to destroy underwater cities."

Next to Ben, Officer Miller drew himself up, as though ready to be outraged. But he seemed to find nothing to say as he considered her words.

"What about borders?" said James York.

"I do not wish to define borders or restrictions."

"Then you guarantee not to attack," he said.

"Of course," said Evagore. "And if you are willing, we can negotiate a trade agreement that benefits us both."

The two men stared. A wisp of triumph passed through both of them. They might as well have had dollar signs flashing in their eyes as they considered all the potential of deep-sea mining. After what Lysi had told me about Medusa's trade agreements with humans and how rich and vibrant the Atlantic was, this sounded like a promising start to fixing the impoverished Pacific Kingdom.

James York straightened his coat. "Given our situation, I think we're best to negotiate a ceasefire. Are you willing to meet with the White House about this, Your Highness?"

I rolled my eyes. Lysi gave me a half-shrug that said, *Well, they got there eventually.*

"If Queen Medusa agrees, I would like to model our treaty after that of the Atlantic," said Evagore.

"I am willing to advise," said Medusa.

During the exchange, Lysi quietly rushed over to me. In our short time apart, I'd missed her smile so much that it ached to see it again. She grasped my hand under the water.

Behind her, someone's head popped through the surface, and I gasped. Nilus.

Automatically, I twisted around to look for my parents. They were trying to navigate around the lava without stepping in it.

"Stay there," I called. "We'll come to you."

I waved Nilus over, and we swam around and rose to the beach to meet them.

My parents' arms wrapped around me the moment I surfaced.

I tried to speak but my voice came out muffled.

After a long moment, I said, "Mama, Papa, there's something you need to know."

I glanced back to Nilus, who waited at a distance like he was afraid to come near. My parents followed my gaze.

I drew a breath. Part of me resented having to be the one to drop this bomb on our parents. But I knew how scared he must be to come here after all these years, and the other part of me felt a rush of sympathy for my big brother. I wanted to help him with this moment.

"Nilus didn't die on the Massacre. He ... he was transformed into a merman."

They stared at me, and then at Nilus, for what felt like several minutes. I wondered if I'd forgotten to speak in Eriana.

Then Nilus drifted closer and said, "Hi Mama. Papa," in a way that was so reminiscent of how he said it as a boy that my eyes sprung with tears. His appearance had changed since becoming a merman, but his voice seemed to trigger something that set time back in motion.

"Oh, Nilus!" said my mother, dissolving into sobs.

She ran forwards and threw herself at him. They splashed into the water. Nilus laughed, holding her above the surface.

My father advanced more haltingly, a dazed look on his face.

Then all four of us were hugging. I lost track of time as we held onto each other. I'd never thought this would happen again—my mother, father, me, and my big brother, together and whole.

The sun dipped past the horizon, casting the beach into a soft glow.

Behind us, I heard James York say, "We'll be in contact, then."

"Until then, you can always find me upon the throne in the Moonless City," said Evagore.

"Er—right. Reeves, you coming?" said Officer Miller.

Ben looked furtively in the direction where he'd left the other helicopter.

He gestured vaguely. "Uh, I've got ..."

"Well, then, get that thing back where it belongs before I have to write you up for stealing it."

"Yes, sir." For some reason he looked immensely relieved.

Without another word, the two men left for their helicopter, where their armed and vested team waited obediently.

Ben watched them for a moment, then looked around, seeming to process where he was and what had happened.

Blondie and Fern appeared out of nowhere on either side of him.

"Want to stay for tea?" said Blondie.

"We have strawberries," said Fern.

Ben glanced from one to the other. He ran a hand over his short hair. Then he smiled. "Why not?"

Fern looped an arm through his and dragged him away.

I shook my head, turning to Evagore.

"Your Majesty," I said, "what about all of Adaro's supporters? What about the anti-human beliefs? Will a treaty be enough?"

"I believe that once his supporters realise the atrocities Adaro committed—from the labour camp to the Nereid prison—they will start to understand how misled they were under their former king. It will take work, but I am confident we can rebuild the Pacific Kingdom."

Dione placed a hand on the queen's shoulder.

"If you'll excuse us, Meela and Lysithea. We have to get the queen into proper care."

"Of course," I said.

"Your Majesty," said Lysi.

She cast us a gracious smile, looking more queen-like than ever beneath her pale blue crown.

Medusa was nowhere to be seen. She had gone. I wondered if we would ever meet again—and whether Lysi or I would ever be welcome in the Atlantic.

My parents and Nilus were deep in conversation, sitting in the retreating tide. Everyone else waited on the beach, chatting excitedly about the dead leviathan. My friends were climbing the lava rock, poking at the molten streams. By the looks of it, Tanuu had melted a shoe. He caught my eye and we exchanged a grin.

Lysi and I drifted a little ways away from everyone else, our tails brushing under the water. I looked with relief into her sapphire eyes, having been terrified of never seeing them again, and she leaned in and kissed me.

I drew back a moment later, eyes burning with tears.

"What is it?" she said.

"It's ... a lot."

She gave a sad smile. "Tell me. What happened?"

I hesitated. Everything Adaro had said to me before I pulled the trigger was prickling in the back of my mind.

"Adaro told me something before he died."

Lysi raised an eyebrow. Without meeting her eye, I told her what he had said about setting us up. I told her how the fishing net she'd gotten stuck in as a kid had been part of his plan, and Panopea had been an innocent victim, and worst of all, how this meant every piece of both our lives had been

354

determined by Adaro. When I finished, I felt sick and angry all over again.

"Mee," said Lysi.

She didn't continue until I raised my eyes to meet hers.

"Mee, I don't care whether we met because of him, or a random pull in the tides, or because I was being a cod and got stuck in a net, or—"

"I don't want him to have anything to do with us!"

"Who cares? It doesn't matter how we met. The point is that we did."

"But—"

She covered my mouth with a pearl-white hand. "Think about it."

I was silent for a moment. I supposed she was right. Adaro had steered my fate like a ship—my brother, the Massacre, my friends and enemies, and my relationship with Lysi. He was part of my past, whether I liked it or not, and I could choose to let that bother me, or I could accept it.

The beach was growing dark, but Lysi's eyes were bright as the moon to me.

"You're the best thing that ever happened to me," she said. "You need to understand that."

"I do."

I raised a hand, and she pressed her palm against mine. We looked at them for a moment—brown skin against white.

"I'll introduce you to my family," whispered Lysi. "My parents and brother will love to meet you."

"I can't wait."

"And then we're going on a date."

I smiled. I plucked a piece of seaweed out of her hair, thinking of two kids who used to play on the beach and wear matching shell necklaces.

So much had happened since then, and so much had changed. Yet under the light of Lysi's gaze and the laughter of friends and family echoing down the beach, I felt like today was the beginning of a lifetime together.

CHAPTER THIRTY-ONE - Ben
The Port of Eriana Kwai

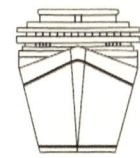

Ten Years Later

The HMS Rozina, a luxury cruise ship, departed Vancouver every week between May and September. It sailed the coast of British Columbia and Alaska, stopping at major ports along the way so tourists could explore the richness the landscape had to offer.

But the real allure, and the reason the cruise had attracted not only tourists from North America, but also those worldwide over the last ten years, was the new destination in its itinerary.

The Reeves family stood inside the Eriana Kwai Cultural Centre, gaping at the enormous serpent overhead. The original corpse had been restored, calcified, and suspended from the ceiling by thick cables. It encircled the main hall, one set of open jaws welcoming people at the entrance and the other descending in the middle of the hall as if it might snap closed over the dais.

"You feeling all right?" said Fern, grasping Ben's hand.

He gave a half-smile. "It's dead, so yeah, I'll be fine. You?"

"I expected panic when I stepped off the ship, but you know, it feels good. I never appreciated how green everything—" She looked down at Spencer, who was tugging relentlessly at her pant leg. "Yes?"

"What does it say?" Spencer pointed at the plaque on the dais.

The family walked over.

"Sisiutl," said Fern. "It tells the story of how it was found, and how your daddy fought it."

"What are those letters?"

"That's how you say it in Eriana."

Spencer turned away. "I wanna go to the beach."

"Now wait a minute," said Ben, picking up his son before he could escape. "We waited two hours in that line to see this thing. We're going to look around, all right?"

"But—"

"Spencer, stay still and smile for a picture," said Fern. "We'll buy you a toy from the shop when we're done."

Ben whispered something in Spencer's ear. Spencer laughed and nodded.

"Ready for our picture, mom!"

Ben hefted his son higher as though offering him to the leviathan's jaws. Spencer opened his mouth and clapped his hands over his cheeks in a pretend scream. Fern took a few pictures and shook her head in exasperation. The boys laughed.

"Listen to this," said Ben, reading the plaque. "'The leviathan was said to play host to the soul of Eriana, goddess and discoverer of this island thousands of years ago. The chasm in the middle of the island formed when the earth split to release this ancient monster. Only by killing the monster could the soul of Eriana be freed, permitting the island to return to peace once more."

"Who killed it?" said Spencer, eyes wide.

"Why don't we keep looking and find out?" said Ben.

The family pushed through the crowd to see each exhibit, learning about the leviathan's birth, reawakening, and death. They agreed to hike to Skaaw Beach later to explore the famous lava swells.

Though Spencer pretended not to care about mermaids, Ben caught a glint of awe in his eyes at the mention of pretty girls turning into sea demons.

Fern covered Spencer's ears. "Ben, you're going to give him a complex."

Ben waved a hand. "It'll give him a healthy respect for women."

They left the museum and headed for the beach, where Blacktail and Tanuu were due to meet them with a picnic.

Spencer watched the kids playing in the water with open envy.

"I want to do that," he shouted, pointing at a young couple parasailing.

Fern laughed. "One day."

Ben couldn't help thinking of the fishing trips he'd get to take his son on in a few years' time.

Fern found a clear patch of beach and set up the blanket and umbrella while Spencer pulled out his toys.

As Ben wandered the shoreline, he watched the families swim in the cool Pacific water. Something caught his eye in the distance, and he stopped. Far across the waves, he swore he saw two women surface—one blonde, one dark. The faint sound of laughter carried towards him on the wind. But when he raised a hand and squinted out at them, he saw only waves.

Ben liked to believe in legends more often these days. He believed everything about this one. He believed a girl and a mermaid, through a stubbornness to believe anything but what their hearts told them, had made all of this happen.

Looking around at the smiling families, Ben decided he would live by their example. Because of them, the ocean was again free and pure, a place of innocent wonder. Eriana Kwai, this Pacific Northwest paradise, finally had the peace it deserved.

Acknowledgements

You'd think, as a writer, I would be able to find the words to express my gratitude to everyone who has been by my side throughout this trilogy. I can't. My family, friends, colleagues, and readers have given me so much support these last five years that I wonder how anyone could possibly be as lucky as I have been. Thank you to each of you for your enthusiasm.

Every author needs a group of friends going through the same struggles. Sometimes this involves late-night rants about how hard writing is. Sometimes this involves conversations made entirely of GIFs and rainbow emojis. Sometimes this is honest feedback, promoting each other's books, or just drinking wine and talking about everything except writing. To my crit bitches: I'm forever grateful to have you in my life. Hugs and unicorns to each of you.

Thank you, thank you, thank you to my readers. To those who have connected with me on social media, who have created artwork, written reviews, or shared the books with your friends: this series would not be a fraction as successful without you. Your posts make me laugh, smile, weep a little, and give enthusiastic fist-pumps. I hope one day I get to meet and hug every single one of you.

What's Next?

If you enjoyed this series, you'll also enjoy Tiana Warner's other books:

The Valkyrie's Daughter, a YA Fantasy with a sapphic enemies-to-lovers romance set in the nine Norse worlds.

Mermaid Huntress: An Ice Massacre Graphic Novel

Find all Tiana Warner's books at tianawarner.com.

Note from the Author

Thank you for reading Ice Kingdom and supporting an indie author. If you enjoyed Meela and Lysi's story, please consider spreading the word and reviewing it online.

To stay up to date with new releases, exciting announcements, and giveaways, please sign up for my newsletter!

tianawarner.com

www.ingramcontent.com/pod-product-compliance
Lightning Source LLC
Chambersburg PA
CBHW020519260626
47156CB00006B/2055